A Bit Much

A Bit Much

Sarah Jackson

PENGUIN
an imprint of Penguin Canada, a division of
Penguin Random House Canada Limited

Canada • USA • UK • Ireland • Australia •
New Zealand • India • South Africa • China

First published 2022

www.penguinrandomhouse.ca

*Publisher's note: This book is a work of fiction. Names, characters,
places and incidents either are the product of the author's imagination
or are used fictitiously, and any resemblance to actual persons living
or dead, events, or locales is entirely coincidental.*

LIBRARY AND ARCHIVES CANADA CATALOGUING IN PUBLICATION

Title: A bit much / Sarah Jackson.
Names: Jackson, Sarah (Author of A bit much), author.
Identifiers: Canadiana (print) 20210309407 | Canadiana
    (ebook) 20210310529 | ISBN 9780735242159 (hardcover) |
    ISBN 9780735242166 (EPUB)
Classification: LCC PS8619.A244725 B58 2022 |
    DDC C813/.6—dc23

Book design by Kate Sinclair
Cover design by Kate Sinclair
Cover image © CSA-Printstock / Getty Images

Printed in Canada

10 9 8 7 6 5 4 3 2 1

Penguin
Random House
PENGUIN CANADA

For Derek

Chapter One

I've always thought that dogs don't like me because they can sense that I have no athletic ability. The pinky and thumb on my left hand are double-jointed; this was my icebreaker in high school. I can tie the stem of a maraschino cherry in a knot with my tongue—if you give me about twenty minutes and promise not to watch me struggle. I feel like a pervert when I pull down the plastic wrapper on an English cucumber. I have a freckle on my bottom lip. I can put my right leg behind my head but not the left one. The sound of someone scraping their fork on their plate hurts my teeth. If I listen to music with lyrics after 8 p.m., I can't sleep because the words get stuck in my head and play over and over. For me, a lemon is an aphrodisiac. I like the feeling of the inside of my cat's ear—it's like cold velvet. I'm always thinking about this—the texture of a personality. These traits, whether common or not, that people believe define their individuality. I'll be walking down the street or sitting on a subway train and I'll notice some small detail about someone

I'm watching. I'll imagine what they're like, what they're better at than I am. And then the self-loathing kicks in because women are conditioned to believe thinking too much about themselves is an exercise in narcissism.

A young woman with lilac hair is my current fixation. Her eyes are painted black and occupy the majority of the upper part of her head. She's wearing leather shorts and a matching tube top. I recognize something in her face: the way she purses her lips and narrows her eyes like she's holding in a sneeze. I know her. Lauren Whitby from high school. The subway station is scorching, and my body temperature is rising even higher out of fear of an encounter with Lauren. The under layer of my hair is soaked with sweat. I see my reflection in the screen of my phone. My bangs are so drenched that they look like squiggles drawn on my forehead with a brown marker.

I scan the platform for a place to hide. A man slightly shorter than a street lamp is standing about five feet from me; he will act as sufficient coverage. Peering around Lurch, I have a clear view of Lauren. She and I were acquaintances in high school; we weren't close, but we had mutual friends and a few classes together. She seemed kind of dim but in a non-threatening way—the type of dim person who admits when they don't understand something and seeks an explanation rather than the type whose ignorance leads to aggression. I didn't recognize Lauren at first because she looked nothing like this when I knew her; she was a GAP kid. She was the type of girl whose favourite colour was pink, and she'd often find a way to let you know this, as if it's interesting to have a favourite colour. She pronounced *pink* "peeenk." She had a curly blonde bob and never wore more makeup than a roll of lip gloss and a light dusting of blush. Lauren's new appearance suggests she has new friends. She and I haven't seen each other since high school, and nothing happened between us to make me dislike her, though I don't want to talk to her now. This is mainly because I don't want to have to acknowledge her new look or tell her what I'm up to.

Lauren is attracting attention from others on the platform, which, I assume, is her intention. She looks straight ahead like she doesn't know they're watching her, but I can tell that she's pushing back her ears and forehead with her cheek and jaw muscles, sucking in her cheeks slightly because she knows that it accentuates her cheekbones and jawline. An unremarkable man walks by me, glances at me, and keeps walking. He is wearing one of those newsboy hats that were on every man's head in the 1910s and then were briefly cool again in the early 2000s, a time when ugly things were considered beautiful. He looks at every girl he passes and spots Lauren. He stands in front of her and pulls out a wrinkled, pale pink tulip from his shirt pocket. I'm close enough to hear him say, "You are looking very elegant. I am looking for an elegant lover." He reaches out to hand her the flower and what looks like a business card. She doesn't take either and walks away from him.

Lauren catches me staring at her.

"Alice?"

Instinctively, I turn away. But she said my name, so by turning away, I make myself look stupid and rude—two things I aim not to be, though occasionally I don't try hard enough.

"Alice?"

As Lauren makes her way over, I can't think of a reason to explain why I turned away. Now even my wrists are sweating.

A man sitting on a bench nearby shakes out his newspaper and it sounds like distant thunder rolling in. We really need the rain.

"Lauren?" I try to put on a convincing smile, but it feels heavy.

"I was trying to figure out who you were. I knew you looked familiar, but I didn't think you were *you*," she says.

"Yep, I am me. You look so different but in a good way," I submit to her ostentatious garb.

"Thanks. You look good too," Lauren says.

She's lying. I look terrible, but compliment mirroring is expected. Although I'd prefer never to cross paths with Lauren, this is a particularly unfortunate time to run into her as I am saturated in perspiration, and she can't see my post-high-school physical improvements. I wasn't much to look at then, but I wasn't treated like an outcast either. I was just "okay" (that's a quote), although I did become more attractive later. But in the last few months, my looks have gone downhill.

"You grew your hair out and dyed it!" says Lauren.

"This is my natural hair colour actually." Is the train delayed? The screen had said it was arriving in four minutes.

"At prom, your hair was black and short. You had that bob. We were hair twins but also sort of opposites, remember? Mine was curly and blonde, and yours was straight and black. You said we were good and evil."

Did I say that? I must have. I had inside jokes with a lot of people in school. Like this one, the jokes weren't always funny or even clever, but they created tenuous connections that I mistook for friendships. They felt important at the time. It was how I appraised myself. Most of these threads are now broken, and I'm down to much fewer friends. Maintaining those relationships became exhausting, and I think it's better this way.

"Oh, yeah. I remember."

My hair is shoulder length now and an ordinary shade of brown. This is the first time in eleven years that my hair has been my natural colour. In my final year of high school, I was into Uma Thurman in *Pulp Fiction*, so I dyed and cut my hair to look like hers. Soon after, someone online called Tarantino derivative, and though I didn't know if I agreed, I felt embarrassed about trying to look like Uma. My hair was already black when I discovered early German cinema after watching *Pandora's Box*, and I cut it shorter to look like Louise Brooks. It didn't take much to change this hairstyle into the Anna Karina look I tried to pull off during my French New Wave phase. I loved asking people if they knew who Anna Karina was and then acted smug when they thought they knew but were thinking of Anna Karenina. I felt this made me cultured, but now I realize this sense of superiority was a product of insecurity. After high school, I saw *Rosemary's Baby*, and I copied Mia Farrow's look and dyed my hair blonde and got a pixie cut. Brutal decision. In the last couple years, I've decided to stop trying to look like other people.

"I guess we're not twins anymore." Lauren says this as though she's congratulating herself for noticing.

"I guess not."

"So, are you in school? What are you doing in the city?"

"I graduated last year and I'm just figuring stuff out," I say while picking the last bit of blue nail polish off my nails. How is she not sweating? Maybe she's not only become good-looking, but she's also gained superhuman powers. She gained the power to not sweat while wearing leather in summertime. Or maybe it's full-body Botox.

"Cool. What did you take?"

"English."

"So, you're working in the city then? Where do you work?"

My mouth moves faster than my brain, and I lie. "A publishing house. Doing editing and stuff."

"That's impressive! Where?"

I pause. "You probably don't know it. It's a smaller indie house. On Elm."

"Seriously? My friend Gwen works there. She's a publicist. You must know her."

"No. Well. I don't work there anymore. I'm on kind of a break right now. Doing stuff." I know I don't sound even slightly convincing.

"Oh. Cool." Lauren's eyes wander. She can tell I'm lying and she's being kind about it.

I'm on the verge of panic and I don't know what else to say.

"I'm a DJ," she says.

"Oh, cool. Music is cool." I sound like this is the first conversation I've ever had.

"Yeah, all over the city. I'll text you next time I'm spinning."

We do not have each other's numbers. Why are we doing this?

"So, are you still close with Mia?" she asks.

My insides tighten, and heat shoots up my back and burrows into my shoulders and neck.

"Yeah," I say, breaking eye contact.

"I heard about her. *So sad*. How is she?" Lauren puts out her hand without making contact. Her hand falls away.

"She's great. She's good. She is good." I look everywhere, except at Lauren. Lurch is eating a green apple—it looks like a grape in his giant hand.

"So good to hear. I was worried."

She gives me a doleful look, and I return the expected hardened-yet-grateful look.

"If she wants the contact for my reiki healer, let me know, okay? Heather is amazing."

I just nod.

"So, Alice, I know I haven't seen you in forever, but I know how honest you are. So, I want to ask you something."

I don't remember anyone thinking of me as honest.

"What do you think of my hair? Is it too much?"

I give her what she wants. "No, Lauren. I really like it. Only you could pull it off."

She beams.

We both nod and exchange flimsy grins. I break eye contact when we hit a wall of silence. The suffocating kind of silence, not the peaceful kind.

Lauren removes her phone from her bag and starts texting. I know there's no service at this station. But I was about to do the same thing. I don't know why it's more uncomfortable to stand beside each other saying nothing than pretending to text while there's no service. I realize I'm going to have to talk to her on the train. What if she gets off on my stop? That's close to thirty minutes. I bite the skin at the sides of my thumb. The train will be here any minute now. Lauren starts checking herself out with the camera on her phone. She's using a filter that makes her look like a gorgeous cartoon dead girl. Now's my chance.

"I have to go! It was nice to see you!" I wave, so I don't have to hug her, and I start backing away. She looks confused. "I just realized that this isn't the right train. I'm such an idiot!" I know I'm not pulling this off.

I wait at the top of the stairs, out of sight, until I know Lauren has got on the train, then I go back down to where I was standing and wait for the next train.

I'm not sure how much longer I can endure this heat. I'm feeling so weak that I can barely stand up straight or support the weight of my head. I wipe the sweat off my face and commend myself for being wise and not wearing any makeup today. Even though I would have preferred that Lauren see me in some makeup, I think of how skin can't breathe under all those layers. Mia tells me that I let people know how little makeup I wear to suggest I'm not shallow and spend my time doing Things of Importance, which she says makes me shallow in a different way.

Looking down at the tracks from the platform, I spot a subway mouse. It must be so hot down there for the mice, the gigantic bodies of the trains speeding over the electric rails. How can they stand it? But I don't know anything about science, so maybe it's not so hot down there. I'm also thinking about how quick I was to put out poison when I had a mouse problem in my apartment.

The subway train speeds by me before it stops. I step on the train. Air conditioning, I'd make love to you now if you had the parts to do it. I ease myself into a seat. There is a great satisfaction in getting a seat during rush hour.

Twenty-five minutes later, I get to my stop. A few blocks, and I am at my destination. I walk through the revolving door that is wide enough for wheelchairs and slow enough for the wounded, then I step into the elevator and push the 4 button.

The receptionist tells me I can't go in yet because Mia's doctor is with her. In the waiting area, I open Twitter. I learn that an extremely rich celebrity wore an eco-friendly dress that cost less than $100 on the red carpet. This celebrity never made her political stances known over the years, but a few months ago, she publicly called herself a feminist, and now she's wearing an affordable dress around other rich people, so everyone is happy with her. After twenty minutes in the waiting room, I walk into room 432.

Mia looks so pale that her face blends in with her pillow. She's becoming an extension of her hospital bed. Her blueberry eyes and her violet-painted lips are a stark contrast to her skin. They look like they're floating just above her face. With her head still on her pillow, she glances at the opened door, and when she realizes it's me, her dark lips break into smile. She sits up straight, crossing her legs in bed.

Her veins are showing through her skin. I almost tell her they are a lovely shade of blue, but I know she'll tell me I'm creepy and laugh when really it might exacerbate her insecurities about looking less like herself each day.

Mia usually shares a room with other patients, but there's no one else here right now.

"I have something for you," I tell her.

"What is it? I'm losing my mind in here." Her eyes become electric, and she seems almost desperate.

"I was thinking about something in the waiting room. Something I want you to know. It's really important. So, I wrote it down."

"Is this going to make me cry?" She rolls her eyes. "I don't want to cry, Al."

"Just read it."

She reads the note and laughs. Mia has told me more than once that I'm the funniest person she knows (something no one else has ever told me, though I'm always waiting for them to).

The note reads, *You are the sexiest human on the fourth floor.*

"Fuck yeah, I am," Mia says as she refolds the note and tucks it under her pillow.

I watch the colourless liquid drip out of the IV bag and move through the tube connected to the hole in Mia's chest. My mouth goes dry and my upper lip starts to sweat like when I'm about to throw up, but I focus on my breathing and the nausea settles a bit.

"So, how are you?" I ask her. I know it's a ridiculous question.

"Oh, perfect," she says. I know she's not going to give details unless I get very specific.

"The nurse said you were having stomach issues?"

Mia groans. "They're obsessed with me. One of the drugs I take is this red drip that constipates me and then gives me shits the size of a softball. I have to bite a washcloth while I'm pushing it out." She says this with a bored expression. She doesn't leave room for emotion or prolonged compassion.

"Jesus. That's awful."

"Hope you've found a replacement for me." She closes her eyes and crosses her hands across her chest like a corpse in their casket at a funeral. There's a faint grin on her face. I hate when Mia makes these jokes, but I force a smile and shake my head as if it's all lighthearted and fun. I know she wants me to distract her from her illness when I'm here instead of asking about her treatments and side effects. This isn't how we usually are, so much pretending and censoring. I don't usually have to protect her feelings or watch what I say. But she's the only person who has ever been able to comfort me, so I have to try to do the same for her now. I think this is the only time she has ever truly needed me.

"I ran into Lauren Whitby today."

"Who?"

"She went to high school with us. Bit of a follower, girly, not the smartest."

She looks at me blankly. "These descriptions are supposed to set her apart?"

"She did a back handspring in gym class and her boob came out of her shirt. First year of high school."

"Ohhh right. Jason Daly got the other dickholes to call her Lauren Titby."

"Yeah, well. She is completely different now. She is like a full-on cül now."

Cüls are what Mia and I call people who are too cool for anyone except other cüls, and famous people. Cüls are all pompous artists of some sort, or models. They dress to grab attention. There's nothing wrong with expressing yourself through clothing. I try to, though not as confidently as I wish to. We spell it *cül* because many of them alter the spelling of their names, choose entirely new and more interesting names, or add accents and diacritical marks to them in order to distinguish themselves from others with the same name. *Cul* also means ass in French.

"Really? I didn't see that coming. I would have thought she was, like, two kids deep at this point and married to a man who thinks girl on top is kinky."

"Well, she's definitely a cül."

"What exactly are you basing this on?"

"Her hair is purple, she was wearing a shitload of makeup, and she was in a two-piece leather outfit."

"In this heat?!"

"Exactly."

I once asked Mia if I could sleep in the hospital room with her on a cot and she laughed, but I was serious. I hate leaving her here. Each cycle of her treatment involves a long stretch where she's hooked up for nearly a week at a time. Sometimes the cycles are extended, depending on her vitals and bloodwork. She also comes in for shorter sessions, where she's hooked up for only a few hours. She says she's getting used to being here all the time, but I notice how agitated she gets. I know she can't stand staying in bed all day and feeling her muscles become soft and limp. Anyone would start to unravel being in the hospital for days, but it really wears on Mia because she's the opposite of a homebody. She's the kind of carpe-diem asshole—though she would never say *carpe diem*—who goes on a run before breakfast. She also plans all her outfits for the week on Sunday, consulting weather apps. Mia used to try to make her own clothes too, during an environmentally conscious phase in first year, but gave up when she realized making sleeves was beyond her skill set, and she couldn't wear ponchos every day. Since we were teens, Mia has dragged me to parties and shows I didn't want to go to. I hate shows—all that standing around and trying to figure out what to do with your body. I default to staring straight ahead, perhaps vaguely tapping my foot if I've had something to drink. Mia doesn't get in her head like that though, she's comfortable socializing. She's constantly dating someone new; she says she can't sit still with anyone for too long—well, other than me. It doesn't make sense for me to like Mia so much because we're so different, and I have generally despised people who *do* a lot of things, but there's no one I like more than her.

I'm trying to remember if Lauren was friends with Anne in high school. I want to ask Mia, but I try to avoid bringing up Anne as much as possible around her. I've known Anne almost as long as I've known Mia. I met Mia when I was four, and we met Anne right before middle school. Anne has been odd ever since Mia's diagnosis. She visited her a couple times at the beginning, but now it's been months, and she won't even see her in between treatment cycles when Mia's at her parents'.

I decide to ask Mia what she's reading lately, a safe question. I look at the pile of books on her bedside table, which is littered with gum wrappers, balled-up tissues, a yellowing phone that used to be white, and small paper containers for pills, which look like what I put my ketchup in at McDonald's. She's usually tidy, so this mess is surprising.

"Are you trying to read *Ulysses* again?" I ask as I pick up the book. I put it down when I spot another tome in the pile. "Mia? Is there a spiritual awakening I need to be made aware of?"

Mia explains that her current roommate, Wendy, who's in her eighties, has been getting treatment for close to a year and said that Mia is the youngest patient she's seen in here. Wendy asked Mia if she has accepted Jesus in her heart, and Mia told her she's not religious but her parents are. Wendy's daughter visited, and though the curtain was drawn and they were whispering, Mia heard Wendy tell her daughter that Mia turned her back on God and is now ill at a young age.

"And then she gave you the Bible."

"It was on my bed with a note on it that just said, *God bless you. Wendy.*"

"Religious people are fucked. Who would blame you for getting sick?"

"You know, it's pretty hateful to think you're better than people who need God."

At first, I think she's joking, but then I realize she's serious. She has no problem changing the tone of a conversation to tell me when she thinks I'm wrong. She isn't always kind when she's trying to make a point. I want to defend myself, but she continues.

"You're as bad as Wendy if you think they're all alike. My parents aren't like that. And it's not only old religious people who blame me. Remember that girl from my gym who's super into crystals? She suggested that maybe I did something bad in another life. And a few months ago, I went to save Dylan from boredom at some work event, and his boss told me maybe I'm sick from too much stress."

"Mia, these people are trash. Don't listen to them."

She gives me a look that says, *why would I?* But I wonder if they get to her. I also wonder why she didn't tell me until now that these things were said to her.

Mia mentioning Dylan reminds me I owe him a text. I've been ignoring him. I'm about to ask her if she's seen him recently when I notice her eyes are fixed on my arms, and she is running her index finger along her bottom lip. Now her finger is purple from her lipstick, and it looks like a bad bruise.

"Al," she pauses, "you're looking thinner. Are you okay?"

"I think I'm the one who's supposed to be worrying about you." I intend to sound protective, instead my tone is cutting. I feel kind of guilty, but I will not talk about my body right now. I know I've lost weight, and I think I look gross, but the only thing worse than looking at my body is talking about it.

I can tell she wants to press me on this, and it's tough for her to drop it, as if betraying an instinct.

"Any job prospects?" she says instead.

"My degree does nothing for me." I'm irritated by myself because I say this all the time. "Whatever though, I shouldn't complain."

"Yes, you should! Our whole generation is getting screwed."

"But what's the point of trying to find a job in the middle of the sixth extinction? I'm trying to carve out a career to make money when in a few years there won't be bees, whales, water— you think money will matter?" I sit on the bed with her.

Mia laughs and her icy hands stroke my clammy palm.

"I'm not joking."

"I know you're not. But you're bumming me out."

"Want to watch a movie? I brought *Romeo and Juliet*."

"Oh, yeah, so uplifting. You can put it on, but I may fall asleep. Don't wake me if I do—my sleep has been shit."

"But I can't do the double suicide scene alone."

Nearly an hour and a half later, Mia is asleep. I turn off the movie before Leo and Claire die. Mia's wig has shifted slightly in her sleep; it's not lined up to where her hairline used to be. I don't want to wake her, so I don't attempt to fix it even though I know she'd be upset to see herself exposed like this. When she was starting treatment about half a year ago, she was told her hair would start falling out two and a half weeks after her first treatment. Mia grieved for the coming loss of something that made her feel confident. She had often received compliments for her long, thick hair that would cause her arms to ache when she put it up. After the first few days of treatment, she was sitting in bed with her hair blanketing her shoulders, and she told me she hoped she'd be an anomaly and her hair wouldn't fall out. But then exactly two and a half weeks after her first treatment, she started to see strands of hair on her pillow in the morning, and more than the usual few hairs clinging to her feet in the shower. And soon after that, she'd gently tug on her hair while washing it and collect dense clumps in her fists. She expected the hairless spots on her scalp to be bloody and scabbed, but they were smooth—a clean separation. There was something unnerving to her about that. She felt betrayed, she wanted blood.

Since her diagnosis, Mia has stayed with her parents. They rented a house in the city when they learned she'd need treatment here. Mia and I share an apartment, but she hasn't been to our place for months. At first, she wouldn't leave her parents' house except for treatments. She wouldn't let me see her. One night,

I heard the lock open in the door to our apartment, and it was Mia in a cherry-coloured winter hat. Her eyes were pink. She asked me to come to the bathroom, and she sat on the edge of the tub. She said a lot of people shave their heads when the hair loss begins, but I don't want to do that. I can't handle this in-between stage. There are strands of hair all over my bedroom, the bathroom, they're in my clothes, and it's so itchy. She handed me scissors. Can you cut it as short as you can? She took off her hat and my stomach dropped.

She still had a lot of hair, but there were patches missing all over her scalp. I started cutting, slowly, far away from her face, as if I were giving her a shoulder-length haircut. Chunks fell down her back and onto my thighs. You need to get closer to my scalp, she said. As much as you can take off. I bit the inside of my cheek and started closer to the scalp. Cutting through the thick pieces was tough on my wrists, and they began to ache. Mia started to cry silently, I could see wet lines on her cheeks, and so I cried too, both of us trying to stay contained as if to shield the other. When there were only a few inches left of her hair, I told her I had to stop, and she said that's okay, and she put her hat back on. The short hairs that fell out were easier for her to deal with. When she lost all her hair, she couldn't look at her reflection without a wig on for a full week.

She picked a synthetic wig even though her parents offered to buy her a wig made of human hair. Mia thought the expense was too much for something temporary. She chose a blonde bob because she had always considered cutting her hair like Nastassja Kinski in *Paris, Texas*, but she wasn't sure she could pull off shorter hair. She told me a nurse explained that sometimes after a patient finishes treatment, their hair grows back entirely different. The texture changes, even the colour. The nurse thought the possibility of her hair looking different when it grew back would be appealing for Mia, but it upset her. When her eyebrows and eyelashes fell out, Mia said she hadn't considered that she might lose hair everywhere and then said she felt stupid for thinking it would affect only the hair on top of her head. Her eyelashes and eyebrows have always been pale, nearly white in the summer, but having nothing there drastically changes a face. She pencils in her eyebrows and glues on fake eyelashes most days, and she puts on lipstick too because the makeup distracts her—it's as if she has somewhere to go. But sometimes she doesn't have the energy to put it on. Before she was sick, she didn't know a lot about makeup. She wore it every day, but she rarely tried anything complex. Since getting sick, she's been watching tutorials and practising, and she knows all about it now. Her eyebrows look real until you get close and see they have no texture.

Movies don't show the hair loss extending to your whole body, and they always show sick people with skeletal bodies, but Mia has gained weight since treatment and is retaining fluid. She said the movies don't get it right.

I hate seeing Mia worry about her appearance. When I was a kid, I was picked on for being short and chubby, for having a big nose, for not wearing the good brands, and for not having a dad. It sounds so generic and tired, but that's how it is when you're a kid. They hated me for having the wrong things and not having the right things. I begged my mother to get me Nike and Adidas clothing like the other kids, but she said it was too expensive. Once I found Tommy Hilfiger overalls at a second-hand store where my mom bought me most of my clothes, and I was so excited to find something name-brand she could afford, even though they were too big. We weren't poor, but the kids at school made me realize we had less than most of them. The kids were not kind to Mia either since she was bigger than most of the boys. She didn't cower like me though. She defended herself. She'd picked up swearing before the rest of us since her cousin showed her all the Scorsese movies, and she told the ones taunting us to fuck their mothers, which really made them scared of her. She asked me why I cared what they thought if I didn't like them. I didn't have an answer, but I knew that I did care. When a boy called me ugly, she pushed him and he fell on his face and bled. When I was about nine, I went on a class trip to a lake and we all went swimming. Mia was sick that day. Two girls from my class grabbed me and pushed me underwater, held me down, and kept pulling me out for a second and pushing me down again. I don't know how long it went on before some teacher intervened, but I can still remember how it felt to try to suck all the air out of the sky. I felt the same when I found out about Mia.

I haven't exactly handled her illness well. Since I found out, I haven't been able to keep much food down. Most food makes me nauseated. I'm having trouble chewing things, I find it exhausting and repulsive. I stopped returning texts, and I stopped going out. I lost my job recently. I barely paid attention to my boss. I bought the wrong grapes—seedless, he'd demand, always seedless. Let him choke, I thought. My boss would ask me to book him flights and I just wouldn't. I hated that job anyway. My mom is freaking out, saying I can't just hide out. She's worried that I'm going to kill myself or something. I've told her I don't want that. I wish I could just sit with Mia, wait out her illness until she's recovered.

Though it's not only Mia. I've always felt a kind of heaviness inside, wanting to pull away from people, though I've struggled to articulate why. Lately, I haven't been able to compartmentalize like I have in the past. Mia has always been so healthy. She's twenty-three years old. I know she's not the first young person to have a serious illness, but she's the first one I've been close to. A girl named Dinah from my middle school died in a car accident three years ago. I didn't know her well, but every day she used to ask me for a pencil in math class. She would bite the pencil, and when she'd give it back, I'd look at the teeth marks. It's unthinkable to me that she just stopped living. My mom kept all my school stuff, and when I went home to visit her for some holiday, I found a pencil, saw Dinah's bite marks, and I put my teeth where hers had been. I considered sending the pencil to her mom, explaining these were her impressions, but I thought it might not go over well.

As I step outside the hospital doors, I see the sun burning low in the distance. The sky is an ashy blue with a muffled pink flush. I hear a *click*, *click*, *click* sound as a tall guy with dark hair hanging in loose waves walks by. With each step, I hear the clicking sound. It's irritating. What is making that noise? I notice he's wearing a denim jacket. The temperature has dropped since I was last outside. In a few months, it will be too cold. I like the in-betweens, spring and fall, but they don't last long here. I feel like I'm always waiting on another season.

In the spring and summer, white fluff from the trees floats around in the air. There's so much fluff right now that it looks like the early days of winter. I see one straight ahead that looks like it's frozen in place.

Chapter Two

It's 5 a.m. and the birds wake me with their morning screams. Eventually I go back under. I wake up at 9:14 a.m., then fall back asleep. I wake up again at 11:37 a.m. Not bad—the morning is basically gone. I can't force my body to sleep anymore, but I don't want to be up, so I stay under my sheet and stare at the wall. I'm thinking about not wanting to shower, put on clothes or makeup. I really should shower because I stink. Why is it that our bodies reek so much after no exertion? Especially mouths—even after a nap, the mouth smells like a decomposing hamster has made a bed on the tongue. I press my cheek against the wall; the wall is cool throughout all seasons. I'm not sure how long I've been necking with the wall, but I can't find the motivation to move. I look at my phone—12:27 now—I'll definitely get up when it's 12:45. I point the fan toward my hair and let it cool my scalp. I open my eyes and look at my phone: it's 12:44, not even a second later it's 12:45. That snuck up on me. I'll listen to one song, and then I'll go shower right after. After the song, I tell myself I need to get out of bed and achieve things. I'd let myself just stay in bed, but I've made a new rule for myself: I can't stay indoors for more than three days straight. It's day four, so I have to go out. Usually, I only go out to see Mia, so oddly she is still the force behind getting me to leave my home.

After I shower, I dry off in front of the mirror. For the last few weeks, I have avoided looking at my body. Today I make myself look; I face my shrinking self. I know people can tell that I'm thinner in my clothes, but being naked now, I can really see how much I've lost. Like most people, I have a fucked-up relationship with my body. I've been called fat a bunch of times in my life, mostly in middle school, and it stays with me no matter what my weight is. I absorb all the bad things and forget the good. When I was in high school, I tried pretty hard to lose weight—tried to convince myself that salads didn't need dressing to taste good, and that if I ate cashews very slowly, eight of them were a filling snack, and walnuts were even better because it takes time to crack them out of their shells. As I got older, I had no clue if I was still fat or chubby or whatever you want to call it, and I wondered if people didn't mention it to me anymore because they weren't as honest, and cruel, as kids can be.

I'm not even sure I thought the skinny girls looked better, but I knew I didn't like my body being bigger. I've never been skinny—people let you know when you're skinny—but now I've lost weight even though I didn't mean to, and I'm thin, lean, for the first time. My collar bones are more pronounced, like waves on the surface of the water, and some of my rib cage is visible when I suck in. I run my finger along a bone. My belly button looks like an open mouth when I stand up straight. Before it looked more like a frown. I used to be a B cup, but my breasts have been drowning in my regular bras, so I've been using a bra from when I was thirteen. I still have hips, and thighs, but I'm trying to figure out where my ass went. I think I'm nearly as thin as I used to hope to be, but it doesn't look good on me. Even my face looks off—I look older than twenty-four. I liked how thin I was when I started losing weight a few months ago because people were telling me I looked good. They asked what I've been doing differently and expected to hear a workout routine, not that I'm staying in bed and not eating. Now I don't like how I look smaller—I look half-assembled. I miss the softness and shapeliness of my former body. But I wonder, if I gain all the weight back, will I hate it again? I have clothes that I ordered online that were too small for me when I bought them—puckering buttons over my chest and material stretched too thin and tight over my hips and ass. While the clothes fit now, they're outdated and look cheap. I bend at the waist and collect the fat from my stomach in my hands, squishing it. I find it oddly comforting. I wonder if there's a weight that I'd like my body at, or if I'm doomed to be unhappy with it, for the sole reason that it's mine.

I sit down on my bed, think about looking for a job, or maybe even writing, and then I lie back down in bed, and cover myself with my sheet. My hair is soaking my pillows. I hear my phone vibrating. It's Dylan. I ignore the call. It's usually only ever Mia, Dylan, my mom, or sometimes Anne. The list of people who used to contact me was longer, but they're probably sick of trying. I'm surprised Anne hasn't given up. I rarely respond to her.

I spend the next forty-five minutes scrolling through accounts on Instagram of girls who have the lives I want. They have twelve-step skincare routines containing vitamins and oils I've never heard of but are deemed by influencers to be crucial if you don't want to be an ugly crone. These women have musical friends and go to book launches of writers they know; their jobs are important and creative and they act like it's no big deal. Their bedrooms are lit like a film set, so a photo of the top of a dresser with vintage perfume bottles and delicate jewellery looks like a still from a Sofia Coppola film. I realize people share only the best of their world from the most flattering angles on Instagram, but there is no lighting that would complement the cat hair, cracker crumbs, and crusty nail polishes of my bedroom.

My bedroom is so small that it is really a bed-room; my bed takes up almost the whole room. There's a narrow space between the bed and wall, so there's a black mark on the wall left by my shorts because my butt hits the wall every time I go past the foot of the bed. I used to wash it off with soap and water, but it builds up again every few days, so now I just leave it. There are piles of clothing throughout my room: some of the clothes need to be washed and others aren't dirty enough for the dirty pile but aren't clean enough for my closet or dresser. There's no on-site washer and dryer, and the laundromat is such a trek, so I've really lowered my standards when it comes to determining if clothing is clean or not.

There's an unopened package on the floor by the door. It's been there for months. An ankle-length red satin dress is inside the box. I was so excited when I bought it. I'd look at the dress online multiple times a day, zooming in on the model and clicking play on the video to watch her long slight body move in ways I imagined myself moving—ways I've never moved before. She was smiling—but not too much. She looked confident, and the wind found her hair in a flattering way, and I was sure it would find mine too once I had this dress. I pictured myself wearing it to a book launch, maybe even my own book launch. I don't have a book deal, and I haven't written a book, but this dress is meant to be worn by someone who has accomplished things. I followed the tracking of the package closely. When the dress finally arrived, it was too hot inside my apartment to try it on; I didn't want to sweat on the delicate fabric. Every day, I thought of excuses not to try it on because I knew it wouldn't look right. It would be too tight in some places and too loose in others. I'm definitely not tall enough for it. So now it sits by my door, still in the box, collecting dust, and I feel guilty every time I look at it.

On my wall, there's a small gold mirror that Mia hung for me. It's too high for me to look in, so I see only the top of my head reflected in it. There are postcards from an Impressionist exhibition taped thoughtlessly all over my walls. They make the room look even smaller. I stare at these paintings for hours; they're beautiful with all the soft blues everywhere, calming sedative blues and warm pink tones. But something is kind of frightening about them too, the blurring and the uncontained colours, everything spilling into everything else—faces blending into backgrounds as if everything could be wiped away.

Feeling the bumps and divots in the wall with my fingertips, I think about all the time I've wasted today. I should be looking for a job. I got almost nothing for severance pay, but I get a little in employment insurance each month. I don't think I can look at my resumé right now. I should try to write. I haven't submitted my stories anywhere for months, not that I've ever been published. I open my laptop and my face suddenly feels hot, so I close my laptop and crawl into the fetal. It feels like there's static on my face, and my throat feels tight. It's happening again. I feel on the verge of tears for reasons I can't fully understand or articulate. If you tell someone you feel like a worthless loser, they'll say you aren't. If you tell them that Earth is a bad place, they'll say yeah, kind of, let's get margaritas.

My phone vibrates again. It's Dylan. *hello alice. Are you dead? Text me either way.* I worry he'll come over to confirm I'm not dead if I don't respond soon, so I text him back and we plan to meet up for lunch tomorrow. I do kind of miss him, but I don't think I have the energy for conversation. I'd rather not go, but I've been avoiding him for weeks, and I have to keep up appearances or else he'll worry, and that's something else to deal with. I grab some Melba toast off my dresser and take two bites. My chest is decorated in crumbs. I wash it down with water that has probably been sitting too long—yes, it tastes like metal and eggs. I touch my head, and notice that my hair is almost entirely dry. I open the dating apps Mia added to my phone. I haven't opened them in about six weeks because dating apps are a fruitless hellscape. Guys asking if I've listened to early Incubus albums, scores of uninvited dick pics—the veins! the nests of hair!—and many messages that just say *hey*. Why would I respond to that? The message at the top of my inbox says *I can tell by ur face you have a tight pussy.* Okay, that was a mistake. I know not all men are bad, but a lot of the bad ones message me. I've initiated contact only twice on these apps. Both times were rare moments of late-night slightly drunken confidence. Both times, I received no response. I wish I could tell them that I tend to make bad first impressions, but that you might start to like me after four to six weeks.

I close the app and start looking for jobs. I find my old job listed among many other administrative jobs, and it makes me feel like shit, especially because the only thing I've achieved today is charging my phone to 100 percent. I decide to go visit Mia.

As I step outside, I'm blasted by a wall of heat. The humidity makes me feel like I've been drinking rum for days. Music and films try to convince you that summer is a sexy time when everyone is wet, the sounds of cicadas climaxing fills the air, and that should also make you want to fuck for some reason. In the '80s, wild sax represented summertime eroticism. Is everyone only acting like they love summer because other people do and they're trying to fit in?

It's only a four-minute walk to the subway, but the sun is so bright that it sparks a searing pain in my head. My mother would say that the weakness could be caused by my poor diet—I don't think there's loads of protein in Melba toast. The sky is the colour of a blue freezie. I reach the station and descend into the subway.

I see the sad flower guy from the other day. As he walks by, he stares at each of the four women on the platform without trying to be inconspicuous. He stops in front of me. He moves so that he's directly in my eyeline. He smiles. His teeth are only a few shades from Dijon. I pretend to text someone, but his next action is one that I can't ignore. He reaches into his shirt pocket. He pulls out a crushed pink tulip with a tiny stem and a small card.

"You look elegant. I'm looking for an elegant lover."

"This must be a slow day for you."

"What?" He looks confused, but he pushes the flower toward my hands.

"No, I don't want it. Thanks." I look away, but he doesn't give up.

"So, can I have your number?"

"Well, I don't have a phone right now. I'm in between phones."

He looks at the phone in my hand.

"Yeah, this is my friend's phone. I really needed one today for a job, a job that I am doing, where I need a phone, so I can't really give you her number, since I'll only have it for, like, a day,

26

and it's not even mine." I am ashamed at my inability to concoct something more convincing.

"Okay, well, can I have your email address for now? I guess I can get your number when you get a phone."

I'm trying to think of a way to say no when I feel a hand graze my lower back. Confused, I turn around and see a man, probably in his thirties, with heavy Marlon Brando–like eyebrows.

"Hey, babe."

I don't say anything. I don't understand, but flower guy has fled the scene.

"Just doing you a solid. That guy is a creep. I saw him earlier approaching women, like a lot of them."

I note that he has said *women* and not *girls*. Even I forget that I should do that. I thank him for intervening.

He picks up the card that the flower guy dropped on the ground. "Certified lover, trained in the art of seduction and lovemaking."

The man who helped me is still standing beside me, but I don't know why. I notice him looking at my legs and I look down to see if there's something stuck to them. He asks my name. I tell him Alice and he laughs and tells me his name is Alex. Is he hitting on me? I can't be with a man who saved me—he'll end up holding it over my head in arguments. If we were together, people would call us Al and Al. People will say "Al," and we'll both turn; we'll have a joint email address; we'll name our kids Alan and Alana. He probably thinks that I think that would be cute. He probably thinks that I think this is fate.

"Really? Your name is Alex?" I ask a little too aggressively.

"Yeah?" His dense eyebrows knit in confusion. "You think I made it up? Why would I lie?"

I don't think I should answer.

He smiles and asks, "Do you want identification?"

I consider. This is the kind of thing I would kick myself for not doing if he ended up being a cannibal, and I find myself waking up in a makeshift cage made of human femurs in his basement.

"Sure, if you're offering."

He doesn't look convinced that this is a normal thing to do, yet he gets out his wallet and hands me his driver's licence. His name is Alex, Alexander. What's wrong with me?

I walk into room 432, and Mia's lips are Barbie pink. She has her weaving loom out, which is a good sign because it's only when she's feeling okay that she can weave. If she's too nauseated, she can't focus on the patterns. She's making a wall hanging for the living room in our apartment and said she'll hang it there when she's finished her treatment and is out of her parents' house.

I bend over to give her a hug, but she blocks me by putting up both her legs and her arms to protect her body.

"You're so sweaty!"

"I know. I caught a glimpse of myself, and I look like the damp meat they serve you here."

Mia laughs and says it's true. "I'm kidding, you look so hot right now. I've never been so horny." She knows I hate that word.

I step into the bathroom inside her hospital room. The bathroom feels muggy. There's a plastic container bolted to the wall filled with syringes and other bloody wet things. I turn on the shower and stick my head under to cool off. I take a towel and dry my hair. I look in the mirror and mascara has collected under my eyes. I look like a bandit. I leave the bathroom.

Mia scrunches up her nose at my wet hair and laughs. "You're just not one of those people who looks sexy when wet."

"I guess that's subjective because I met someone this afternoon who would probably disagree with you, Mia."

"Were you harassed on the subway again?"

"Yes, twice actually, but the second time was kind of nice."

Mia looks confused.

I summarize the episode to Mia and she responds to every beat with wider eyes and pantomimes an excited child by clapping her hands.

"You have a date? When?!"

"Tomorrow. Mia, calm down."

"Aw, your first date!" She's kidding about the first date thing, but I refuse to laugh. It's tough for me to talk about relationships and sex with her because she almost always treads into condescension.

She opens her arms for a hug and expects me to come to her.

"I'm not hugging you. Am I really that hopeless? Is it that shocking that I'm going on a date?"

Mia drops her arms. "Oh, come on. Don't act like you don't know what I'm talking about. You hate everyone!"

"I'm not that bad." I walk over and sit on the end of the bed.

"Alice, you give people, like, three seconds to impress you, and if they're not everything you've ever wanted, you're done with them."

I shrug. I haven't had much experience with relationships. Every time I develop feelings for someone, I discover some vital flaw in our pairing. That's not always a failing on their part—sometimes there's something I know they want that I can't provide so I give up. Mia is the person I'm the most honest with, but I won't tell her this, not all of it. I tell her that I'm selective, which I am, but it's a reductive way to describe my problems with intimacy. She thinks I'm just too critical. She prides herself on her advice-giving and on her ability to parse others' desires and insecurities, so she would feel wounded that she hadn't got this right about me. Mia never dates anyone longer than a year as she gets bored easily. She can be cold when she ends things. When she tells me I dismiss people quickly, I want to tell her that at least I don't leave them suddenly when we've already formed a real relationship. Sometimes I find her advice on dating and sex a bit smug, and while she wants to help, I think she finds it amusing on some level that I can never make anything work.

"You know how I hate pigeons?" I ask Mia.

Mia looks exhausted before I even begin. "Yes, why?"

"I hate them because they're ugly, uninteresting, and not unique to our neighbourhood—"

Mia cuts me off. "No, I'm not asking you why you hate them, I am asking why the fuck are you talking about pigeons?"

"Because, Mia, I had a moment with a couple of pigeons last week. And they really were a couple. I like pigeons now."

She looks bored, but I carry on with my story.

"I saw two pigeons necking with each other, but it was more like one pigeon trying to coerce the other into necking with it. It rubbed its ugly neck on the identical ugly neck of the other pigeon. The pigeon resisted and wanted nothing to do with the pigeon making the moves. And I immediately thought, do you have the right to be picky? And then it climbed on the other bird's back as it was hunkered down, you know, all vulnerable. The bird was standing on the other's back, legs completely straight! The under-bird almost gave in and settled for the bird it didn't want. But then—it shook that squatter off, it tumbled onto the pavement. I thought, yes, I admire this bird. That's my whole philosophy on love and relationships right there."

Mia was silent for a moment. "I realize this is not the solution to most things or maybe to anything, but I think you desperately need to get laid. When is the last time you had sex?"

"Did you even listen to the story?"

"How long?" she presses.

"It's been a while."

"I've had sex more recently than you, and I've been a mutant for months, so you need to get on that."

"You're not a mutant."

Mia brushes off my last comment. "It's good you have a date tomorrow, you should probably have sex with him."

"I just met him!"

"You don't have to be so sentimental about sex."

I want to say *seximental* but I bite my tongue.

"I'm not sentimental. I could go months longer. Sometimes I think sex is overrated and people are only looking for a confidence boost."

Mia looks horrified. "That is not why I have sex. It's the friction—don't belittle friction. And if I have feelings for them, then it's the intimacy and love or whatever."

"Maybe I just haven't had great sex."

"I know you haven't. So, try tomorrow, for me. If you get laid, it's kind of like I'm getting laid. You're fucking for two now."

I've been at the hospital for hours. It's almost dusk. Walking to the subway, my body feels weighed down. Lately I get this heaviness in my legs, shoulders, and head, and it's a struggle to move my body in a simple way, and then I feel pressure in my forehead like I'm going to cry, and sometimes I do. A breeze brushes over my face, and I feel a little lighter. The time right before dusk is almost perfect—warm and cool at the same time—and the sky is more than five colours, and everything seems slowed down.

Lying on my bed with my cat, Gus, my phone rings, and I see that my mom is calling. I'd better pick up because I ignored two of her calls earlier today. I answer. The gist of the conversation is that I tell my mom that I'm being productive and getting lots of writing done and have applied to many jobs, and that I'm eating, and working out, and enjoying the weather, and seeing lots of friends, and that I'm breaking out into song regularly like a character Julie Andrews would play. The problem is that my mom knows me fairly well, and she knows that even at my best, I'm never that cheerful, and I never work out, so I'm pretty sure she knows everything I just said is bullshit.

After the call, I lie in bed hoping to fall asleep. I've never had an easy time falling asleep, but in the last six months, my insomnia has become much worse. I've been so desperate to cool down that I've started to soak my sleeping tank top in cold water and wring it out before I wear it to bed. I've also started to go to bed with wet hair and to moisturize my entire body, especially my feet. When that doesn't work, I sleep with an ice pack on my chest.

But it's not only the heat that keeps me up. Turning off my thoughts is crucial. Sleep is impossible without this action, or inaction. I try to place a black sky in my mind, to stop my thoughts completely, but it's difficult. Any successful compartmentalizing I do during the day falls apart at night and thoughts push through. Sometimes when I close my eyes, I see violent images, like a wolf tearing apart a rabbit, and I panic and don't want to close my eyes. The image just came to me one night, and

I've had a hard time forgetting it since. I know I have to focus on the black, but sometimes it isn't possible. I worry about everything and everyone. I worry about living incorrectly. I think about conversations from years ago and wonder if I hurt someone, gave them a complex, and maybe they've lost sleep fixating on the dumb thing I said. I worry my heart will stop working. I think about time passing as I lie awake, and the rest I'm missing. I calculate the hours until I have to wake up and then I think about how I'll never sleep and then I think about how tired I'll be in the morning. I won't sleep tonight.

Chapter Three

Last night I clawed the wall so hard that I broke right through, and on the other side, it was autumn, and Mia was there with hair down to her ankles.

My heart was beating so fast last night that it felt like it was swelling, becoming too big for my body to contain, like it might crack my rib cage or ooze between my bones. I put my cheek against the wall—it didn't help. I took two Gravol and felt nothing. I put my hand to the foot of the bed, to feel around for Gus, and felt that he was there—that helped a little. I began to think of other things that make me scared like sexual assault, and I felt agitated and had to assure myself that my apartment was safe. I turned on the lights in my room. I grabbed the baseball bat that I keep by my bed, and I looked under my bed and in my closet. Then I went into Mia's room, looked under her bed and in her closet, and I checked the bathroom, and the kitchen, and living room—okay, no violent men or rabid animals. I started worrying about fire and checked the stove and unplugged the coffee maker and toaster.

I got back into bed and turned off the lights, but then it was too dark, so I plugged in the blue string lights that I have hanging up on the wall above my bed. Blue has always calmed me, and the lights, though dim, have a way of making things look safe. An hour later, I drank some water and assured myself that I wasn't dying, though I kept my phone close, in case I started to, not that I'd know what it would feel like. I thought, maybe I am dying now, or am about to, and my heart is warning me to call someone. I went to sit in Mia's room, but it wasn't any better in there, so I tried the living room, but my heart was speeding in there too, and my eyes felt like they were burning. I sat on the counter in the kitchen, and that didn't work, so I got into the bathtub. I do this when I'm panicking at home. I travel from room to room, thinking that something there will make me feel better, but I feel the same in every room.

Last night was a bad night, but no night is ever an easy sleep. I'm definitely a high maintenance sleeper. I listen to the same song while I try to sleep, sometimes I listen to it multiple times. It's nearly twelve minutes long and is mostly instrumental with soft singing. The noise of the fan is also a must as it's a consistent and reliable sound. I'm not sure if I'm afraid to hear the sounds that my apartment makes, or if I'm afraid to hear nothing at all.

Usually, I prefer the room that I sleep in to be as dark as possible, but some nights I need to be able to see my room and see outside when I look out my window. When I was a little kid, I was afraid of the dark, and my mother used to say that even the sun is afraid of the dark and that's why it runs away before night comes. I guess I can also blame her for my poor grades in science.

I check my phone and see I have a text from Dylan asking if we're still meeting at 12:30. He knows he has to confirm many times with me because I've been breaking plans with him a lot. I forgot we had a lunch today. I was hoping to lie in bed all day to conserve my energy for my date with Alex. It's been weeks since I've seen Dylan and I know I can't cancel on him again or he'll really start to worry. After my shower, I put on clean clothes, blow-dry my hair, and put on a bit of makeup. I look in the mirror and decide that I look all right.

As I approach the restaurant, I see Dylan coming toward me. He's smiling, but then his mouth sinks into a frown. He says, "Hey, Nosferatu, I think we need to feed you." I know he's kidding, but his comment stings. Dylan's never been great with comedic timing.

His insult is followed by a hug, and I'm sure he notices how much more compact I feel than usual. Dylan looks professional in his white dress shirt and grey tie, and I suddenly feel sloppy in my old jersey dress that's fraying at the hem. He's come a long way from when I met him on the first day of undergrad. He was wearing a grey hoodie, which was plain but looked like it was made of expensive soft material, and tight black jeans with the ankles rolled up imprecisely, as if he had followed a tutorial but failed. We had to pair up to discuss a poem by John Donne about a flea that was also about sex, because everything is, and then tell the class our impressions. Dylan kept fidgeting in his pants, pulling at his thighs. I tried to pretend I didn't notice. He must have been aware that his restlessness was quite conspicuous because he told me he didn't usually wear pants so tight, but he knew the types of girls he likes want guys to wear tight jeans. I tried to suppress a laugh, but I couldn't help but let it out. He then said I don't know why I told you that, and I said perhaps the jeans are cutting off blood flow to your brain. I told Mia what he'd said to me, and she was certain he was hitting on me. I told her no, he is too good-looking to be into me. I said he was trying to get advice from me and was hoping I was friends with the types of girls he liked. That's the role I often played in high school.

Later that day, I saw him in another one of my literature classes, but he was wearing Nike sweatpants tapered at the ankle. Mia was in that class too, and the three of us soon became close. Dylan is from a small town, and he grew up playing basketball at school. He was considered a jock, but he was always pretty bored by his friends. He had girlfriends all throughout high school, and he was attracted to them physically, but he found their conversations lacking the depth he had seen in films. *Before Sunrise* kind of fucked up his expectations for romance. He felt bad telling his girlfriends that something was missing between them, so when his girlfriends would tell him they loved him, he'd say it back to spare them hurt feelings. One weekend, Dylan went to see some bands in a bigger city about an hour from his hometown, and he met girls who wore thick black eyeliner and band T-shirts, and he realized these were the girls he was looking for—the artsy types who conversed about Topics of Substance, like arthouse films and philosophy, and could speak, vaguely, about politics. I came down on him hard for lumping women into categories based on their appearance even though I often make the same assumptions about people. During that first year in undergrad, Dylan slowly fell out of touch with his friends from high school, and he, Mia, and I formed our own circle.

We walk inside the restaurant and sit at a burgundy booth with tears in the seat cushion. There are paintings on the walls of fully dressed people in various sexual positions, and these are accompanied by high contrast black-and-white photos of sewer grates and stop signs. The menu is one page, one sided. Dylan's menu is laminated and mine isn't. I'm assuming Dylan doesn't come to this place with his colleagues.

Dylan runs his fingertips down the length of his tie. His clothes look exactly the right size for him, and I realize he probably had them tailored.

"Look at you. You look like Michael Douglas in every Michael Douglas movie. About to get caught in some mysterious woman's web."

He smiles slightly without making eye contact with me, still looking at the menu, rubbing his facial hair, which is not full enough to be classified as a beard. His hair looks recently cut, but he's kept it how he usually keeps it—short back and sides, longer on top. Dylan always looks clean. I guess that's a rich person thing. Most people probably wouldn't call him rich, but he puts money in a savings account each paycheque, so he's rich to me.

Even though it's the afternoon, Dylan still has pillow creases on the side of his face. I am envious of how deeply Dylan must sleep to get those creases. I bet he slips into unconsciousness as soon as his cheek touches his pillow. He trusts that it's safe to shut himself off and be vulnerable in his bed. I would pay to be able to do that.

Dylan pulls me out of my fixation on his sleep lines. "I'm sorry for that Nosferatu comment. That was a dick thing to say. I haven't seen you in weeks and that's what I say?" He rubs his neck and shakes his head.

"Don't worry about it." I look down at my menu.

"I think I was surprised to see you looking . . . Were you sick or something?"

"Yeah, I had a flu and couldn't really eat," I lie, feeling slightly guilty but knowing he won't press me on it.

He touches the tips of my fingers. "You okay now?" Dylan's nails look freshly clipped and buffed.

I pull my hand away to put my hair behind my ear. "Yeah, I'm fine, but I still have to eat lightly, so I'm just going to get a soup to not upset my stomach too much." Also, it's less than six dollars.

Dylan looks back down at the menu and I see the tiny indent in his nose that never fully closed up after he took his nose ring out. The tight jeans weren't his last aesthetic attempt at attracting the art girls he was attracted to. Mia and I went with him to get it pierced, and Mia got a labret piercing right under her bottom lip, which she took out two months later, and I got second holes in my ears because I didn't want to emphasize anything on my face. I thought Dylan was good-looking the first day I met him, but I became extremely attracted to him after he got the nose piercing, which is embarrassing. I tried not to show him that I was develop- ing feelings for him. But Mia could tell. She said she knew because I seemed to make fewer dumb jokes and choose my words care- fully when Dylan was around. And also one morning I freaked out when he stopped by our dorm room before I had showered.

After we order, I try to think of something to say so that he won't ask me about my body or about what I've been doing (nothing) for the weeks I've been avoiding him.

"So, is work good?"

A smile creeps across his face. "Alice," he says flatly.

"Yes?"

"You never ask me about work."

"I do!"

He laughs quietly. "You don't."

"Well, I am now."

"You think my job is boring."

I grin but try to force it away. "No, I think your job is smart and practical!"

He covers his face with his hands. "That means boring."

Dylan was not a big reader as a kid, but when his older sister came home from university on the weekends when he was about sixteen, he looked through her books from her contemporary American fiction class. The required reading in high school didn't interest him, but he realized he enjoyed books. He started taking English courses in first year, but he switched to a business focus in second year after doing research into the kinds of jobs and lack-lustre salaries he could get with an English degree. Dylan is one of my closest friends, but I don't understand what he does at his job. I only know it involves money and he needs to wear a tie every day to work. Even though he's been successful in his career and he's only about two years in, he seems deeply insecure about his job because he doesn't work in *the arts*. He doesn't want certain people to think he lacks artistic sensibility or empathy, and it seems like every time we get together, he makes a point to talk about books and films. I always tell him that people who work in the arts are insecure about their jobs when speaking to people in other fields because they often don't make much money and some people view their work as trivial. Not that I work in any field at all.

"Most of the people in my office are pretty boring though. I know we complain about art snobs, but the boring office people are brutal too. Can you believe that someone from my work who's our age saw me at the grocery store, obviously out of my work clothes, and asked me if I was *alternative*?"

"What does that mean? Do people still say *alternative*? Did she mean your clothes or something?" I ask.

"I guess."

"What were you wearing?"

"A black T-shirt and jeans that I cut off at the knee because it's so hot out and I needed something to do errands in."

"Well, that *is* pretty alternative."

He gives me a fake annoyed look.

When our food is delivered, the soup is too hot to eat.

"So, why are you at work in a suit on a Saturday?"

"Clients from Finland are here, and they could only meet today. They fly out tonight."

I make a face at him to show him I feel for him and also that maybe his life sucks.

Dylan's watch catches the sunlight, and it captures my attention. I wonder if he noticed the threads coming loose from the hem of my dress.

"Yep. Working life is pain," he says.

"I wish I were still in school. I feel all my knowledge draining out of me. I forget things, like the endings of books. And the other day, I forgot what the word *incredulous* means."

He finishes chewing a bite of his enchilada and nods. "Yeah, we didn't know how lucky we were as students. I guess Mia is the only one out of us who actually gets to avoid work hell."

I turn my head away from him and focus on the way a man is chewing with his mouth open. "That's a fucked-up thing to say."

"Come on, she's the one who always says that. I didn't mean it seriously."

I look down at my soup. "I don't want to talk about this anymore."

I hear Dylan say sorry, and I can tell he means it. He seems like he'd do anything to take it back.

After a long, weighty silence, I ask Dylan how things are with Eva, the girl he's been dating for a while.

"We broke up like a month ago."

"What? Why don't I know these things?"

"Because you ignore my texts, and you only ever leave the house to—"

I cut him off. "I know I've been weird lately, I'm just . . . *off.* I'm sorry about Eva. Why did you break up?"

"Oh, come on, you know I wasn't really into her."

"Why would I know that? If you're dating someone, I assume you're into them."

He smiles thinly and rests his head on his palm with his elbow on the table. "I think I was just lonely." He looks at me.

I pick up a napkin to wipe my mouth even though I haven't eaten anything yet. "So, I guess you're okay about the breakup then."

"Yeah, she wasn't my type."

"You used to talk about having a very specific type, but you've dated all different types of girls."

"I have a type—but they're just not very accessible, so I settle."

"Oh, come on, Dylan, you don't exactly have a hard time getting laid."

"No, but, like I said, I can get lonely."

"Lonely and looking for the company of sensitive art girls?" I tease him.

"Don't hold dumb things I said and did when I was eighteen against me. I don't do it to you."

I smile. "Okay. So, you are interested in certain girls, but they're just not *accessible*?"

"Right."

We both say nothing for nearly half a minute. I think he's in love with Anne but will never tell me. They slept together years ago and dated for a few weeks. My feelings for Dylan started fading after that.

My eyes search the room for something to comment on to kill the silence. Our server thinks I'm trying to get his attention and comes over.

On the way home, I walk into a store new to the neighbourhood. The name is ordinary with a minimalist window display of rocks and old vials and bottles, which are blue, white, and brown. There's a wire-haired dog by the door who looks like it has a complex and expensive diet. I walk inside and the store doesn't have much in it: mostly candles, various tinctures in delicate vessels, planters, books on tarot and tarot cards, totes with breasts or political messages on them. I pick up the most gorgeous bowl I've ever seen; it's ceramic and cream with blue speckles all over it. It's big enough for a bowl of cereal but not big enough to be a fruit bowl. Adults have bowls like this. When I have money, I will buy this bowl, so people know they are in an adult's home and that I have a full life and care about the space I live in, selecting things, carefully, to fill it. I turn over the bowl to see the sticker with the price on the bottom: $88. I try to make a face that communicates that I think this is a reasonable price and will consider buying it since an artfully dishevelled woman in an oversized ivory blouse, who I assume is the owner, is watching me. I pick up some soap and lift it to my nose. I make a note to myself to also buy some adult soap someday soon. People will come over and wash their hands in my bathroom and think, wow, what taste she has. And later on, after they've left, they'll get a whiff of the soap and think of me and how impressed they were with my soap, and with me.

"French lavender and rosehip," says the owner. "It's divine."

I nod. I imagine trying to say the word *divine* in a sentence, out loud.

I feel pressured to buy something, but I don't have the money. I pretend to feel a vibration from my phone. I leave the store, not sure if I seemed believable.

In front of the store, I feel a hand on my shoulder. I look at my accoster's face and see a tall girl with her hair cut short and dyed silvery blonde. Her bangs are long, skimming the tops of her arched eyebrows. She has a full face of makeup on, but somehow she manages to look subtle and effortless. She's iced like a cake, one that would win money on one of those cake shows on TV. This is Anne, but she introduces herself to new people as Anastasia since Anne is too plain for *someone like her.*

When Anne moved to our city, no one tried to be friends with her because the groups had already been established, and there wasn't any place for her. For the first couple weeks during recess, she sat alone in the field behind our school, eating a green apple. She'd eat it the same way each time: she'd first bite a line around the centre of the apple, and it would look like the apple had a white belt on—a defined waist. Then she ate all the green away at the bottom, and then the top. Then she'd throw it on the ground behind her. I tried eating apples like that after I saw her doing it, to see if I had been missing something. Mia and I and our friend Jenny watched Anne. We thought that we were witches after constantly watching the movie *The Craft.* We had assembled our own prepubescent coven, and we needed a fourth witch because everyone knows there have to be four witches to call the corners (North, South, East, and West). Mia recruited Anne as our fourth. I was hesitant about her, but Mia convinced me to give her a chance. We tried to perform spells; we were all pretty sure we made Anne levitate one night, and we think we made Ashley Rankin, eleven-year-old sadist, get acne. Jenny's family moved away when we started middle school the following year, and even though our interests veered away from witchcraft and refocused on whose breasts were growing the fastest and how the fuck you use a tampon, the three of us remained close.

But three is a tough number. A ménage à trois makes no sense to me. I imagine two people are having a good time pleasuring each other while the third is forgotten at the side of the bed, and maybe one hand of the other two is lazily, thoughtlessly flicking or rubbing something on the third person's body. This problem isn't solely a sex problem—there's always someone left out in a group of three.

When Jenny moved away, it was tough on Anne because Mia and I were closer and we had a history. She felt alienated sometimes, not understanding our inside jokes but laughing anyway. Mia and I would squeeze each other's hands when this happened, silently acknowledging to each other that it was weird for Anne to laugh at something she couldn't possibly understand. Mia called her out on it once, and Anne didn't talk to her for a week, but she had no one else, so she eventually forgave her.

Anne and I both relied on Mia. She defended me in elementary and middle school, and she did the same for Anne. Anne got a lot of attention from guys and was often called a slut regardless of how she behaved. Mia threatened anyone who hurt us. Mia's fearlessness got us into trouble sometimes, like when she declared tampons should be free and stole them from a pharmacy even though none of us had our periods yet. We got caught, but she took the blame. She also pierced her belly button and mine and Anne's when we were bored one night. I never planned on wearing anything that was navel-revealing, but when Anne said she was in, I didn't want to be left out. I was nervous, and Mia said on three—one, two, but then I said, No wait! And she stopped, and she said okay, I have a plan. Close your eyes (I closed them), picture a field, a serene field. Then she said, What do you see in the field? And I said deer and flowers. She said describe the flowers, and she jammed the needle through the skin of my belly button while I was distracted talking about the dark centre of the flowers. All of our piercings got infected, and we had to wear loose shirts. In gym class, Anne got hit in the stomach in dodge ball and fell to her knees in pain.

When we got to high school, we met new people and these people had parties. At first, I refused to go to a lot of these parties, thinking everyone was so pathetic to desperately want to fit in, even though I was also afraid to not be liked. But Mia was so outgoing, and Anne, though shy in middle school, gained confidence as she began to get a lot of compliments on her looks. Mia and Anne started going to parties together, and that's when they realized how much they had in common. I worried they'd become too close and decide that they didn't need me, so when Mia would beg me to go out with her, I started to say yes. And sometimes it wasn't awful and I made some other friends who I thought of as backups for Mia, but most of the time it was all overly sweet drinks and greasy boys pushing themselves against girls, any girls. Mia didn't seem to mind that I followed her around like a needy shadow, but I made sure to have another friend at parties to talk to so I wouldn't have to stand alone if there was somewhere I couldn't follow Mia. The best parts of those nights were the shaky, drunk walks and bus rides home when I would do mean impressions of the assholes at the party and Mia would laugh and pee a little. Anne would walk home with us too, but eventually she started to leave with other people.

Mia did everything first. She got her period first, drank first, smoked weed first, learned to drive first, had sex first. She discovered masturbating first, asking me and Anne, Do you ever wipe yourself with toilet paper after peeing and it feels really good, so you keep going? She would find the weirdest videos on the internet. I remember one time, she made us watch this video of all these snakes fucking in one giant, tangled, undulating mass; she explained there was only one female but a ton of males vying for her attention. As she recounted the fine details of snake sex, I begged her to stop saying the word *cloaca*.

Mia and Anne talked about sex and dating a lot, a topic I had nothing to add to, other than the occasional dumb joke, which often got me laughs but also sometimes elicited a *how would you know?* response from Anne. I listened to them talk about who they went on dates with and who they hooked up with, and I guess I listened with envy. The people I liked didn't like me back, and I didn't want Mia and Anne to encourage me to try to go for it when they had little to lose if I got rejected, so I rarely told them who I liked. But sometimes they would look at me when I had been silent too long. They'd ask me questions like who I liked and if I was nervous about having sex for the first time. Everything sex related happened later for me than them, but I wouldn't tell them about anything until months later, so I had time to assess my feelings, get some distance from it, and so I could prepare for their reactions. They often made me feel ridiculous by saying things like, Alice, you're becoming a woman, with huge grins on their faces. Their reactions felt condescending, like I was behind and couldn't possibly know what I was doing, like it was entertaining to them that I was trying.

One night, we had a sleepover at Anne's, and I told them about a guy from work who felt me up after my shift at McDonald's. I wanted to ask Mia if I was supposed to feel pleasure from someone squeezing my tits because I didn't, but I refused to ask while Anne was there. I also admitted that I gave him a hand job. Anne asked me if I used two hands, and I couldn't remember. She said it's like a pepper grinder, one hand on the shaft and one on the head, but don't like twist it or anything like that, she said laughing.

Stroke the tip in a circular motion and move your other hand up and down, slowly then faster. She asked me to show them how I did it and she handed me her plastic water bottle as a stand-in for a dick. I refused. Mia joined in and said, Oh, come on, Al. Just show us. I got up and left the room, with them shouting my name down the stairs while I walked out the front door. That night, I stayed up, imagining all the things they said about me even though Mia had sent me a ton of messages apologizing. Anne sent me one saying *sry* and I suspected Mia forced her to send it, or maybe Mia even sent it from Anne's phone. The next day, we went to the mall, Anne and I pretending nothing happened, while Mia tried to level things out by making fun of Anne for buying a thong with glitter on it. That will shred your ass, she said, forcing me to make eye contact with her so that we could share a laugh.

When Mia and I went to the same university and enrolled in some of the same classes, Anne moved to the city too, but she didn't go to school with us. I found out Anne applied to our school only after she told Mia she didn't get in. Anne told me she moved to the city at the same time as us to focus on modelling; she had done a bit of work after being scouted when she was fifteen. Once we became close with Dylan, she felt really excluded, and I guess I could see why—we talked mostly about people in our classes and what we were studying, and she had nothing to contribute. Mia told me that Anne worried we thought she was dumb and said Anne accused me of making a face after she told us she hadn't read something I thought everyone had read. I acted shocked when Mia said this, but I did feel a little superior to her for being accepted to our school when she hadn't been.

I never told Anne that I had feelings for Dylan years ago, around the time she slept with him, but a part of me thinks she knew. When they were dating for those few weeks, Anne said to me I swear I thought he had a thing for you and it worried me, but he promised me that you're not his type and he isn't attracted to you. That sort of killed my crush on Dylan. It was second-hand rejection, but it felt just as discouraging. I promised myself I'd stop wasting time thinking something might happen.

In the last three years, Anne hasn't been hanging around us as much. She has new friends—mostly cüls, and sometimes they like Mia and me, but sometimes they don't, so Anne doesn't always take the risk of inviting us out with her. Since Mia is more of a party person than I am, Anne asks her to hang out more than she asks me to. When she does invite us both out, Anne seems to gauge whether her friends think we're cool or not, and if they decide not, she'll pay less attention to us. Anne is one of those people who wants to have as many friends as possible. I don't trust people with that many friends. It seems so careless. Do these friend collectors confide in all of their friends? Imagine leaving your personal belongings all over the city. You wouldn't remember where you left everything.

Before Mia's illness, Anne used to ask her for advice, and if she didn't like Mia's take, she'd come to me. Even though we don't hang out together as much as we used to, Anne still calls or texts me when she needs advice, probably because she's been avoiding Mia and can't ask her. She values my opinion, but she doesn't always want me around her other friends. She has been having trouble with her boyfriend and texting me about it frequently, though I don't often respond. I'm a little nervous to see how this interaction will go since I haven't been very responsive to her texts. It's hard for me to feign interest in her love life these days.

"What's going on, Al?" Anne asks.

"I just had lunch with Dylan. What's going on with you?" I ask lightly, as if things between us are normal.

"No, I mean, what's really going on with you?" Anne asks sternly. I assume she's referring to how I've been hiding out, or how I lost my job, or maybe my weight until she continues. "Are you mad at me?" She looks like a baby bird, but one that I'm afraid of. She has a hold over me, and she knows it. Old friends are tricky because you may find that you have little in common after years of knowing them, and maybe you don't even really like them that much anymore, but your shared history makes it complicated and harder to turn away.

"No, no, I've just been busy."

"You don't answer my texts or my calls. I know you've seen that I've called you."

My instinct is to apologize because she seems hurt, and it would be a way out of this conversation, but it would give her what she wants—confirmation that she's still liked and not at fault. She's good at making people say what she wants to hear, to make them conform to the shape of her palm. I'm not sorry, so I won't do it. I tell her again, with no sweetness in my voice, that I've been busy.

She turns from me, squinting her eyes, and makes a show of searching for sunglasses in her bag. When she finds them, she doesn't put them on.

"Want to get a drink or something? It's after noon, so we're allowed," Anne says.

"No, I'm really hot. I could go for a popsicle or something though."

"I could go for a popsicle." Anne says it in a surprised way, like she had forgotten about the existence of popsicles.

Sitting on a bench in a park, eating popsicles beside Anne, both of us sweating in slightly see-through clothing, I feel like I'm in a Harmony Korine film.

I stop licking my grape-flavoured popsicle and ask Anne, "How have you been?" Purple sugary goo drips down my wrist, and I shamelessly lick it off.

"Max is being a dick."

"In what way?"

"Mostly I'm annoyed with the way he flirts with girls when we're out together, and I feel like a lot of people don't even know that we're actually together. I'm pretty sure they just think I'm someone he fucks. But, like, we've been together almost eight months now." Anne's boyfriend is usually called *Maxwell*. This is the name that he prefers, but I notice that when he does something that Anne disapproves of, she refers to him simply as *Max*. It's like she's demoting him.

"That doesn't sound good." I don't have the energy to pretend I care.

She looks disappointed in my lazy counselling. "So, where have you been, Alice? You've been a fucking ghost. I feel like you're avoiding me."

"I've been with Mia." I intend for this to sting.

"Is she okay?" She sounds genuinely concerned.

"Have you seen her much?" I ask even though I know she hasn't.

Anne pushes her bangs off her forehead. She runs her finger along her knees. Anne's eyes are striking, but she is the kind of person to go into detail when describing her eye colour. She can't only say brown or green. She says, Ohh, you know they're a milk chocolate kind of brown with flakes of yellowy gold in them, but then when I'm in the sunlight, they look green. I can't deny that she's beautiful though, so some of that haughtiness is warranted, I guess.

"I'm afraid to see her, Al. I don't want to see her like that. It's hard to talk about that with her. What am I supposed to say?"

Suddenly she looks so young, like a frightened kid who put on mascara for the first time. I decide it's not innocence in her eyes, but selfishness that seems inseparable from cruelty.

"There's really not much you need to say or do, Anne." I say her name so she knows I'm frustrated.

She starts to bite her nails then says abruptly, "Some people are going out for drinks tomorrow night, want to come?"

"Maybe," I say.

"Come on. No one ever sees you anymore. You should come out with us." Anne stumbles on this last sentence and I think we're both remembering the last time I went out with Anne and her friends about three months ago. Anne promised it would be a casual time at a casual bar, but we ended up going dancing. It is difficult—no—it is painful for me to force enthusiasm for dancing, and I just don't feel it unless I'm drunk with all of the other drunk dancers. So, I drank, but I felt out of place and wanted to be alone. I danced with Anne and her friends, but then I felt my face go stiff, and my teeth began to hurt, and smiling was painful. I pushed myself so hard to pull my lips open and curve them upwards, and to show my teeth, but it hurt, and the stiffness in my face took over. I became so frustrated and uncomfortable that I felt my face twitching, and my throat tightening, and I tried so hard to not cry, but it all broke through. The rest of my body wasn't in check with my head though, so my body was still moving, still dancing, while my face was crying. It must have been a terrible sight because Anne's friends stopped dancing and stared. Anne started yelling my name over the loud music, and she started touching my shoulders, and then I realized what was happening, and I stopped moving, but I kept crying. Anne took me into the washroom and asked me what happened, and I couldn't explain, so I left and got into a cab.

"They're your friends, not mine," I correct Anne.

"Claire is your friend too. She misses you."

I shoot her an unconvinced glare.

She drops her popsicle stick and lights a cigarette. I try to think of a topic that will make me seem more interested in Anne's life. I ask, "How's modelling going? Your hair is different. It looks good. Is it for a job?"

When Anne was nineteen, she was making some decent money from modelling, and she even got to walk in some shows during fashion week. Everyone thought that we would all see her in *Vogue* or *W*, but that never happened. I'm not sure why it didn't happen for her because Anne is the quintessential model: willowy with a face so symmetrical it makes you hate your parents. She still models, but it's mostly for hair salons in the city and new local designers. When someone asks her what she does, she says she models even though the money she lives off is 75 percent from bartending. She assures everyone that she still has a chance to break out in modelling, but I don't think that she even believes that. There used to be a brightness in her eyes when she talked about it, but now there's just a vacancy.

She hauls on the cigarette then releases grey smoke out of her nostrils. "It was supposed to be for a job, but it didn't work out. Long story."

I feel I shouldn't press her for further explanation, and I know it was cruel to bring up modelling at all.

Anne eyes a bus waiting at a red light across the road, and she says, "Oh shit, I should jump on that bus. I have to meet Maxwell, and that bus is super unreliable. It will be like twenty minutes 'til the next one. But I loved seeing you." She hugs me. "Come out tomorrow, Al. I'll bug you 'til you say yes," she warns me.

"Okay, I'll go." I relinquish. "Text me."

"You text me." Before she starts to walk away, she laughs and says, "Your teeth and lips are purple by the way." I look at her blankly, not understanding, as she walks backwards, still facing me. "From the popsicle."

Anne waves to me, steps on her cigarette, and then runs across the road to catch the bus. The doors close right as she arrives, but she waves at the driver and makes a distressed smile, and he opens the door to let her on. I can see from where I'm sitting that the bus is packed with people and that there are no seats available, but a young man sees Anne and gets up so she can sit down. I look into my compact mirror and see that the spaces separating my teeth are stained from the popsicle. My lips are purple and swollen. I don't know how Anne managed to keep all of her lipstick on.

Chapter Four

I showered twice today like I'm someone who goes to the gym. I intended to put some effort into styling my hair for the date tonight, but after I got out of the shower and wrapped myself in a towel, I got into bed and stared at my phone for a long time and now my hair is completely dry and flat. I got caught up reading a Twitter thread of people trashing a book that came out recently, and though no one is saying the name of the author or book, I'm pretty sure they're talking about a guy from a creative writing class I took. He called my short story "sentimental" and at first I thought it was a compliment, but I soon learned it wasn't. I try to tell myself I'm just staying up to date on current literary discussions, but I know I'm full of shit when I search Twitter for his name, the title of his book, and the word *sucks*.

Gus is chewing on an elastic at the foot of the bed, and this gets me out of bed to hold open his jaw and pull the spitty mess out of his mouth.

I look in my closet. As I step closer to push aside my clothes, I stub my toe on a heavy book that's covered in clothing. I forgot about the flowers I was pressing in the book—I meant to frame them, show my mom and Mia all the hobbies I've been trying. I pulled a few forget-me-nots from my neighbour's garden—she has a lush garden, she wouldn't notice. But I left them too long and their blue petals are now brown and folded in the wrong spots. I'm not good at this Martha Stewart shit.

I turn my attention back to my closet. I used to collect vintage clothing but never had the courage to wear any of it. I've never worn my black-and-white checkered mod dress or my pink chiffon blouse with loud, flowing sleeves. If I saw someone wearing these items, I'd probably think they were superficial and attention-seeking, but really I'd be jealous they had the confidence to wear them out. Mia often wears loud things—lots of colour, white denim, big organza sleeves. I don't think she's an obnoxious jerk when she wears them, so, yeah, I see the flaw in my logic. You can dress to grab attention only if I like you.

I put on a navy dress with white polka dots, but it doesn't fit the same as it used to, hanging too low over my breasts. It might look sexy to someone, and I don't want Alex to think I'm going to have sex with him or even that I like him, so I put on a long-sleeve black shirt over the dress and hope it looks all right. The temperature is supposed to go down tonight, so I don't think I'll be too hot.

After applying my makeup, I assess my primping job in the mirror. I look a little plain, so I take some inspiration from Mia and decide to put on lipstick. I want to be the girl who wears lipstick and pulls it off, but I have several lipstick-related concerns: I fear that it draws too much attention and that I look desperate, I fear that I'll choose the wrong colour for my skin tone and look like a clown, I fear smearing. Also, it is impossible to eat with lipstick on; the bottom lip hits the chin, leaving a lipstick soulpatch.

One time in class, while wearing a deep red lipstick, I pulled a sweater off, up over my head, and smeared my lipstick all down the front of my sweater, and it left a streak from my philtrum to my nostril. Of course, I had forgotten I was wearing lipstick. To make this truly mortifying, a professor that I had recently been fantasizing about pulled me aside as class was beginning and let me know what was on my face. I don't think that I'm cautious enough for lipstick. It's been three years since that happened, so I decide to give it another go. I salvage four old tubes from my drawers. One has been separated from its lid and is covered in some kind of crusty white film, and there are unidentifiable hairs stuck to it. I remove the lid of another tube, the deep red I wore to class, but it's half melted. Moving on to the final two: both appear to be in good condition—one is a subtle pink gifted by Mia, and the other is an orangey brown. So pink it is. I carefully apply the lipstick and try to stay within the lines. As a reflex, I press my bottom lip to my top lip and rub them together—the result of miseducation by cosmetic ads and movies. I now have lipstick all around my lips, outside the edges. Mia would be ashamed. I take off my lipstick with the towel from my shower, begin again, and resist the urge to press. Mia taught me another lesson: she told me to put my index finger in my mouth, following the application, and then to pull it out while lightly sucking on the finger, so that lipstick does not get on the teeth, and the excess lipstick comes off on the finger. She advised me never to do this final step in public as I would surely attract undesirable males.

Looking in the mirror, I think that I look pretty good, and I like the idea of being on a date. It's a story to tell. I am a young woman who dates. I pucker my lips and then smile. I remind myself that I have good teeth. Then I picture Mia lying in her hospital bed, with her painted lips, waiting for her night drip.

I don't have to go tonight. I can come see you if you want. I type the text but delete it. I look in the mirror again and decide the lipstick no longer looks subtle. I wipe it off on the towel.

Sitting on the train, I think about getting off at the next stop and going home. My shoulders are up around my ears, I feel so tense. My hands are slick with sweat. Why am I even doing this? I'm not going to fall in love. I'm not going to have sex with him. I don't even remember what he looks like other than thick eyebrows. I just want to be in bed, or to sit with Mia. I imagine myself on the date, and my tongue feels swollen like I'm unable to speak.

I text Alex. *Family emergency. I'm not going to make it. So sorry to bail.* I feel guilty, but the relief is stronger. I get off at the next stop and transfer to another line. When the doors open at a stop, I can hear a woman yelling, "Fucking kill me. Please just kill me!" as she runs along the platform. She gets on and everyone she tries to make eye contact with looks away. I worry she'll come toward me and then I feel bad for wanting her to stay away.

I walk through the hospital doors to the elevators and pause. I don't want to explain to Mia why I've bailed on the date. I don't think I can explain it. She'll be upset. She thinks I use her illness as an excuse to disengage from everything and everyone.

I turn around and exit the hospital. I sit on a nearby bench. It's getting dark. The dying light casts a blue wash over everything, making the hospital grounds look like a haunted place. I sit here until the sunlight fades entirely. I try to figure out which room Mia's in. The hospital is lit up even though it's late. Mia's machines pump all night, making it hard for her to sleep. Even with the lights off, a blue light burns on her IV machine throughout the night. A pale face appears in a window, and for a second I think it's her, but it's not. I get a notification that Alex has texted me. I don't open it. I delete it. I block his phone number.

I head home on the subway. I spot a small insect on the floor of the train and worry it's a bedbug. I check that all the zippers on my bag are closed, so nothing can get in. Out of the corner of my eye, I see a large, bear-like hand wrap around the pole right by my head. The hand moves up and down, right in front of my face. It moves slowly and then faster, in a rhythm. The bear-hand man and I are the only two people on this car of the train, so I'm afraid to look up. But I do because the hand gestures have become impossible to ignore, even with my headphones on, and I see small light eyes peering down at me. My stomach knots up, and my mouth tastes coppery. The train halts and even though I'm three stations away from my stop, I get off and run up the platform steps, almost crashing into a group of teens. I continue running until I reach a crowded street. There's a chill in the air, but I'm soaked in sweat. I lean against the side of a convenience store and try to catch my breath. I hate being out after dark. People become so volatile at night, and I don't know how to feel calm around strangers.

It's not even ten yet, but my street is deserted. Flying insects are worshipping the light of the street lamps, even if they're not sure why. Cool air drifts through the treetops in a slow rhythm that settles me.

Click, click, click. I hear a clicking sound, and on the other side of the street is the man that I saw in the denim jacket when I was leaving the hospital the other day. We are walking at almost exactly the same pace. He's going in the same direction that I am, and we are nearly parallel. I slow my pace, and I stop under a street lamp to take my phone out of my bag. At this moment, he looks back at me, and my chest burns. But he turns back around and keeps heading in the same direction. The clicking man is soon swallowed by darkness. I have my phone in one hand, and my keys in the other, with my largest key positioned between my index and middle finger in case I need to jam it into an eye, temple, jugular, or scrotum. I regularly arm myself with my keys. Nothing major has ever happened to me to make me so afraid, but the endless stories of girls and women being attacked constantly put me on edge while walking alone at night, including what happened to Anne.

Anne was attacked by a man about two years ago when she was walking home from her boyfriend's apartment after a fight. Around 3 a.m., she stormed away dramatically, but at a speed that would have allowed her boyfriend to catch up to her if he wanted to. I picture her making her way through each room in his apartment, as if searching for something, when really she wanted only to make a mess of his things and slam as many doors as possible.

Anne had lived only a short walk from her boyfriend's apartment. She glanced over her shoulder frequently on the walk home to see if her boyfriend was coming after her, but she soon realized that he wasn't.

There is a large park with tall trees close to Anne's apartment. Street lamps line the sidewalk, but the actual park remains dark. Anne knows not to go through the park at night, so she walked close to the perimeter on the sidewalk. Three street lamps in a row were burnt out that night. As Anne walked through the dark area, she told me later that she felt a kick to the back of her calf, and she fell over onto her knees. Shocked and disoriented, she didn't try to scream until she felt arms grab around her ribcage, attempting to pull her into the park. A single crackling scream escaped her throat. She tried to shout again, but she couldn't scream a second time. She felt like her voice was too far away, down deep in her stomach, and she couldn't get anything out.

Anne, and likely her attacker, figured no one else was out on the street, but what they hadn't noticed was a driver in a parked taxi about fifteen feet ahead. The driver had turned off her car to have a peaceful cigarette. The driver heard Anne's scream and saw the struggle in her rear-view mirror. While Anne was being dragged off the sidewalk, the driver swung open her door and yelled, Let her go, motherfucker! I'm calling the fucking cops right now. And I've got a fucking gun!

The attacker ran into the park, and the driver rushed over to Anne, who remained frozen on the sidewalk. She helped Anne walk to her cab, and they waited for the cops to come. She offered her the only things she had in her car—Starbursts and cigarettes. Anne said yes to the cigarette, but her hand was shaking too much to smoke it, so it just burned and ashed between her fingers. After the cops came, the driver confessed to Anne that she didn't actually have a gun. Anne filed a report. She told me that experience was another layer of trauma and thought the cops were fairly useless. As far as she knows, the attacker was never caught.

Ever since Anne told me about this, I have feared every man when I'm alone at night. I see every man as a potential attacker, and my anxiety spikes. For the first couple months after the attack, Anne had been frantic and on edge, never wanting to leave her apartment, but eventually she seemed fine, and continued on walking alone at night but only on busy streets, and avoided parks. She started carrying a small knife in her bag. She was attacked and I wasn't, but I haven't been able to stop fixating on this attack. I continue to think about it every time I'm alone outside at night.

When I make it inside, I lock the door and attach the door chain. As I'm lying in bed, my anxiety blooms, and I look out my window to confirm the clicking man isn't there. I grab my phone to call Mia. Maybe I should tell her about bailing on the date. I check the time and see it's after midnight, and I think it's too late to call her room because she's probably sleeping, and if not, I'll wake up her roommate. I don't know if she's sleeping or trying to get to sleep. Maybe she's reading or watching a movie because she can't sleep. Maybe she can't sleep because she's in pain. She said she hasn't been sleeping well, but she didn't give me many details. Maybe she gets woken up when they change the drugs in her drip, or maybe she's too nauseated to fall asleep. She told me that she tastes the drugs or maybe it's the saline they run through her between the drugs, but it's made her obsessively chew gum and suck hard candies, and she brushes her teeth more than ten times a day to get the taste out of her mouth. She says it's like how she imagines cleaning products taste.

I go to check my email and I see a new one from my mom. I open it, and the words that stand out are *I want you to try therapy.*

Chapter Five

Only three hours of sleep. Tylenol for breakfast. I try to imagine myself in a therapist's office. Do they make you lie down, or is that an antiquated practice? Do they watch to see if you lie down and make assessments based on your choice? Would lying down display my willingness to be vulnerable? Or would it reveal that I'm relying on outdated depictions from TV and films to inform my behaviour in therapy? I decide to read the email from my mom again. I open it on my laptop and see that I have an email from Mia delivered at 3:26 a.m. I wonder if I was awake at that time.

Hey Al. I'm unplugged from my IV for a bit, separated from my ball and chain and out of my room. I don't want to lie to you and I feel like I did the other day, and that really freaks me out. Because I feel like I'm kinda losing it, and you're the only one I'm honest with. When I was complaining to you about being super horny (I know you hate that word) and saying you were fucking for two or whatever . . . that was just me trying to sound normal. The truth is that I'm fucked up right now. My body has changed so much. Not just my hair, but my whole body. After being in bed all the time, and all the drugs, swelling, scars, needles, and all these nurses and doctors constantly touching me . . . I haven't even told you about the swabbing . . . I don't even think of my body as a sexual place anymore. I can't even imagine having sex again. I don't really want to talk about this in person but I needed to tell you. Please don't talk to me about this. Please don't even write back. They gave me a sleeping pill, and it's not making me sleep, just making me feel light and heavy at the same time. I think I'll probably regret this email.

xox Mia

I put my cheek against the wall and ball the duvet up and press it against my stomach. My gut is telling me to write her back, or to go to her and tell her all this is temporary, though I have no idea if it is. I have no clue if her body will go back to how it was, and I consider that she'll always have scars. But they'll lighten and turn from pink to white. I read the email two more times. I need to be cautious, even more cautious.

I look at the email from my mom again and decide to call her. Did you just get up? she asks. I lie and tell her I've been up since eight, adjusting my voice to make myself sound very awake. She says something in a sarcastic tone, but I can't make it out because there is loud banging coming from her end. I ask her what's up with the noise. I can tell she's walking through her house because the hammering sound becomes distant and dull, but she over-compensates and says too loudly that it's someone installing new tiles in the bathroom. I grumble about this—I loved the seafoam tiles. She says they're out of date, and I tell her they're classic. Now she's chewing something. Maybe a pear. I think everyone hates the sound of their mother chewing. She tells me she is re-doing the bathroom, taking out the clawfoot tub and putting in a Jacuzzi tub. I tell her it had character. She asks if I got her email. I say yes. She asks me what I think. I tell her I know she thinks I'm crazy. She exhales heavily into the phone and says, Of course I don't. She says she wants me to talk to someone. She tells me she made an appointment for me tomorrow and will email me the address. I tell her no way, that's too soon, I need to prepare. She says if I go once and decide I don't like it, she won't ask me to go again. I ask her if it's even legal for her to arrange this for me since I'm an adult. Then I accuse her of pretending to be me to make the appointment. She says she knew I wouldn't go if she left it up to me. I tell her that's a huge violation and I'll be telling the therapist about this. She ignores my threat and says, So you'll go tomorrow? I agree so I can get it over with. She asks me how I'm doing for money, and I tell her I'm going to find a job soon. She tells me I'd probably feel better about myself if I had a job. I tell her I have to go because I have to take something out of the oven. She starts to ask what I'm making, but I say see ya and hang up before she completes her sentence.

I feel bad for being salty on the phone, but she can be so inva-sive. My mother and I are quite different. She's the kind of person who can't watch a movie without feeling like she's wasting time, and if she makes it through the whole thing, she has to do some-thing while she watches it, like fold laundry or check her email. I tell her that watching films helps me with writing. This makes her sigh. I know she's worried about my career prospects and thinks I'm unfocused. She says she's proud of me. I think she might say it only to reassure herself that she's a good mother. She knows that mothers who never tell their children they are proud of them have made a vital error.

Mia was supposed to leave the hospital yesterday, but her doctor wanted to monitor her because she was very weak from treatment. I wanted to visit her around 1 p.m., but she wasn't allowed to have visitors. I've been trying not to worry about them keeping her longer even though it's happened a few times now. I've attempted to write and to apply for jobs, but I haven't been able to concentrate. I look through my social media and begin to think I'm not very smart, and even though I think of myself as being funny, maybe I'm really not funny at all. I look at photos of myself and stare in the mirror. I find myself repulsive. My features appear disproportionate. I try on some of my clothes and see that nothing looks good on my body, so I decide my body is a mess, and I'm shallow and greedy for having clothing I don't like or wear often. I assume no one likes me—they find me annoying or dull and ugly, and they all talk about these things when I'm not around. I know I should try to make plans, but the thought of having to talk about myself, especially when I have nothing going on makes me tired, so I stay in bed with my cheek against the wall.

I get an email from a literary magazine. I sit up straight in bed to give it the attention it deserves. The subject line is the title of my short story. I forgot I'd submitted it. I think that was about eight months ago. My heart is beating fast. I open it. It's a rejection. It says something along the lines of "Please stop wasting our time with your trash, you self-absorbed hack. If you subscribe now, you'll get 30 percent off a year's subscription."

I delete the email. I call the hospital and ask about Mia. They say she's feeling better and think it would be fine for her to have a visitor.

Inside the hospital, a middle-aged man in a red T-shirt that says VOLUNTEER points to the hand sanitation pump. I just sanitized my hands, but I dutifully pump while he smiles.

Mia has blue lipstick on today. She seems energetic, so I know I should mirror that. I tell her it's a nice blue, and she calls me basic, telling me it's not blue, it's cobalt. I correct her and say more like Yves Klein Blue.

She gives me a kiss and reflected in the window, I see a ghostly blue print on my cheek. I ask her why she had to stay two extra days and she tells me it was bad nausea, but she doesn't want to talk about it.

"Well?" she says.

"Well, what?" I think she's talking about the email, but I don't want to bring it up and break the rule she set.

"Your date. How was it?"

I forgot she'd ask about the date. "Not good. He was pretty boring. I won't be seeing him again."

Mia closes her eyes. "Hard for me to take your word for it because you're so damn picky. What did you talk about?"

"His work and my lack of work. Honestly, it was so dull."

"What does he do?"

"I don't even remember. Something incomprehensible like Dylan. Bank something?"

"God, you are a snob."

I let my mouth hang open, pretending to be offended.

"Where did you go?" she asks.

"The Persian place—the one beside the swimming pool we broke into last summer."

Mia's face turns hard. "You're lying to me. That place is closed for repairs from a fire."

I'm caught in my lie. "I bailed on him. It's hard to explain."

"Try."

She looks disappointed, and I want to distract her, make her laugh, but she's being stern with me now.

I tell her I'm not at a place where I want to be meeting people, how I don't like myself right now. She asks when I will like myself and I don't know the answer.

"You're a really frustrating person," she says.

I look away from her because I can't argue with that.

"You know you're not the one who's sick, right?"

I grab her hand and ask her to please not be mad at me and tell her I promise to try harder and push myself. I cringe at how pathetic I sound. I wouldn't act like this around anyone else. She doesn't say anything, but she squeezes my hand and it isn't forgiveness, but I'll take what I can get. Usually, she's tougher on me. I can tell she's exhausted.

She lets go and tells me she needs some gum from the hospital gift shop. I tell her I'll get it for her. I take longer than I need to, picking my split ends in a washroom stall. When I get back to the room, I notice her mood has changed. She thanks me for the gum and asks if I want any. I don't want gum, but I say yes because it makes me seem amiable and I want to keep her in this good mood.

"So, I heard you and Dylan had a lunch date?" A half smile creeps up one side of her face.

"Mia! I know what that Katie Holmes smile means."

"You two just need to let love happen, or fuck or whatever."

I'm surprised she'd bring up sex after her email, and I try to meet her eye to see if we're allowed to talk about it, but when she looks away, I know the answer is no, and so I move on.

"Do you have a calendar reminder to bug me about this, like, every three months? It's never going to happen."

"You've been weird around each other for years. I'm not making it up. You two are so annoying."

"I don't have feelings for him anymore, and I haven't for a long time."

"Since he had sex with Anne. Like he's a tainted Victorian woman or something."

"That's not true. But he is in love with Anne."

"He is so not! Anne's hot, but who cares? Your ego is bruised because she got there first."

I stare at Mia. I know you're not supposed to be angry at sick people, but I am. She thinks she knows me better than I know myself. I know better than to think about Dylan in that way now. And it's not because he slept with Anne. I don't think I'm meant to be in a relationship. I don't know how to do it. And it doesn't matter because I'm almost certain Dylan still cares for Anne. They dated briefly, but Anne met a new guy and stopped talking to Dylan. At first, neither of them would show up if the other was around, but in the last year or so, they have been more mature about enduring each other's company. I catch Dylan looking at her from time to time when he's not in her eyeline.

I tell Mia that I know she's trying to help, but she has to believe me when I say I don't want anything more with Dylan. I'm considering telling her that I don't think having a partner will make me happy when her machine starts beeping.

I panic, run out to the hallway, find a nurse, and bring him back to the room. Mia tries to tell me to relax—she says it's probably just an air bubble in the line that interrupts the infusion, and that happens all the time. The nurse looks half-asleep and confirms it's a small air bubble. He tells me to chill and tells Mia he'll be back in two hours to change her drip.

A clock with a timer on her bedside table goes off, and she puts her fingers into a little white paper cup and removes a large green round pill, a small blue round pill, two long rectangular white pills, and a translucent red fat oval pill and drops them into her mouth all at once, and takes a big swig of water. She grabs an aging banana from her tray, peels it, and eats half, and then puts the remaining half of the banana back on her tray. After swallowing, she explains, "I have to eat food when I take the white ones." She adds, "Can you believe I can swallow all the pills with one sip of water now? I used to do them one at a time." She's acting oddly peppy now. I want to ask her if she's okay. Before I can say anything, she continues. "So, Alice, are you doing anything tonight? I bet my plans are better."

"Not much, actually."

Mia looks disappointed.

"Well, Anne wants me to go out with her. I ran into her. But I really don't want to go."

"Oh," she says flatly. There's something humming under the surface of her skin, but she's trying hard to conceal it.

I shouldn't have mentioned my plans with Anne. I try to redeem myself by telling Mia I don't want to see Anne.

"I don't care if you see her. You can see whoever you want."

I know her casual voice, and that's not it. I feel like I should say something more, but I don't. She's told me before that Anne doesn't know how to focus on someone else. I agreed with her, but she didn't seem comforted. Every time I try to talk about Anne, she changes the subject. I'm not supposed to talk about her illness or Anne. She told me once that everyone has a limit for compassion and eventually reaches capacity—that they get worn down by feeling bad for you, reassuring you, seeing you suffer. I told her I don't believe that, trying to make sure she knows that I'll never get to that point. I know she tries to prevent me from exerting too much solicitude.

We sit in silence. I want to ask her when she's being released and if her family's trip to a cabin they've rented is still happening, but I don't in case they had to cancel. My stomach makes a strange gurgling sound and she laughs. I see blue lipstick on her teeth and wipe it off with my finger. I guess it's good I double sanitized.

Chapter Six

I peer out of the door of my apartment. I step onto my porch, and my street is so dark. Why did I agree to this? Excuses flood my brain: I have food poisoning; I can't find my keys, so I can't lock my door; Gus broke a window (that one's especially weak); I think I have a tick bite. Anne isn't going to buy any of these, but I'm still going to try.

I don't think I can make it. I feel shitty, I text Anne. A few minutes later she texts back, *If you're not here in an hour I'm coming to your place.* I doubt she is serious, but I'm not taking any chances.

I get to the edge of my yard and look down my deserted street. Beads of sweat form under my bangs and on my neck. I look at my phone to see how much a rideshare would cost, and it's over $15, and I decide I can't spare it because I'll need money to spend at the bar. I put my keys between my fingers and keep my phone out. I cross the street every time a man walks too close to me. I also try to walk near other women and stay on the side of the street that doesn't have cars parked on it since it's tough to see if anyone is in the cars, sitting in the dark. Or maybe there's someone crouching between the parked cars. My heart beats quickly most of the way there until I hit a busy street and there are people everywhere, though now my social anxiety is ready to take over and shine.

I don't think that I've been to this bar before, but a lot of these places look quite similar, so it's difficult to remember. It's dimly lit, probably to encourage romance, but it's so dark that I can't really make out the colour of the walls. I would say it's definitely somewhere between deep red and aubergine. A few weak overhead lights and four kitschy lamps (one is a ballerina caught in the middle of a fouetté; one is a stag's head; one is the Statue of Liberty, and of course its bulb acts as the light from the torch; one is a panther with the bulb in its mouth) are responsible for lighting the entire bar. There are wooden rectangular tables that have been painted white all around the room. There are also two sunken-in black couches with little white polka dots on them and a baroque-style chaise longue that looks light blue, but the poor lighting leaves the true colour unidentifiable.

Anne is sitting at a table with two young women and one man. As I approach the table, I try to get Anne's attention by doing a kind of crouch walk to get in her eyeline. She doesn't see me, so when I stand right in front of the table, I crouch even lower, which invites unfriendly head-to-toe staring by everyone at Anne's table, and when Anne finally turns around, she gives me a small smile and says flatly, "Oh, hey, Alice. What's up?"

Her reaction makes it seem like she's surprised, and not necessarily pleased, by my presence. I have to assume that her lukewarm reaction has something to do with an impression she's trying to make on these people whom I've never seen before.

Anne is wedged between one of the girls and the guy, and was engrossed in conversation with the girl, with her back to the guy, so I take the seat on the other side of the table beside a pretty girl with long dark hair. Her hair is perfectly parted down the centre, and even though it's dark in here, I can still tell her hair is shiny. I wonder if she has any of those short pieces, the fly-aways, that stick up from my hair when I'm trying to make it look smooth. She's wearing a loose men's T-shirt tucked into very short but high waisted denim shorts. Her body is curvy and soft, and I want mine to look like hers, and I think maybe it used to but not filled out in the right places. Girls this pretty intimidate me and make me feel ridiculous for even trying to look good. If I hadn't been friends with Anne for years, she'd make me feel the same way. When these beautiful girls talk to me, they're probably only thinking about how much prettier they are than me. I feel like a toddler in my blue denim pinafore dress and white-and-black striped T-shirt. I wonder if Mia has ever met these people. Mia and I can never keep track of Anne's network of friends, acquaintances, and sycophants.

The pretty girl turns to me and says, "I love your dress. Where did you get it?"

"It was actually my mom's."

"Vintage. Awesome!" She's so animated she's a fucking Care Bear. She tucks her hair behind her ears, and I see she has silver earrings and cuffs all up her ear and only one tiny stud in the other. How do people know to do this?

I say thanks and try to sound energetic, but I flail. There is a pause in conversation. "I'm Alice by the way." I put out my hand to shake hers.

She takes my hand into her velvet palm. Of course she's smooth. "Hi, I'm Zoe." Zoe looks at Anne. "Anastasia is a terrible friend and forgets to introduce people."

Hearing this, Anne breaks from her conversation and says,

"This is Alice. Alice, that is Zoe, obviously." Anne touches the back of the other girl, who's short with a long low ponytail. "This is Naomi." Naomi smiles, without teeth, but does not make eye contact while doing so. Anne then lays her hand out in front of the curly haired guy to her right, palm up, like how Vanna White would reveal the lit-up puzzleboard on *Wheel of Fortune*. "And this is . . ."

He looks at me nervously, then looks at Anne. "Craig, my name is Craig."

Anne leans against Craig in flirtatious defeat. "Oh shit! Sorry, Craig! I'm terrible with names."

"It's okay. I don't mind." Craig is far too accommodating. I wish I could tell him Anne's had many nameless admirers, but I don't know if that would make him feel better or worse.

Anne looks at her empty glass, frowns performatively, and says, "I need a drink. Anyone else?"

"Yeah, I'll just have a pitcher of sangria," says Naomi.

"Al, what about you?" asks Anne.

"No, I don't think I'm drinking tonight."

"You're at a bar. You're with me. You're drinking," Anne insists.

"Okay, gin and tonic, I guess."

"You're having a double G&T," says Anne.

"Okay, sure, whatever," I say.

Anne turns to Craig and nudges him with her shoulder. "Do you want a drink, Craig?"

He looks at his nearly empty beer glass. "Yeah, yeah, I could use another."

Anne keeps staring at Craig, and then she asks in a voice noticeably higher, "Would you mind, you know, getting them for us?"

Craig jerks his head backwards. "Oh yeah," he says while standing up. "Of course, no problem!"

"Thanks! You're the best," Anne says to Craig while staring at a photo of a woman in a bikini on her phone, zooming in on her stomach.

"I'll come to help, Craig. You can't take them all by yourself," I say.

Craig looks relieved and is about to respond when Anne reaches across the table and gestures at me to sit down. She says, "Don't insult him, Alice. Craig works at a restaurant, right?"

"Yeah, it's no problem. Vodka water, right, Anastasia?" Craig asks.

"Yes! You have such a good memory!" She looks at everyone at the table, and says like a proud mother, "And we've only met once before this!"

The look on Craig's face makes it seem like they've met a few more times, but he just turns around and walks toward the bar.

Naomi laughs. "Oh god, he's going to fall with all those drinks! By the way, Anastasia, Craig said that he is a *line cook*, he isn't a server."

Zoe covers her mouth to pretend to hide a laugh, and Anne says, "Well, I mean, he is in a restaurant, and he's seen how servers balance drinks"—she pauses—"I believe in him." The girls laugh while I glance over at Craig.

Naomi and Zoe are both looking at me, but in different ways: Naomi has an icy glare fixed at my face but has yet to make eye contact with me, and whenever I look at her, she turns away. Zoe, on the other hand, is also observing me, but in a less lethal way. When I catch her, she says, "Sorry for staring, I just really like your hair."

Me? I hope she isn't saying this only because she thinks my hair is bad and I've caught her staring, so she thinks she has to compliment it to explain the staring.

"Oh, you have nice hair too," I tell Zoe. Maybe she really does like my hair. I know I shouldn't question compliments so much. I should say thank you instead of fighting them. Mia told me to stop doing that. I like that someone with nice hair thinks that my hair is nice. I can't help but think that compliments from attractive people feel more valuable than those from unattractive people. I like myself less for thinking this.

Anne adds, "Yeah, Al, your hair is looking good these days. Much better than that blonde pixie cut you tried a few years ago." She laughs. "God, what a mistake! Some people just can't pull off short hair." She tucks a strand of her short hair behind her ear.

I laugh coolly. "Yeah, you've seen me through some awkward hair phases." I don't know why I help Anne make fun of me. I wonder who else thought that I looked bad with that hair.

"I really like your bangs—I've been thinking about getting bangs for, like, a year now," says Zoe.

I'm growing weary of this hair talk, but I humour Zoe. "Well, these are a pain in the ass, but I need them because I have a total five head."

"What's a five head?" asks Zoe.

"It means your forehead is huge—takes five fingers to cover it," Naomi explains.

"I have a big forehead, it's true," I confess.

Anne says, "She does need bangs, but you're adorable other than that, Al." Anne actually pinches my cheeks. "We all have our imperfections. I'm a total freak—in comparison to the length of my thighs, my calves are way too long."

"Yeah, I've been meaning to tell you that you should never wear shorts," I say to Anne.

Zoe laughs and Anne glares at me.

Craig returns with a vodka water in his left hand, my gin and tonic wedged between his left wrist and his chest, and a pitcher full of Naomi's sangria in his right hand, and an empty glass held between his arm and torso. Craig quietly asks Naomi to move her bag off the table so he can put the drinks down. I notice that Craig was unable to get a drink for himself. Craig slips back to the bar to grab himself a drink.

Zoe's eyes are on me again, and she asks me, "So, Alice, where do you live?" Usually, Anne's friends aren't so friendly, so Zoe makes me nervous; it makes me think she wants something from me. I try to ignore my suspicions and accept that she's kind.

"Actually, I live about a twenty-minute walk north of Anastasia. I've lived in the city for six years."

"God, I haven't been that far north in forever. What is even over there?" Naomi asks. I pretend not to hear.

"So, how have I never met you?" asks Zoe.

"Alice is a hermit. She doesn't leave her apartment. Tonight is a big step for her," Anne says.

"I don't think I've quite earned hermit status. I'm just busy doing other things. I don't spend that much time at the bar." I mean for this to insult Anne, but I don't think she caught the dig.

Anne smirks and it's a cunty smirk. "Alice wants to be a writer. She's working on a novel. Alice's goals are a little ambitious, but I think they're sweet."

When people find me interesting, or compliment me in any way, Anne usually finds a way to insult me in a backhanded way. She knows she's being mean but gets caught up with trying to impress people. The next day she texts me and asks me if I'm okay because I was "being weird" and she was "worried." That's her lazy way of apologizing.

Sensing the awkwardness in the air, Zoe says, "A writer? That's cool. What's your Twitter handle?"

"Oh, I don't have one. I look at tweets, but I don't post anything."

"Oh, okay. I thought all writers had them."

"They should," says Naomi.

In a moment of uncomfortable silence, we all take a sip of our drinks. Craig returns with a beer in his hand, and announces sheepishly, "My sister's best friend is here, so I'm going to talk with her for a bit, but I'll be back, okay?" Craig sounds as if he is asking permission, and I think that he might be.

"Okay, see you later," Anne says indifferently.

"Craig kind of sucks," Naomi declares shortly after Craig's departure.

"He is sweet though. And I never have to pay for my drinks with him." Zoe defends him, kind of.

"Sure, but what's his deal? You know?" Naomi asks.

"I know, I don't know," Zoe agrees.

I don't understand what they've agreed on.

A girl with stringy bleach-blonde hair, wearing a sheer black top with a see-through bra underneath, paired with neon-green vinyl shorts over fishnet stockings, walking on five-inch black patent leather heels walks by our table, toward the DJ's booth. Seconds later, her clone walks over to the same area.

"Do you know them?" I ask Anne.

"That's Fine and Dandy. They're DJs. I can't believe you've never seen them, they DJ everywhere. They have a residency at Dick's Pussy," Anne explains.

"What's that?" I ask.

"You don't know it?" Naomi wrinkles her brow.

"Do you know Richard's Cat?" Zoe asks.

"Oh yeah, that's by my old dorm. I know Richard's Cat."

"No one calls it that." Naomi sounds annoyed.

"Clearly someone does," I say.

"They're twins," Zoe informs me.

"No, no, they're a couple," Naomi corrects Zoe.

"Honestly, I've heard both," Anne tells us.

I look at the time on Zoe's phone when she answers a text and wonder if I've been here long enough to consider it a proper night out.

One of the lamps in the bar, the Statue of Liberty, has burned out, so the bar is even darker than before. I have to pee, but I can't see anything that looks like it could be a washroom.

I'm about to ask Zoe if she knows where the washroom is, but before I can, a woman with a billow of gold hair arrives at our table sobbing. Her back is turned to me, I can't see her face. Across the table, Anne stands up and the woman embraces her with force, almost knocking her over before burying her face in Anne's shoulder. She's close enough now that I can tell it's Claire.

Claire always said she looks like Jayne Mansfield. I don't think anyone other than Claire has made the comparison, but I guess she supposed that her giant tits, hourglass shape plus curly blonde hair (not like Jayne Mansfield's at all, more like Glenn Close's in *Fatal Attraction*, which is still pretty cool) equal Jayne Mansfield. She could have suggested she was a Marilyn Monroe look-alike, but I think in her mind, she took the more modest route by proclaiming Jayne Mansfield her doppelgänger. She is so used to being hit on that she often mistakes everyday activities and actions for come-ons. Once we were out walking, and a man was riding a bike, and he signalled with his hand to show that he was turning left, but Claire mistook this as a wave to her, and she smiled and announced to the rest of us that he was a babe and she hoped he'd come back. Claire is the type who thinks doing drugs and fucking ugly men make her deep, and I often wonder if she enjoys doing these things or just likes how they sound.

Claire's face is reddened and her makeup smeared. In between sobs and sniffles, Claire manages to spit out, "Marcus fucking cheated on me!"

The music has progressively got louder in the last twenty minutes, once Fine and Dandy took over, so the volume of conversation has risen, and Zoe looks puzzled and asks me to repeat what Claire said, and although Naomi most likely did not hear either, she says, "Marcus fucked up, probably."

I tell them both, "She said Marcus cheated on her." I try to look sympathetic, but I didn't even know that she had a boyfriend, so this news doesn't make me feel much. Regardless, I should show Claire some compassion, so I go to put my hand on her arm, but I'm thwarted by Anne who leads her away from the table. A string of multi-coloured lights hanging from the ceiling has been plugged in and leaves an odd bruise of colour on everyone's faces; the colours look like they're crawling over their faces as they move.

"I wonder if I should go with them, to see if she's okay," I say to Zoe. Naomi heads to the patio for a cigarette.

"She probably just wants Anastasia there. It's just that she doesn't even know you, so she probably doesn't want to talk about that in front of you, you know?" Zoe says.

"Actually, I've known her for years."

"Really? Did you meet through Anastasia?"

Anne and Claire met through me. I met Claire at the bookstore on campus where she worked. We had conversations about books, but now that I think about it, I had been talking, and she had been agreeing with me. I didn't even notice because I was trying to be a very serious scholar with original insights about literature, and I was too nervous to ever speak out in class, so I would test out my theories on Claire. I thought that her great mind had similar ideas about literature as my great mind, but she was merely an ass-kisser. She was friendly to me because she saw me with Dylan, and once she found out that we weren't a couple, or even sleeping together, she thought the route to Dylan was through me. I didn't realize that Claire was using me until I had known her for about three months. Dylan was not interested in Claire and felt uncomfortable about her attempts to wrangle his attention.

Claire never had any trouble winning male attention, but she seemed to recognize that this attention was purely sexual and fleeting, whereas men were enchanted by Anne. Anne was usually cold, and sometimes cruel, but she knew when to be sweet, and she could do anything she wanted because she had a face that seemed to make people think she was special. Claire and Anne are both attention-seekers, and Claire is an attention-seeking opportunist. She thought that by being seen with Anne, she would get more attention. Claire attached herself to Anne through me, and once she became bound to Anne, Claire and I unravelled. Claire and Mia have met a couple times at parties, but Claire was always aloof around her. I wonder if Anne has told Claire about Mia's illness, and if she has, was it only to elicit sympathy for herself?

I know Zoe is waiting for my response to her question, but I suddenly feel the energy draining out of me. I attempt to speak, but it's as though the words get stuck on the bumps and grooves of my tongue. The music sounds muffled, and I can still feel the bass. All the colours and light in the room move in waves like some electric ribbon. Something hard and heavy is pressing against my spine, and the pressure becomes unbearable, and it's searing hot now and travels up my back, burning it, all of the hairs go up on my arms, the pressure rests in my throat, and I can't breathe, and then it shoots up into my head, as fast as a bullet, and I can feel hot wetness in my eyes.

"ALICE!"

I open my eyes and see Anne, Claire, Zoe, and Naomi all staring at me holding shot glasses filled with liquor.

There is one in front of me.

"We're doing breakup shots, Alice. Come on."

"I'm not drinking tonight," I say quietly.

"Did she say she's not fucking drinking?" Claire, her makeup now fixed, asks Anne.

"Alice, breakup shots. Claire is hurt. Drink," Anne orders.

"What is it?" I ask.

"It's good. Drink." Claire lifts her tiny glass. "Fuck you, Marcus!"

She drinks, Anne drinks, Naomi drinks, Zoe drinks, and I drink. This happens three more times in the next twenty-five minutes. I'm a little drunk now, and it gets easier to socialize.

"Who is that girl Craig is with?" Claire asks.

"It's his sister's friend or something. He's not into her if that's what you're wondering," Anne says.

"Why isn't he over here with us? With me?" I guess Claire is into Craig.

"Because he doesn't know where things are with you and Marcus, but he definitely likes you."

This is classic Anne. She encourages Claire to pursue Craig even though she knows he likes her instead. It's like Anne wants Craig to reject Claire and tell Claire that he can't be with her because he has feelings for Anne. I'd like to think that Anne isn't that self-absorbed, but it happened to me in high school. Anne assured me that a boy who worked with her at the mall liked me, and said she'd heard it from his friend. After months of her convincing me to go for it, I messaged him and asked if he wanted to go to a battle of the bands night with me, and he told me he would but only as friends because he liked Anne and he didn't want her to get the wrong idea. I told him yeah, just friends, while sweating from embarrassment. Then when I told her what happened, she made out with him soon after, and he grew more infatuated. She ditched him a few weeks later. That was the last time I asked anyone out in high school.

"I don't know. Should I try to get back with Marcus?" Claire asks.

"Maybe just wait and see what happens. You might end up back together," Anne says.

"I think you should give him another chance. He knows he screwed up, and if you make him promise that he won't do it again, then it should be okay." Zoe rewards herself for her words of wisdom with a sip of her drink.

Claire looks like she is half listening to her friends' advice, while simultaneously trying to exhibit a sort of weepy, sexy look in the direction of the table behind me. She says, "Yeah, I guess. God! I don't know what to do!"

She and I don't talk anymore, but I am a touch inebriated and feel compelled to chime in. "You can't go back to him. If he cheats on you, that's it, it's over. You can't trust him. He doesn't care about you," I say.

"Actually, he's very caring," Claire lashes back.

"Why would someone who cares about you have sex with someone else?" I ask.

Zoe looks shocked but intrigued.

"He does care about me. You've never met him. How would you even know?"

"It doesn't matter if I've met him. I just know that if someone cheats, then they don't care. Why would someone do that to someone they care about?"

"I don't know. It's complicated. It just happens sometimes. It doesn't mean they don't care. They just made a mistake," Anne explains.

"So, Alice, if someone cheated on you, then you'd break up with them? No questions asked?" Zoe asks.

"Definitely. Right away," I reply.

"What if they just kissed someone?" Claire asks.

"Yes, a kiss is still cheating."

"But what if you were really in love?" Zoe persists.

"If they did that to me, then I'd assume they weren't really in love with me," I say.

"But that's not how things work. That's too easy. I'm not saying that everyone has to cheat, but just because someone cheats doesn't mean they're this terrible person who doesn't care. Maybe you're just conceited, thinking that you're so perfect that no one should want anyone else," Anne says.

"I don't think I'm perfect. I just have high expectations, I guess."

"Maybe unrealistically high, which is probably why you've never had a relationship longer than three months." Anne does not break eye contact with me as she says this. I'm surprised she got it exactly right. Three months was my longest relationship. I was twenty and dating Adrian. He was deeply sarcastic, and we hated the same people and the same movies. At first, hanging out with him was fun because I finally felt right about everything. But then I realized he hated *everything*—that was his entire personality. He watched a full TV series that I loved only so he could tell me all the reasons he thought it was bad. I was gearing up to break up with him, but he got there first. He told me he needed to date someone older because he craved "experienced conversation."

I hate Anne in this moment. I want to throw my drink in her face, or maybe even drag her by her hair over the table, but instead I walk to the washroom.

The washroom is exactly how every other bar washroom is after 2 a.m.: it reeks of piss, every toilet is clogged, the floor is littered with paper towels, most of the locks on the doors don't work. I place toilet paper on the toilet seat, and I sit down to pee. On the door of the stall, *DON'T FUCK HIM* is written in lipstick. I look at my phone and see that I have a text message from Dylan asking what I'm up to. There's no music playing in the bathroom, so I call Dylan and find out that he has just left a bar and is not too far from me. I ask him to stop by here to pick me up and walk me home, and he agrees, but when I tell him Claire is here, he asks me to meet him outside. I see a wet twenty-dollar bill crumpled near my foot in the stall. I pick it up with a few pieces of toilet paper and pat it dry, trying not to think of what made it wet.

I know Dylan will be about another fifteen minutes or so, so I decide to wait out the time with Anne and her friends. When I get back to the table, I see that Craig is back, sitting in Naomi's spot, speaking to Anne.

"Hey, where's my chair?" I ask.

"Well, someone asked if anyone was using it and I said no, so they took it," Claire explains.

"But I was just in the washroom. I was coming back."

Anne breaks from her conversation with Craig to listen.

"Yeah, I didn't know that. You seemed pissed. I thought you left."

"Okay, well, I am leaving now. So, I'll see you around." I leave the twenty on the table.

"What, you're leaving?" Anne asks, looking concerned that I may actually be angry at her.

"Yeah, I'm tired."

Anne, still looking worried, says, "Okay, well, text me, okay? Let's hang out next week?" She stands up and hugs me. I don't hug her back.

Waiting outside for Dylan, I watch girls teeter on their high heels, and slop shawarma down their bras. A man who looks like he's in his late thirties stops in front of me and says suggestively, as all comments made by strange men after 2 a.m. are, "Hey there." His eyes are wandering, and I'm thinking he can't even see me clearly.

"You look like my dad," I respond.

Wounded, he walks away. That line always works.

I'm shaking from a chill in the air and wish that I had brought a sweater with me.

Being outside makes me realize that I'm more drunk than I thought I was. Everything sounds slightly obscured like there's something over my ears, and I'm feeling a little dizzy while watching boys and men staring at girls and women, trying to collect them and take them home like kids collecting shells on the beach.

"How's your night been?" I hear behind me. I turn to see Dylan.

"I swear, Dylan, if Anne could clone herself, fuck herself, and marry herself, she definitely would."

"Was she being a dick again?"

"No," I respond. "She was being a total cunt."

"Should I even ask?"

"Please don't."

Dylan sees that I'm shivering, takes off his Nike zip-up, and puts it over my shoulders.

"Did the cunt make you drink?"

"*Man*, that sounds so wrong coming from you."

He laughs.

"I'm a bit dizzy." I can think straight, but movement is making me nauseated.

"Just lean on me, if you need some balance."

We walk along a messy street, and every few minutes, we see abandoned after-bar meals littered along the sidewalk and suspicious streams and pools that one hopes are beverages but are more likely urine. We wade through a sea of idiots: girls walking home barefoot, holding impossibly tall heels in their hands, with bloated bellies exposed in their tight dresses; muscly guys attempting to provoke a reaction from other guys by shouting derogatory words at them; a man in a bus stop shelter rubbing his girlfriend's back while she cries and pukes in her hands, the boyfriend looks rocky himself, and ends up spitting up a bit on her back.

We turn off the main road onto a quieter street.

"Do you know that everyone looks at your face?" Dylan asks.

"What do you mean? Like, as we've been walking down the street just now? They're all drunk sexual deviants, sounds about right."

Dylan laughs. "I didn't mean just now. I notice it whenever I walk with you, the people we pass by, they all look at your face."

I'm embarrassed, and I can tell he's tipsy. I don't know what to say, so I avoid his comment by bending down to pet the belly of a tuxedo cat rolling on the pavement.

The stars glint above us.

"I never see stars in the city. This is crazy," says Dylan.

"Bright star, would I were steadfast as thou art—

Not in lone splendour hung aloft the night

And watching, with eternal lids apart,

Like Nature's patient, sleepless Eremite."

I recite these lines dramatically, mocking myself.

Dylan rolls his eyes. "You're such a nerd. Remember when you had to read that out in class, and Professor Wynne told you that you accentuated the incorrect syllables?"

"She was such a bitch, *and* she was wrong. I understand Keats. She was soulless."

"She was probably jealous of your youth."

I hear a crunching sound and realize I've stepped on a snail. "Oh, shit! I hate when I do that. Sorry, little guy!"

"Alice?"

"Yeah?"

"This is your apartment."

"Oh, right. Wow, that was fast." I take off Dylan's zip-up and hand it to him.

"Do you want to hang out a bit longer?" Dylan asks.

"I would, but I'm super tired. Thanks for walking me home. You're a nice person."

"I know, but don't tell people that."

I'm dizzy and want to get some water. I'm waiting for Dylan to leave, but he's just standing still. I say goodnight and hug him.

"Goodnight. I'll text you next week." Dylan touches my elbow. "You should probably have some water, and maybe some food."

"Goodnight, Dylan."

Lying down on my couch, I scroll through my phone as Gus rubs his face against my toes. I read an email from my mother reminding me of my appointment tomorrow. I should maybe try puking now, so I don't puke in the morning. I'm not sure that this makes sense.

In an attempt to sober up, I fill a glass with water, and drink it on my porch, in one of Mia's blue wool sweaters. It's going to be jacket season soon. Summer is almost over. I hear a *click, click, click* and see that same man, walking down my street. He is wearing the denim jacket again. He looks over at me and sees me staring at him. I frown, look away, and go back inside without checking to see if he's still looking at me. I put an extra weapon, a hammer, beside my bed before I close my eyes.

Chapter Seven

A cool breeze enters my apartment through the bathroom window. It's the kind of freshness that a tampon commercial tries to evoke. The woman in the commercial would be wearing natural-looking makeup, a white cotton sweater, white jeans—as if she herself is an extension of the tampon. She'd open the window and smile at the fresh air coming through it, seemingly unbothered that her uterine wall is shedding like mad, she's bleeding heavily, bloating, cramping up, and having massive shits. That's how amazing the tampon is.

I check my bank account and regret buying organic tomatoes last week, but I stepped into a grocery store to avoid someone from my last job whom I saw walking toward me. A writer I admire posted a photo of panzanella she had made, and I bought the tomatoes to make one too, but I know I'm not going to do all that chopping.

I open my resumé. It's just generic teen jobs like McDonald's, babysitter, and clothing sales clerk, plus my first office job out of undergrad as an administrative assistant. My resumé is written in Word's default setting, in Calibri, a bodyless font, slim and dull. I prefer a serif—I want something to hold onto. I change the font to Times New Roman, the professor's choice, then I change it to Cambria. Cambria is pretty and has curves, but it doesn't have a sense of superiority like Garamond.

I find several job postings for administrative assistants and receptionists and send nearly identical cover letters to more than twenty postings. I promise myself I won't work more than a year at any of these offices.

I really don't want to go to this appointment. I'll do it to appease my mother. She likes to remind me that I'm covered under her benefits only until I turn twenty-five, which is less than half a year away. So, I have little time to become an adult with a healthy mind.

The psychologist is Dr. T. Eccles. I looked him up and his name is Timmy. How am I supposed to trust someone with my mental health when his name is Timmy? Timmy is a child's name. Timmys wet the bed.

I put on a wine-coloured dress with a white Peter Pan collar because I think it makes me look put together and also inno-cent. But then I worry it makes me look too infantile, and maybe Dr. Timmy would deduce that I'm having trouble enter-ing adulthood, and he'll jump to a lot of conclusions based on the no dad thing. So, I ditch the Peter Pan collar and opt for a pale green dress with a pointed collar. I put my hair in a bun, but after deciding I look like Laura Ingalls Wilder, I wear it down. I put on mascara and some blush. No lipstick because I worry about the associations there. I almost put on my old leather ankle boots, but I remember that Mia told me they cut my legs in a way that makes them look short. She said this to me privately, and I appreciated her honesty even though it stung a little.

On the bus to my appointment, I read an essay by a writer a few years older than me whose career I follow closely. She has the same plain middle name as me, but it seems classic and smart and not boring on her. She tweets a lot about politics and art. Well-known people in the literary world like her posts and share her pieces. She never makes self-deprecating jokes. She thinks she's pretty. And she is, for sure. But I'm not just assuming she thinks she's pretty based on how she poses in photos on her Instagram. I mean I know she knows she's pretty because she's mentioned her beauty in essays she's written. Sometimes I hate her and want other people to criticize her for not hating herself or not pretending to not know that she's pretty and smart. But I know this is me being jealous and petty, and I realize I really admire her. I think she's actually doing it right. Never let them see you hate yourself.

I click on a Twitter account of a middle-aged woman who posts about the dreams she has. *Last night I dreamt I went on a date with a guy I met online. When he walked in the restaurant and introduced himself, I realized he was my golden retriever but my first thought was this fucking liar said he was six feet tall.* I wonder if she is making these up, or if she actually has these dreams, but I decide that it doesn't matter. I wonder if Dr. Timmy will ask me about my dreams. I definitely won't tell him about the one I had a few months ago where Mia and I were stranded somewhere without food, and after days of not eating, she told me that I could eat her, and I took a few bites out of her arms and legs while she smiled at me. Her flesh was soft, white, and kind of salty, reminding me of buffalo mozzarella.

Dr. Timmy, a man of average height, in his sixties, dressed from head to toe in beige, surprises me with some of his methods.

He hands me an illustration of a woman's body (with much bigger breasts than mine—how am I to relate?) and asks me to circle the parts of my body that hurt or where I most often feel pressure or pain. I look at him confused, and he explains that he wants to know where I feel that my emotional pain is being stored, or if I ever feel physical pain at highly emotional and stressful times, where on the body do I feel this pain. I circle my knees because I figure that that would be the least worrisome, and I guess that therapists would be concerned about patients who circled the head, the stomach, the crotch, or the heart. Dr. Timmy keeps saying the words *depression* and *anxiety* as if they are an inextricable part of me. He asks me to rate my depression and anxiety on a scale of one to ten. I was expecting that because I've seen it in movies. I have never felt as depressed and anxious as I have the last few months, but I don't feel that I have earned these big words. I can imagine much more stressful and depressing situations, and I know people have much more difficult lives than I do, so should I use the same words? I try to avoid talking about Mia, but I last only twelve minutes. I almost say *I am really sick*, but then I pause and tell him Mia is really sick. Every time I say her name in a sentence, I follow it up with "but she's going to be fine." And I wait for him to agree with me, but he never does, he just nods at me, but in a polite way, not in the way someone would nod if they agreed that what you said was correct.

Perhaps my preconceived ideas about Dr. Timmy and therapy prevent me from finding the session useful. I don't know if I'll go back. I worry that attending only one session won't satisfy my mother even though she said it would.

A social worker at Mia's hospital suggested group therapy for her family. Mia told me they didn't need it. Mia and her family are very close, like the kind of family who has secret recipes and runs marathons together. They were like this even when Mia was getting in trouble at school for threatening people who fucked with us. I've never seen her get heated with her parents. Anne says this is because she's an only child, so they don't have to love other children and are very patient with her. Anne says this as the third daughter in her family who feels she doesn't benefit from being the baby and is considered last or even as extraneous—her sisters are much older and her parents weren't trying to have more kids. But I'm an only child too, and I'm not close with my mother. When she tells me she loves me, I feel annoyed, and I can't articulate why. I know it's a bad quality. Mia and her parents rent a cabin up north together every year, and she insisted they continue the tradition even while she's sick. They're up there now since she has a bit of time until her next round of treatment starts. I texted her a few hours ago, but she hasn't responded. I wonder if she's canoeing. It would be good to see her outside in nature. I call her phone. It rings several times and goes to voicemail. I don't leave a message, but I send her a couple more texts.

I need to distract myself from the scenarios my brain presents to me when she doesn't answer: she had a dizzy spell and hit her head on a rock, she went on a hike too close to bears, she tried to prove her good health to her family by shooting rapids in a canoe and broke her femur like Burt Reynolds in *Deliverance*. I try to focus on writing since I haven't done much of that, at all really. I start from the beginning of my manuscript and get three pages in, and the screen appears blurry. I decide to lie down and close my eyes for only fifteen minutes, and get back to my manuscript right after. Forty minutes later, I wake up to Gus lightly batting my nose with his paw. How is it that I can't sleep at night, but I pass out in a room full of sunlight? Gus is meowing and asking for more attention. I move one hand over his head with my eyes still closed.

I close my laptop because I know I'm not going to write. I have wasted the afternoon. I have wasted many afternoons.

I heat up a box of lentil and black bean soup. It's hot but tastes like nothing, it's just hot mush. I pour it all in a container and put it in the fridge even though I know I'll never eat it. I turn on the TV. Another wedding show. Women crying because their dresses don't fit properly. Other women crying because they're not the ones getting married. I watch for twenty minutes. My mom is calling me. I ignore it. She leaves a message; she's just checking up and hopes my appointment went well.

Dylan texts me: *hey! I got tickets to some band's ep release party tonight. Want to be my plus one? You'll probably say no, but there'll be lots of people there for us to make fun of so you should say yes.* I respond: *sorry. Dinner isn't sitting well tonight, i'm feeling off, so i wouldn't be any fun anyway. Some other time.* I realize after I send the text that that text roughly translates to *I'm shitting a lot.*

I try Mia's phone again. It just keeps ringing. My thumb hovers over her mom's number in my contacts, but I decide that will be my last resort. Her parents used to field a lot of my panicked questions in the early days of Mia's illness. I probably overwhelmed them. I became another young woman for them to worry about. I noticed they stopped giving me updates from the doctors.

I put on a bad TV movie to keep me distracted. The title font drips blood. It's about a new woman in the neighbourhood who befriends another woman, and the new woman is nice, so nice that she can't be trusted because she wants to kill the woman and take her husband. These movies are always about that.

I check my email. I haven't received any word from the jobs that I applied to. It might be too soon to hear yet.

I think about writing. Instead, I peel all of the nail polish off my fingernails, trying to pull them off in full sheets. Then I reapply my nail polish. A blue so light it looks white. I look at my kitchen from my living room and see that I desperately need to do some dishes. I do the dishes. My nail polish is already peeling off again.

I wake up in the middle of the night, shivering. A flat sheet will no longer be sufficient coverage. I reach for the blanket at the foot of my bed, pull it over me, and grab my phone. Nothing. I try to tell myself that there's bad cell reception where she's staying. I turn on the blue lights and stare into the bulbs until my eyes slowly close.

The next day, while feeding Elton, my fish, a red male betta, I notice a white bubbly foam clouding the surface of the water in his bowl. The fish was an impromptu gift from Dylan. He was buying socks in some chain store, which also sold fish and hamsters, and he saw the red fish and thought I would like it, so he bought it for me. At first this seemed incredibly kind, but it later occurred to me that this gift was perhaps too impulsive, and maybe even careless. Dylan did not consider that cats like to kill and eat fish. Elton has spent his whole life in Mia's room, and we have to make sure that her door is closed so that Gus does not kill Elton. This can get stressful. We worry: did we close the door when we left? I wish we could text Elton to see if he is okay/alive. The same day that Dylan gave me Elton, I said to him I'm going to be so sad when he dies. I then considered his life: confined to a bowl, a small bowl, alone, never to love or make love. I, someone who claims to be an animal lover, contribute to Elton's captivity. But I also eat dairy and wear leather, so I was a hypocrite before Elton anyway. I can be lazy about my convictions.

I told Dylan how I felt about the fish. He groaned but then suggested that he take Elton. I considered this plan but ultimately decided this would be a form of rejection (to Dylan and Elton). Dylan mentioned something about a fish not having much of a memory and that I was overreacting. I decided that I would never own a fish again after this one, but that I would make this one's life happy. I change his water regularly, I got him a little cave hide-out thing for his bowl and got him two kinds of food. So, when I see the white foam, I assume the worst—Elton is dying. I look it up and the first few hits on Google inform me that the white foam is actually called a bubble-nest and it means that the fish is happy and is ready to mate; the fish blows bubbles, and the bubble-nest is meant to attract females, and it is intended as a place to deposit their eggs. Yesterday, a doctor asked me to rate my depression and anxiety on a scale of one to ten. Today, my fish is so pleased with his life that he feels he is ready to start a family.

Beside the fish bowl, there's a photo of Mia, Anne, and me at our high school prom. An expensive and fairly uneventful night. Anne is wearing a simple silver silk dress with spaghetti straps, looking like a '90s Calvin Klein model; Mia is in a short, purple sequin dress and her hair is wavy and almost down to her waist; and I look gothy and miserable in a black bob and black tulle strapless dress that I had to yank up the entire night. I look at the other framed photos Mia has in her room. There's a photo of Mia, Anne, and me at summer camp when we were around thirteen, the ugliest age for me: sperm brows and a retainer on my top and bottom teeth to correct an overbite. Mia had gone to that camp since she was seven, and Anne joined her after she moved to our town when she was eleven. Mia told me that Anne cried for the first few nights because she was homesick, and Mia found this irritating, telling Anne it's only one week, and what are you even sad about? This upset Anne even more, and the next day, she refused to leave the cabin. That night, Mia crawled out of her top bunk and into Anne's bottom bunk to calm her down. Anne got used to camp at the same time the boys started noticing her. When Anne and Mia came back from camp, I begged my mom to let me go for one week the following summer because I didn't want to be left out. They had matching gimp necklaces and stories about people I didn't know. My mother said it would have to be my one gift for the year, and I'd have to contribute some of my own money. For months, I saved the money I made from babysitting this kid who claimed there was a ghost living in her broken computer.

Camp was mostly terrible for me. I wasn't good with bugs, I hated wearing bathing suits in front of strangers, and I had to go on an overnight canoe trip and shit outside, but not being with Mia and Anne was worse. Mia loved sailing and made us go often. The three of us would take a little Laser boat out on the lake. When the wind would pick up and we would speed through the lake, Anne and I would get nervous and scream, worrying that we would capsize. Mia said that we were babies, and explained that you just get wet, and then you have to step on the daggerboard on the bottom of the boat, and push down with your weight to get the boat back up again. Once she admitted that she tipped us on purpose to show us that it wasn't that bad. We all thought it was fun, and it became a game that we would play; one of us would try to make the boat tip at an unexpected moment. In the photo, we're standing in bathing suits. Anne is in a red string bikini she stole from her sister, Mia is in a neon-pink one piece with mesh over the stomach, and I'm in a white-and-blue striped one piece with straps that tied at the shoulders. We're squinting from the sun, standing in front of the docks.

Gus slinks around my ankles, petting himself with my legs. I guess I didn't close the door firmly and he snuck in, so I pick him up, and he leaps from my arms onto Mia's dresser knocking bottles of creams to the floor. I pick him up and drop him outside of the room, shutting the door. He wails dramatically and pokes his grey paw under the door. I put the bottles back and notice that none shattered. I think they're all hard plastic, not glass. I pick up a small pale purple bottle of cream. I pump some out and rub it over my hands and neck like I've seen Mia do.

Mia has a blue velvet headboard that her dad made her since the Anthropologie bed she wanted was $3,000. Mia and her mom made the quilt on her bed together like they're characters in some Austen novel, prepping her dowry. I lie on the bed and run my hand over the velvet.

Sometime later, maybe an hour, I go back to my bedroom and see that my phone screen has lit up. I rush to my phone and see that Mia's called me. We never leave each other voice messages because we think they're annoying to check, so she's texted me. *Heyyy! Sorry. We were doing this dumb no phones thing all day yesterday and I fell asleep before the ban lifted. Going to see some waterfalls today with the fam a couple hours from here. Hope I don't barf in the car. See you next week!*

I am so relieved that Mia is okay. I realize I've wasted two days worrying about her, so I make a profile on a temp agency's website to try to make up for it. I press my palms into my eyes after applying to a temp agency that would assign me office jobs where I'd have to wear seven condoms on my personality to fit in. I practise my high, friendly phone voice that is so unlike my natural pitch: "Good morning, this is Alice. How can I help you?"

Chapter Eight

For days, I move between my bed and the couch. I think I've broken my rule about not staying inside for more than three days. I've barely slept even though I've been spending all my time lying in soft places.

I haven't received a text from anyone except from my mom—she sent me blurry photos showing the progress on her bathroom renovation. I resist the urge to text Mia. She said "see you next week," which I think means don't contact me until then. Maybe she's testing me to see if I can manage without her. I look at my Instagram account and realize it's been two months since I've posted anything. I look through the photos on my phone, and I find a selfie from about eight months ago. I was in a washroom at a semi-fancy restaurant and the lighting made my skin look smooth and glowing. Mia did my makeup that night, so my eyes and lips looked bigger than they are. I'm making a face that says I don't care my photo's being taken but I guess I'll look right at the lens and maybe, by chance, I'll look hot. I think I look pretty good.

I edit it slightly by increasing the brightness and the contrast. I post it without a caption. I keep refreshing my notifications, and after twenty-eight minutes, only two people have liked it and my aunt didn't like it but commented, *where is this?* I tell myself it was a bad time to post since everyone is at work and not looking at their phones. They'll look at noon when they're on lunch break, which is soon. By 1:28 p.m., only three more people have liked it, so I delete it. I look at the photo again and decide it's not so great.

I run out of episodes of a show about a celibate detective with a shameful secret, and the streaming service warns me it will play another show about another detective it thinks I will like. The show should be campy, instead it takes itself too seriously, but I don't have energy to do anything else, so it continues to play as it gets dark outside and I fall in and out of sleep on the couch.

The next day, I decide I should ask Dylan to hang out. My thumb hovers over the screen of my phone while I think of something to text him. I see the little bubble indicating he's writing to me in that moment, but then he stops typing without sending anything. I stare at the screen for a full six minutes to see if he'll start typing again, but he doesn't. If he's decided not to message me, then I won't message him.

I haven't showered in a few days. I kick off my shorts in bed, preparing to shower. I run my fingers along the grooved stretch marks on my hips. The silver tracks on my skin, charting the growing and shrinking of my body. I feel like such a cliché with my drawn curtains and loss of appetite. I have to get out of this apartment.

I decide to go to the movies by myself. When you go alone, you don't have to worry that someone won't like the movie you've suggested. You don't have to share your movie snacks with them. And I don't have to convince them that the very back of the theatre, in the centre, is the best for movie viewing; you don't have anyone behind you talking, or chewing popcorn, and you have the best view of the screen—you miss nothing.

My eyes take a few minutes to adjust to the sunlight when I step outside my apartment. Whenever I leave after being inside for days, I become panicked at the thought that anything could happen. In my apartment, I am contained.

On the subway, a teen in neon shoes points at me and makes a hand gesture I don't recognize to his friend and then smiles at me. I don't know if the hand gesture is communicating something negative or positive.

At the theatre, I'm deciding what to see. I notice a foreign title. It sounds German, maybe Danish. I haven't seen the trailer, and I'm not sure what the title translates to, but I'm feeling adventurous.

My stomach growls and I know I need to eat. I've always wanted to try the movie theatre nachos, but I've resisted. The artificial cheese looks disgusting and delicious at the same time. I give in and buy the fake cheese.

Like most matinee shows, the theatre is nearly empty. The seats I prefer are available, so I sit there. I surprise myself and eat all the nachos before the trailers begin. It feels good to be full. Guilt often follows this feeling even though I know that's deeply wrong. I don't feel guilty today; I'm pleased that I could eat all the nachos. I wipe my hands on my tights. I drink from my water bottle, but not all the water because I don't want to have to pee during the movie. The lights dim and immediately I feel less anxious than I was outside.

About ten minutes into the film, I can hear the door to the theatre open, and someone carrying a guitar case and a giant umbrella sits down in my row, leaving only two seats between us.

Why would someone choose a seat so close to me when nearly the entire theatre is empty? I can feel a scowl spread over my face. Out of the corner of my eye, I see this close-sitter looking at me. If he is going to ask me what he missed in the first few minutes, I will offer him a silencing gaze that will hopefully unsettle him and teach him to be respectful during public movie viewings. He turns to face the screen. I know I can't look at him directly because he'll see me, so I lower my eyes down and then to the right. I see curly dark hair. A black sweater, black jeans, black slip-on shoes, and a denim jacket slung over the chair. He looks back at me, and I unintentionally let out a sigh. He keeps looking at me, and now I'm nervous. What if this close-sitting stranger is a predator? How will I get away? He's blocking the side of the aisle that leads to the only exit. Usually, I don't feel uncomfortable seeing nudity onscreen in a movie theatre, but when the busty red-haired actress in the movie takes her clothes off, I lean my head against my right hand to create a barrier between the close-sitter and me. Later in the film, the actress is being choked on a small boat somewhere in Europe on a foggy day. I sink low in my seat and cover my neck with my hair in case the man near me gets ideas. I once received a message on a dating app from a man with a veiny forehead that said I had a nice, long, chokable neck. The man reaches into his pocket and I tense up, sliding my hand into my bag to find my keys to protect myself in case he has a switchblade. I hear a rustling and quickly look over to see him unwrapping a Werther's Original. The movie ends. I pretend to text someone as I wait for him to leave. He grabs his stuff and stands up. I look up, but I see only the back of him as he's walking out.

I exit through the front doors of the theatre and feel light rain. I see a grey sky and angry clouds. Then I see the back of the man. I weave around him as he puts on his jacket. I walk fast in front of him. I think that, like usual, I'm overreacting, and then I hear *click*, *click*, *click* behind me. I turn around to look behind me and realize the man that sat beside me is the man I keep seeing around who makes the clicking sound as he walks. Is he stalking me? The rain picks up and I regret not bringing an umbrella. I speed walk, and it doesn't look natural or casual in any way. Still, I hear *click*, *click*, *click* but faintly—the soft pat of the rain stifles the sound of his movements. I almost walk into two women kissing in front of a convenience store under an awning. I'm not going to turn around. I'm grateful it's still daytime. *Click*, *click*, *click*. I have to take a left to get to my bus stop. Hopefully he'll just stay on this street. I turn left. *Click*, *click*, *click*. He is following me. The rain starts beating down now, and it drowns out all other sound. My hair is pasted to my neck and the rain is weighing down my clothes. It's a warm rain, but I feel a chill sink in. I can see my bus stop up ahead, and there are at least ten people at it, so I won't be alone. The bus is coming. The bus gets there. Everyone gets on. Shit! I have to cross the street. By the time I cross the street, the bus has left.

I turn around and scream in my stalker's face. He jumps back. I clutch my bag. There are cars driving by, and I see people across the street, so I should be okay.

"What do you want?" I shout at him.

He steps away from me with one hand holding his guitar case and the other holding a massive black umbrella. "I just wanted to help you out. You're getting soaked. I have this huge umbrella, and I thought we could share it." He holds the umbrella over us. I step out from under it and back into the rain.

"Why me? And not her?" I point to another woman without an umbrella. "Or him?" I point to a soaked man trying to hail a taxi.

He looks stumped and nervous. "Because I—"

"Because you've been following me! I've seen you around, *a lot*."

He looks worried. "No, no, you've got it all wrong. I live in your area, and I've noticed you, but I haven't been following you, only now because of the rain, but I wasn't following you in the way you mean. You always seem so down, and I thought maybe you needed to talk to someone or something."

"What is your problem? You want me to smile while I walk around alone? Do you know how insane that would look?"

"That's not what I mean! I'm not a creep, I swear. I know it's wrong to expect a woman to smile. I get why that's a problem. I thought you seemed upset. I thought maybe I should try to talk to you, but I didn't know how to approach you without coming off as a weirdo. And obviously I still don't know how to do that."

"Clearly not." I turn my back to him and start to walk away. He walks around me, and steps in front of me. "Are you insane? Leave me alone!"

"Please wait. I'll leave you alone, but I just want to say that I can see now that this seems aggressive and I'm just some stranger coming up to you. I'm trying to be nice. I'm really sorry. I feel like an ass. I just wanted to talk to you." He has faint wrinkles around his eyes.

"Did you know that you make a clicking noise every time you take a step? What's with that?"

"Shit, is that really noticeable? I have a tear in the pocket of my jacket, and some coins fell through and are stuck in the lining. I can't get them out. They make this annoying noise when I walk, but I didn't think other people could hear."

"Are you stalking me or what? You say we live in the same neighbourhood, but I see you everywhere, and it's freaking me out."

"I see you all the time because we live on the same street. I moved there a few months ago. I'm not stalking you."

"See! How do you know where I live? That's stalker knowledge right there."

"Well, I've seen you go into your house, and I've seen you sit on your porch. Or maybe it's your friend's house or your boyfriend's house or your girlfriend's house or something, but you seem to go there a lot. You're always alone, so I figured you lived there."

"Okay, and why were you outside the hospital that one time?"

"I'm not sure what time you mean, but I have a friend who lives by a hospital."

"And what about today, at the movies?"

"Do I have to have a reason to go everywhere? I don't know. A coincidence? I like movies."

"Why did you sit so close to me?"

"I left a two-seat buffer, and anyway, you were in the centre back, it's the best place to sit in the theatre. It had nothing to do with you. I only recognized you after I sat down."

"Really?" I think he's being sincere.

"Really. I'm not stalking you. But when I see you, you usually look distressed. And I thought maybe I should ask you what's wrong. But I can see that this has been a huge mistake, and I'm very sorry for bothering you. I promise I'll leave you alone."

He turns and walks about ten feet away from me, and then stands there. The rain has slowed.

I stare at him.

"You know, when wanting to achieve a dramatic exit, I would suggest a storm off, which involves leaving the scene completely, rather than standing just a few feet away," I tell him.

"Well, I need to take this bus too. I'm not stalking you, but I still live on the same street as you," he says.

I wait a second, feeling bad. I walk over to him but not too close. "Hey, I'm sorry. I guess it's nice of you to worry about strangers."

"I know it seems weird. There's not a normal way to approach someone you don't know."

"To be honest, it's kind of a red flag to want to get to know a sad girl or whatever. Like you're interested in their sadness, or think they're deep because they feel this and you want in on it, or—"

"Okay, I get it. I wasn't turned on by your tears or whatever you're trying to say."

Am I being mean? Maybe this is a way people meet. I don't know if I'm being rude to a friendly stranger, or if I'm comforting an asshole.

"So, have you had problems with stalkers or something?" he asks.

"No. I'm just aware of them, the chance of them."

"Right. You're prepared."

The bus is approaching. I feel like he seems harmless, or less threatening than he did. I push myself to seem less paranoid. I ask him if we should sit together, and he tells me only if I want to.

I actually don't trust him yet, but I do feel bad for screaming in his face.

We climb the stairs and pass a group of teenagers who are hiding alcohol in plastic bottles. I choose two seats close to the back. He sets his guitar case beside him on the floor, but it juts into the aisle. We sit silently, looking out opposite windows. My eyes move over to his hands. They're slightly flaky. He needs moisturizer. I look up and I notice his dark wavy hair is a bit long in the front, the longest pieces hanging by his eyes. I wonder if his hair is naturally this way or if this is the work of preening.

As I try to think of something to say, he says, "I'm hungry."

"What?"

"Are you hungry?"

"Not really, actually." I kind of am, but I think he's going to ask me to go get something to eat, and I just want to be alone for a while. Though he seems okay.

"Will you be hungry tomorrow?" He smiles and the wrinkles around his eyes deepen. He has good teeth and full lips, and I decide I like his mouth.

"Yeah, I guess I will be hungry at some point tomorrow. Judging by history."

"Well, do you want to eat something with me? Tomorrow?"

A man in a large sweater, damp from the rain, trips over the guitar case. "Watch where you leave your shit!" My neighbour apologizes to the man. He moves his case so that it's vertical, and holds it between his knees alongside his umbrella, but he's having a hard time with all his stuff, so I take his umbrella and put it between my knees.

"I don't think I should ask him to eat with me."

"No, I don't think you should. I'm pretty sure he wants you dead."

"What about you?"

"No, I don't want you dead."

"That's a good start, but I meant, do you want to eat with me tomorrow?"

I pause. "Yeah, sure."

"Why are you hesitant?"

"Because I don't know you."

"I'm James."

"Okay, James, but I still don't know you. And a lot of people are terrible, I think maybe most people are. Even when I was yelling at you, no one tried to intervene. The bystander effect is real."

"I'm not a terrible person. Or at least, find out tomorrow. You can make that assessment."

I say okay, and he looks pleased. I can't tell if this is sweet or pathetic. Scenarios from movies flood my mind—maybe I'm the subject of some bet he's trying to win, or maybe he needs my blood as a key ingredient to unlock some ancient curse.

"So, will you meet me at three in the park by our street?" he asks.

"Okay. Do you need my phone number or something?"

"You shouldn't give your phone number to a stranger."

I look down at my palms and smirk. "My stop is next," I say.

"Mine too, obviously."

I pull the cord, and a few seconds later, we both get off the bus, and walk down our street. The rain has stopped, but the wind picks up and shakes us violently. I have to hold down the front and back of my dress.

"So, will you tell me your name, or do you have to wait until you know me better?" James asks.

I know he's making fun of me, but I still pause and consider it. There's no way he can use my first name against me. A lot of people know my first name.

"My name is Alice."

"Alice? Okay, good name."

I should ask a question now. That's how conversation works. "So, James, are you in a band? How long have you been playing guitar?"

"This is embarrassing, but I'll tell you the truth. I don't play in a band, I don't even play guitar actually. This is my brother's case, the guitar broke, so now I have the case, but no guitar." He pauses. "I carry my laundry in it. Yeah."

"You carry it so people think you play an instrument."

He shrugs.

"Wow, that is pathetic." I laugh.

"I know. It's not cool."

"No, it's really not. That also kind of makes you a liar."

He looks at me defensively. "Hey, come on. It's good for carrying laundry. Plus I was very forthcoming with that information. I could've lied."

The rain starts again and he opens his umbrella and holds it over us.

"Why is your umbrella so big?"

"It's a golf umbrella. My friend's dad won it in a golf tournament and it was the only one I had around."

"That's such a dad gift. You do realize it's comically large, right? This and the guitar case. You have too many props. It's like you're Carrot Top or something."

He gives me a look like he thinks I'm mean, but I can tell it's lighthearted.

He remembers that he meant to do his laundry after the movie, so he says he has to go do that now, but he'll see me tomorrow. I wonder if his arms ache carrying around the case and massive umbrella. The whole guitar case bit makes him kind of a twee nightmare. He might be too old to have a gimmick. But I also think I'm attracted to him.

"Oh, do you want my umbrella?"

"No, it's barely raining and I'm, like, two seconds away from home."

"I know." He winks.

"Creep!"

I turn to walk away.

This could be a mistake, but something makes me think that James might be safe. I'm nervous, but Mia will be proud I'm trying. As I walk by a neighbour's garden, the wind makes the flowers' heads nod at me.

Chapter Nine

I had a lot of trouble sleeping last night, wondering if I made a mistake about James. I drafted an email to Mia, but I deleted it when I realized I was coming across as self-involved. At 4:32 a.m., I looked at my phone, and I guess I fell asleep at some point after.

My phone vibrates. It's a text from Anne. She's attached a photo of us from Halloween years ago when we went as Bette Davis and Joan Crawford in *What Ever Happened to Baby Jane?* Mia was doing a couple's costume, Siouxsie Sioux and Robert Smith, with someone she was dating at the time. The three of us had just moved to the city together a few months before, so we didn't have close friends here. We were going to do a group costume, but Mia ditched us to do the couple's costume, and Anne and I were stuck together. Anne's text says, *You look so cute here and I look like trash.* We painted on wrinkles to make us look old, but in the photo, I don't have the aging makeup on yet. It's the only photo of us where I look better than her. She must feel guilty about the night we went out. Another text comes in. *Its like weeks away but you have to come to Maxwell's halloween party. Will send you deets later to put it in your cal.*

I check my email. There's one from someone named Meredith at the temp agency I sent my resumé to. She wants to meet with me. I know this is a good thing because I need money, but it feels bad.

As I open my closet door, I remember picking out an outfit for my last date—the date I didn't actually go on. I try to put it out of mind and pull out a burgundy sweater dress and take my clothes off. Standing naked in front of the mirror, I wonder if men have been approaching me lately because I'm thinner. I guess the flower guy was talking to every youngish woman he saw, but Alex and James? I look worse than I did before. I think? It can't be my weight. Once when Anne was drunk, she told me that she noticed guys approached me fairly often, and I thought she was trying to compliment me, but then she told me she thinks that happens because I'm not intimidating. I think she meant to suggest that I'm plain.

I put on the burgundy dress, and it doesn't fit right, so I take it off. I decide on a green velvet sleeveless dress with an oversized black sweater over top to signal that sex isn't happening. James will be disappointed when he finds out I'm not going to have sex with him. I'll probably never meet up with him again after this. I can avoid running into him by walking down side streets instead of walking on our street. I wonder if he approached me only because the proximity is convenient.

I decide to take a bubble bath. I need to relax, and women relax in tubs. Scented candles are usually lit too, but I won't take the risk of Gus knocking them over. Although being trapped in a bubble bath with a fire all around seems so cinematic. I'm out of bubble bath oil, so I take a regular bath. It's hot, and I think my body looks better through the water. Gus slinks along the edge of the tub watching over me.

I put a toothpick in the pocket of my jacket in case I need to jam it in his eye. As I button up the final button on my jacket, my phone vibrates. It's Dylan. *Dinner tonight? Tomorrow?* I respond, *Can't. Sorry!!* I turn my phone on silent.

Walking to the park, the regret is fully sinking in. I'd rather be inside alone watching something mindless and amazing like *Love Island*.

The park is nearly empty, except for two girls sharing a bag of chips on a picnic bench, and a tall man walking his tiny dog down a gravel path.

I hear my name being called, but I don't see James.

"Alice, look up!"

I follow the voice. I see James in a tree with a backpack on. I walk over to the tree.

"You look nice!"

The wind, though mild, has blown my hair around, and strands of my hair are stuck to my Chapsticked lips. I brush them off. "If this is you trying to be different, I have to tell you I hate that self-consciously quirky thing."

"Of course you do! I just thought that you'd be more comfortable up here."

"What? What are you talking about?" I shout.

"You said most people are terrible. This way, we can be away from them, and you can feel comfortable while still enjoying the outdoors."

"Did I say that? You can't take everything I say so literally."

He asks, "Are you coming up?"

I size up the challenge in front of me, consider that I am in a dress, my shoes have no treading, and I lack upper-body strength. "I'm going to be honest. I don't think I can climb a tree."

He looks around the park. "We'll go up there." He points to a jungle gym. "You can climb a ladder."

He climbs down to a lower branch. Charting his next move, he tells me he wishes I weren't watching him, so I turn around for a minute. I hear him hit the ground, and when I look back, he's wiping dirt off his black jeans.

James climbs up the red slide of the jungle gym to show me that he does not require the use of the ladder.

I applaud his slide-scaling skills. We sit on the landing area at the top of the slide that attaches to the monkey bars. Our knees touch, and my palms are moist even though the rest of me is cold.

James removes his backpack and takes some sandwiches out. He asks, "Do you like prosciutto?" The sun hits his eyes and he squints. He's got a defined jawline. I find myself predictable for being drawn to it.

"I don't eat meat actually. Sorry, I didn't realize that you were bringing food. I would have told you."

He looks into his backpack. It looks like a relic with its broken zipper and fraying fabric. "I also have an avocado and tomato sandwich. I bought this fancy meat to impress you, but I guess that's not going to work with you?"

"Is prosciutto fancy meat? I don't think so." I smirk.

"It was in the fancy meat section. What do you know? You're vegetarian."

I shrug.

"So, why don't you eat meat?"

I hate this question.

Once, when Mia and I were sixteen, she stared at me while I was eating a salami sandwich in the cafeteria and asked me how I could eat an innocent animal. Others could hear, and I think she was trying to make a statement. Sometimes she could take things too far when she was trying to prove a point and she'd get preachy and sort of aggressive. She had just watched a documentary on veganism, and I hadn't noticed that she'd been eating vegan for that whole week. I threw out my sandwich and told my mom I was vegan now, and she started to list all my favourite dishes, noting they included cheese, so I settled for vegetarianism. Mia was eating dairy a month later and back on meat three months later. When I asked her about it, she said she read an article that said veganism is classist, and she was on a hunt for the correct way to eat ethically. I continued to not eat meat, though I was unsure if it was for the right reasons.

I wipe sand off my tights. "I don't ask people why they eat meat, but they seem to have an issue with why I don't eat meat."

"I don't have an issue, I'm just curious. You don't have to answer if you don't want to." He lifts his fancy meat sandwich. "I'm sorry, but I'm going to eat this."

"That's fine. You know what? I'm not going to answer that question. I've been answering that question since I was sixteen, and I feel like people ask me so they can argue with my reasoning, tell me I should be vegan if I actually give a shit, and then they call me self-righteous. They assume I think less of them because they eat meat, but I don't. So, if you know that I'm not judging you, can we not have this conversation?"

"Sure, no problem."

Why do I do this?

"It's not you, it's meat," I say.

He shakes his head. "So, you're a dork, huh?"

I pretend to take offence.

"And I'm not huge on kids, so I'm not sure if taking me to a park, and then picnicking on a jungle gym, is exactly the way to woo me anyway." My mouth goes dry after I say this. I shouldn't assume he's into me.

"Who said I'm trying to woo you?"

He's grinning, but I think I've made this weird. I try to think of something to say.

"I don't hate kids. I don't know why I said that. Maybe some-day I'll want them. I don't know."

He hesitates.

"I don't mean with you!" I say.

"Oh, I wasn't offering." We laugh. Kids start climbing on the jungle gym and we agree that we seem creepy and move to a bench.

I busy my hands by punching out sections along the veins of a fallen leaf that seems to have dried and changed colour prematurely.

"So, do you have a job? I'm just wondering because you're not at work, and it's a weekday," James asks.

"I'm a student actually. I don't have classes today. I mostly have night classes." I regret lying, but it's too late.

"What are you studying?" Before I can answer, he says, "Let me guess—English?"

"Are you suggesting that I'm predictable?"

"So, I'm right then?"

I pretend like I'm annoyed but nod. "What about you? School? Job?"

"I was a film major actually, but I dropped out second year

because I was learning how to analyze films and write about them. That's not what I was interested in—I want to make them."

"Why don't you go to film school?" I ask.

"I'm saving for it. I've been saving for a while, but it costs a lot. I feel like I'll be in my forties by the time I have enough."

"So that's in, like, two years?"

James is resting his head on his hand with his fingers covering his mouth, but I can tell he's smiling. We make eye contact, but it feels too intimate, so I look away.

"So, do you want to be a camera man? A key grip? What?" I ask.

"A director." He winces. "Yeah, I try to make it impossible to achieve my goals."

"You sound like me now."

"Oh yeah? What do you want?"

"I like to write." I cover my eyes with my hand for a second. In a bad posh English accent, I say, "I'm writing a novel." I sigh. "God, I hate talking about this. I sound so arrogant and narcissistic."

"So, I guess I shouldn't ask you what it's about?"

"It would not be wise." I kill another conversation. "So, where do you work?"

"I help build sets for plays, operas, ballets, sometimes movie sets. I also help with lighting and other equipment sometimes. I'm only an apprentice. I don't do the design, just the building."

"That's cool."

We're silent for a moment and I push myself to talk more.

"What are some of your favourite movies?" I ask, embarrassed by my token interview question.

"I think it's better that we don't reveal that kind of information, so we know that we're not basing our attraction for each other on shallow things."

I avoid acknowledging that he said *attraction* and say, "What do you mean? Liking movies is shallow?"

"No, but forming an opinion on someone based on the art they like is shallow. We should really get to know each other as people, not just how much we resemble one another."

"A very noble endeavour. It's good to know that you're not at all superficial. But didn't you approach me because you thought I was cute?" I challenge him. My heart is beating so fast. Have I ever been this brave? I wonder if I seem confident.

"Okay! I admit it; my good deed was not an entirely selfless pursuit."

"You men are all the same."

"A sad truth. But it's hard to meet people if you don't want to do it online. Have you ever tried online dating? It's awful. And I'm sure it's even worse for you—I mean—women."

I think of the times I've been ditched by people I've met online. One experience was particularly painful because the date seemed to be going well. Usually, you're aware of every minute. You're drained of any kind of wit you thought you might have, and you ask questions that you truly don't give a fuck about. But this one was decent. We discovered we hated the same comedians. We both got excited when a Whitney Houston song was played at the restaurant. And at the end of the night, he walked me home, kissed me (no tongue), and he said, I had a really good time. Let's do this again.

Why did he say that if he never wanted to see me again? Did he say it because he thinks of himself as a *nice guy* and didn't want to make me feel bad? Did he say it to avoid the awkwardness he'd feel over telling me he wasn't into me? I would have preferred hearing *You are an ugly bore. I won't be calling you, fucko!* than waiting for him to contact me and then spending a full day crafting a text to him only to have it ignored. It made me question if I remembered the date correctly. Maybe he didn't laugh at my jokes, or maybe he didn't think I was attractive. But I guess I'll never know the real reason.

I notice tiny bumps spread over James's arms and ask him if he needs to leave because he's cold. He asks me if I want to go to his place. I want to say no, but I'm trying to fight my impulses, so I say yes.

He doesn't seem horrible, but it's only been an hour.

On the way to James's, the wind picks up. My bangs fly around, revealing my giant forehead, and I try to fix them without James noticing.

James's apartment is one room plus a bathroom. The bedroom area has a double bed in it with a tacky, seashell-patterned comforter that reminds me of the Orlando hotel room I stayed in fifteen years ago with Mia's family. A tall bookcase filled with DVDs and books is oddly placed in the middle of the room instead of against the wall. The living room area has a TV and a beige couch. On the walls, there is one framed painting of a lady with glasses in a fur coat, standing in a field.

"By the way, I can see all the movies and books you like since they're right here."

"I know. My plan to remain mysterious is falling apart."

"Wait, you own *Fried Green Tomatoes* on DVD?"

"What's wrong with *Fried Green Tomatoes*?"

"I've just never met a man who likes it."

"You seem to have a very narrow view of sex and gender," James says.

James orders a veggie pizza and I eat two slices. I thank him for providing two meals for me in one day. I make fun of myself for using the word *providing*, like I'm some grateful Stepford wife.

We watch some episodes of *Veep* on his couch. I keep thinking that he's looking at my legs while we're watching, though I'm not sure if he really is, and I won't turn to look because what will I say if he is? Do you like them? Both? In case he is looking at me, I try not to slouch and sit closer to the edge of the couch cushion rather than rest against the back, presenting straight lines with my body. Anne used to tell me to sit like this because it would be more flattering to my shape. I hate that I'm taking her advice, but I want him to think I look good. I notice when we first started watching the show, we were laughing a lot, but neither of us have laughed during this last episode and it's almost finished. I forgot to keep laughing. I became distracted every time he moved slightly on the couch, adjusting his weight. He seemed to be getting closer to me, or maybe I was moving closer to him. Since he hasn't been laughing either, maybe he's also thinking about how I'm not laughing, focused on my body moving closer, my weight shifting on the cushions, both of us sinking toward each other. I let out a laugh so he doesn't think I'm thinking about his body, and he looks at me. Maybe there was no joke before I laughed. He moves his leg and his knee grazes my thigh, and I freeze. I notice that it's close to 9 p.m., and that we've been hanging out for six hours. I wonder if that's too long for a first date or whatever this is, and I wonder if I've been imagining the bodily tension. Maybe he's just watching the show and he hasn't paid attention to my body. He might want me to leave but isn't asking me to since he doesn't want to make me feel bad. I figure that I should take the stress off both of us, and I lie that I have some readings for class tomorrow.

"What's the class?"

I think of the most intimidating and least accessible literature course I took in school. "Literature and Psychoanalysis."

"Jesus. That sounds awful."

I agree with James and then put on my jacket. I have trouble finding the second sleeve and try to make a joke out of it while he guides the sleeve opening to my hand. I follow him to the door, but before he opens it, I stop him by touching his elbow and say, "Okay, so I'm not actually a student right now, technically, but I was before. And I don't have a job right now either, but I did before." I turn away slightly.

"Why did you say that then?" James asks, trying to catch my eye.

"Because I didn't want you to think I was a loser, since I'm not a student and I'm not employed."

"I don't think you're a loser. You're a bit of a liar though."

"It's not really a lie because I only let you believe it for a few hours."

"Is that how that works?"

"I don't know. Are you buying it?" I look him in the eye.

"No, but it's fine. I've probably lied tonight too."

"What did you lie about?"

"I think I'll keep you guessing," he says as he runs his hand over my upper arm.

I try to not look at my arm, but I can't stop myself. When I look back up at him, I see his other hand rising toward my face and instinctively I grab it. He looks confused, so I try to save the moment by pretending I'm just trying to hold his hand, which is something I would never try to do. He must be buying it because he steps toward me. I look up at him, and he touches my chin and kisses me. The warmth from his mouth makes my forearms and the back of my neck cold. The kiss lasts only a few seconds, but I wasn't expecting it so it seems a lot longer.

He says he can walk me home, and I tell him that I live so close he can actually see my front door from his, and if he's truly worried, he can watch me walk home.

As I walk home, I realize that for the first time in months, my head feels light, and not in a dizzying, faint way. The light of the moon commands my attention and I tilt my head up to take it in.

Chapter Ten

Mia has graciously allowed me to take the only lounge seat of the sectional couch at her parents' while we watch old music videos on her laptop. She pours me some tea and hands me a slice of lemon.

"Don't you get turned on by eating lemons? Should I leave the room?" she asks.

"It's hard to explain. They do something to my brain."

She presses play on the "Thong Song" video.

"He's amazing. I've never had the amount of energy that SisQó has in this video," I say.

"That's because you don't exercise."

I suggest a Miley Cyrus video and Mia plays it.

"I secretly loved her music in high school, but because I was such a punk," she says, mocking herself, "I could never admit it."

"Oh, same. Remember when you failed your math test, and I made you a playlist to cheer you up? I hid the track list, so you didn't know until you listened to it that it was all songs you hated? Though I guess you actually loved the Miley song I put on it."

After I made that playlist, Mia and I had a running joke where she'd play songs I hate when I had a bad day and I'd do the same for her. It usually worked, but I haven't tried it since she got sick.

I hand Mia twenty dollars for the burritos we ordered.

"It's on me," she says, waving the money away.

"No, I have that temp job starting next week."

"Oh yeah, you'll be rolling in it. Are you looking forward to starting?"

"Are you genuinely asking me that? It's going to be terrible."

"But it's money. And it's just for now. Focus on the *temp* in temp job."

I don't want to force optimism, so I ask Mia how the trip to the cabin went.

"It was weird. I wanted to see if I could still solo portage a canoe, and my parents were like, no, you'll hurt yourself, and they kept telling me to reapply sunscreen. I felt like a kid."

"Well, you do have to be careful in the sun right now."

Mia ignores my sun warning and says, "They also took photos of me constantly, like even when I was just sitting on the couch doing nothing."

She asks me if anything else is new.

I know I should tell her about James, but I can't do it. I shouldn't be feeling good while Mia isn't. I know she'd be upset if she knew I felt this way. She'd say *that's ridiculous, I don't want to hold you back*—whether she really felt that way or not—giving me freedom to see James while also showing off my compassion for her. I think it would be self-serving if I told her I worried about this.

I tell her nothing is new.

At home, watching *Funny Girl*, Barbra Streisand's hands keep catching my eye. I've never noticed anything special about hands before, but hers seem so elegant. I look at my hands and wonder if they could be thought of as elegant. I pause the movie and stand in front of a mirror trying to mimic her hand movements. While trying out a dramatic pose with the back of my hand sweeping across my raised chin, I hear a knock at the door.

I usually ignore knocks at the door, but after the third knock, I think I'd better open it. I'm wearing a hot-sauce-stained shirt and underwear with tears in the lace, so I quickly put on Mia's silk robe and walk to the door. I can see the shape of a head through the opaque pink glass on the door, but I can't make out any features. I open it and Dylan is standing there, kind of sweaty, with a basketball under his arm. Dylan hasn't been over in a while. He, Mia, and I used to watch movies here every Sunday. And he would show up a few times a week to go running with Mia. Dylan and Mia kept running even when she first started treatment, but soon she had to stop.

I look behind him, down the street, to see if James is out. Dylan looks puzzled and asks if someone is after me, but he's not serious. He says he was playing basketball with some friends in the park and asks if he can have some water. I invite him in, fill a mug with water, and hand it to him.

I look at his bag suspiciously. "You don't have water in there?"

"Drank it all."

He drinks the water and pulls some tights out from underneath him on the orange barkcloth chair he's sitting on.

"Been busy?" he asks.

I take the tights from him and bunch them in the pocket of the robe and tell him I have been, yes.

"Who were you looking for outside?"

"No one." I notice his shoes. How does he keep them so white? "How was the party?" I ask.

"What party?"

"That band's EP party."

"Oh, right. I decided not to go." He rubs his neck. "So, why couldn't you?"

"I went to see Mia."

He looks at me suspiciously. "She was at that cabin with her family."

I notice my knees are spiky, hairy. I cover them with a pillow. "Oh, yeah. Shit. I'm messing up my days."

Dylan looks away from me, and I can tell it's because he knows I'm not being honest. I start to feel anxious, not wanting to talk about James. "Dylan, I think you're getting my chair all sweaty."

"You got this for twenty bucks at the Salvation Army. Gus has clawed it to shit."

"So what? I like it."

He breaks eye contact with me again and pushes his damp hair back with his fingers. "Okay, I should go, I guess." He picks up his bag and walks to the door.

I start to follow him. I ask him to wait. "I was on a date. Or a hang or something. Just feels weird to tell you."

He leans his back against the door and looks at me. "Why do you feel weird telling me that?"

I focus on the pink textured glass of the window on the door. I can't see out the window, but my eyes follow the ripples in the glass.

"It's weird telling anyone."

"You can tell me stuff." He pauses. "So, who is he?" He runs his finger along the black grooves of the ball.

"I'll tell you, but not now."

He doesn't say anything.

"I'm weird, I know," I say.

"You're a bit unusual, yeah."

Before he leaves, he makes me promise to see an Erwin Blumenfeld exhibit with him before it's over.

I look in the bathroom mirror. I see a long coarse hair on the side of my face—only from one of those odd angles you have to strain your neck to see. I try to determine if Dylan was close enough to see it.

I notice that the back of the toilet is leaking. This has happened before, but Mia has always handled the correspondence with our landlord, Terry, whom I find intimidating because he doesn't start emails by addressing our names or close them by signing his—a man who feels no need to perform even the most undemanding form of pleasantries. The last time this leak happened, about a year and a half ago, Mia was about to leave for the weekend to visit her parents. She asked me to call Terry to tell him the leak needed to be fixed. I said, Can't you? and made a face like *I'm the weak one but maybe you find it charming how we have these roles.* She said, God, can't you do anything on your own? I remember exactly what she said because it stung. I need some sugar-coating. After she said this, I told her I'd handle it. She left, and I put towels on the floor. I wrote a script of my call to Terry, practising how I'd tell him about the leak, making sure to be tough if he tried to tell me it was our fault for flushing *feminine products* down the toilet, something we never did, but something he once accused us of. It was almost 8 p.m. by the time I was done with my script, so I told myself I would call him in the morning because I didn't want to wake up his kids, not that I had any reason to believe he had kids. The next morning, as I was psyching myself up to make the call, I received a text from Terry saying he'd come by to check the leak in the afternoon.

I text Terry about the leak. I open my text history with James. *I hope it's okay that I kissed you and didn't ask.* At first, I thought the text was sweet, but now it kind of bothers me. I don't know if it's the text that annoys me, or the fact that he didn't ask. Although I'm not sure if I'd want him to ask. He's been texting me to hang out again, but I've been making up excuses not to see him just yet. I worry that if I see him again, he'll find things he doesn't like about me. Or maybe I'll stop liking him after discovering some flaw I can't get over.

Chapter Eleven

My business casual sweater is so cheap and brittle it feels like hay. My skirt is too short even with tights. I realize this when I see that everyone else's skirt hems end right above their knees or past them. My first temp job is at a charity to cover for a receptionist who had a mental breakdown. That's not the story my supervisor gave me, but a woman with piecey bangs named Lisa told me this when we were both washing our hands in the washroom. She said Amber is on contract, so she isn't covered for a leave or sick days, and isn't getting paid while away for her breakdown, and her guess is that she'll be back soon because she was saving up to quit this job.

Every day here is the same as the last. When I'm not taking phone calls, I'm supposed to tidy up the supply room, but it's too far from the phone to hear if it's ringing, and I'm not allowed to miss any calls, so I spend my unpaid half hour for lunch cleaning up the supply room. Sometimes people call just to yell about how this charity is a scam, and my supervisor has suggested that I direct them to the website where they can leave comments and suggestions. These comments are sent to an inbox that no one checks. Yesterday, I dropped off a message I took for a man in the office who seems important and clears his throat a lot. Usually, I forward calls directly to the people whom callers ask for, but this important man in the office told me he doesn't like to be surprised and asked that I write down the name, number, and reason the person is calling and hand-deliver them to him. I told him I'm not supposed to leave the phone, but he just repeated his request to me slower and in a deeper tone.

I try to tell myself that I'm doing some good for this sick world by working for this charity, but then I remember that I was placed here and didn't choose it, and I wonder if this organization really is a scam. I decide that writing is a pretty selfish act, and though I still want to write a book, I'll stop after one. I throw out my soda can in the recycling and see that no one here separates their garbage into the appropriate bins. This place is a shithole. Other than the money, the only other good thing about the temp work is that my mother calls me and emails me less frequently to tell me I need a job.

Taking the subway during the peak of rush hour is a nightmare, so I usually stay until 6 p.m. even though my supervisor tells me every day she sees me staying late that my pay ends at 5 p.m. Today there's a delay on the subway. Strangers' bodies surround me, pressing up against me, and a tall girl's ponytail keeps hitting me in the face. My bra feels like it's suddenly six sizes too small, and I feel certain this is where I'll die.

On my day off, I get on the subway to go to the hospital. I see someone from a book club I quit two years ago. I don't think she's spotted me. I thought the club would be fun because I love arguing about books, but people weren't listening to each other, they were waiting for people to finish their thoughts so they could share their own insights that had nothing to do with what others had said. I thought this person from my book club and I got along okay, but after I liked a photo on Instagram of her and her dog (she'd remind you often that the dog was a rescue), I noticed that she hadn't been liking my posts. I checked to see if she was still following me, and I saw that she wasn't. It's not like she follows only a tight circle of friends—she follows eight hundred people. Why not me? It takes effort to unfollow someone. I rarely post and make sure I don't post a photo of my face more than once a month, and I try to not do back-to-back photos of Gus. I don't see what I could have done to bother her. I almost unfollowed her back, but then I thought what if she checks to see if I noticed her unfollow me and then realizes I unfollowed her as a counterattack? So, I just left it as is, following her, so that she thinks that I don't care.

When she gets off at her stop, I see her hug a woman I used to know on the platform. I used to hang out with this woman fairly regularly, but she stopped asking me to do things after I made too many excuses for not wanting to get together right around the time Mia got sick. I don't blame her. I don't chase people either. She takes off her jacket and I see that she's pregnant as the train pulls away.

Mia barely looks up when I enter the hospital room. She's watching a show starring an actress known for her beauty. In this show, she isn't wearing eye makeup, which is a nod to her depression and boosts her chances of being nominated for a big award.

"Don't you hate this show?"

With eyes still on the screen, she shrugs.

Mia isn't wearing lipstick today. Only blush, eyelashes, and she's drawn on her eyebrows. Her lips look chapped, and I wonder if all the lipstick she wears dries out her lips.

I ask her if she's finished any weavings lately, and she waves me off the topic, quickly saying she hasn't been able to concentrate. I try to say some empathetic words and she instructs me with her eyes to stop, like how a cat will tell you with its eyes *now is not the time to pet me.*

I saw on Twitter that this is the weekend of an annual marathon that Mia always ran in.

"Have you been getting a lot of writing done?" Mia asks in a tone suggesting she already knows the answer. "The temp job is just a few days a week, right?"

"I actually brought something that I wrote for you." I hand her a piece of paper. "I was trying to think of the worst beginning to what I thought would be the worst novel ever."

Mia reads aloud, "He trembled with ecstasy and unrivalled pleasure as she wrapped her arm around his torso; his coos of delight increased in volume as she stroked him with another arm, and another, and another, and another, and another, and another, and another; entangled in her tentacles, and in love, he knew that this was more than a dalliance, but he couldn't escape the dysphoria that reminded him that America might not be ready to have a half-human, half-octopus as their first lady." Mia tries to hide a smirk, and then drops the piece of paper on her lap. "What about your book, Alice? When am I going to read that?"

For most of university, Mia would ask to see my writing. I would tell her "when I'm done." She pointed out that I'll never feel like I'm finished. Finally, a couple years ago, I caved and showed her a short story I hadn't shown anyone. I had been alone with unfinished short stories and a couple chapters of a novel, wavering between telling myself I'm very, very special and very, very stupid. I was scared to show her, but I had hoped she would confirm a mild burning suspicion I had that I might be talented. When I handed Mia my story one night in her bedroom, she started reading it right in front of me. I was staring at her eyes and mouth, searching for some sign of approval, but she gave nothing away. I decided I couldn't watch and waited in my room, counting my teeth with my tongue. When Mia finished, she didn't knock down my door in the middle of the night to declare that I was a literary master.

She gave me back my story in the afternoon the next day, marked up in blue ink. She told me she thought I had potential for sure, but that my story needed work. She could tell I was disappointed and asked me if I thought I was a secret genius or something, which sounded harsh. I said no, of course not. She told me those people don't exist, or there's, like, very few of them who are naturally brilliant. She said you're a B student—why did you think you wouldn't have to work on something to get really good at it? Sometimes her rationality comes across as cruel, though often it's something I need to hear. I tried sending some of my stories to literary magazines, so that I could prove her wrong. I've had a steady run of rejections, but I've also thought maybe I just haven't found my audience yet. Then I hear Mia in my head, imagining her saying *maybe you just haven't honed your craft yet because you spend more time fantasizing that you're a writer and weaponizing it against people who've never believed in you rather than actually writing.* Mia asked a few times to see the next draft, dropping in a few compliments to encourage me, but she stopped asking after I kept telling her I wasn't finished yet. I'm sure she knew I hadn't begun revisions. I started showing my stories to Dylan instead of Mia because his critiques were gentler and he offered more compliments. I never fully absorbed his praise though because his advice wasn't as thoughtful. I knew Mia was right about most of her notes, but if I took her comments seriously, I'd have so much work to do.

"Mia! You've lost your sense of humour? I had you in mind when I was writing this. I'm so disappointed."

"I'm disappointed in you," Mia rebuts. "You don't have a full-time job. You should be writing."

"But I've been working."

"For, like, two weeks! And that job is up soon. You've been unemployed for months."

She tells me she thinks I don't want to commit to writing because I'm afraid of rejection. She says I'm afraid someone will call it false or bad, and that's why I'm critical of people who do share their art.

"Are you saying I'm so afraid of being seen as pretentious that I'm actually kind of a philistine?"

"I mean, that's kind of a lot, but like a softer version of that, yeah."

I don't think she realizes how brutal she sounds, but I know she's right. I'm some lazy girl who talks about being a writer, but then doesn't even try. And now I have some new distraction—dating? I'm afraid to tell her about James. I don't even know if anything is happening with us. If I talk to her about it, then she'll feel sorry for me when it ends, and then I'll seem weak.

"So, why did I have to hear from Dylan that you went on a date, like, weeks ago? You came over to my parents' and didn't say anything about it."

Is she reading my mind?

"I was going to tell you."

"So, do you like him?" Mia asks.

I say nothing.

She gasps. "Alice! My god. You do."

I'm about to say I don't know him well, but I already know what she'll say to that.

I answer her questions about where we met, what he looks like, and where he works. She can't help but slap the bed with delight when I tell her he lives on our street.

"So," she says, sitting up straight and folding her hands together like she's about to perform in a choir. I know she's preparing to make fun of me. "Coitus?" she tries to say with a straight face, but she shakes while suppressing a laugh.

"No! Why do you keep pushing sex with strangers on me?"

Before she can respond she winces and unwraps three cubes of purple bubble gum and puts them all in her mouth and starts chewing.

"Gross medicinal taste in your mouth again?" I ask.

Mia nods as she chews the sugary wad. She then spits it into a tissue and crumples it up. "I hate that." Mia takes a sip of water and asks me, "So, you didn't have sex with him, but did you at least kiss?"

I cover my mouth with my hand and look away. She erupts into laughter and I feel like we're fourteen again.

As we watch *Young Frankenstein*, I notice that Mia's not laughing during the parts of the movie that she usually laughs at. I'm also noticing that I'm the only one making comments while we watch the movie. I feel her mood changing again, and I ask if she's okay.

"I'm fine," she says without taking her eyes off the screen.

"Are you sure?" I ask.

"I just said I was," she says.

I feel my phone vibrate in my pocket. It's Dylan. It's a meme of Benedict Cumberbatch as an alien, pretending to be human. His eyes and neck are Photoshopped. It's old, but to lighten the mood, I decide to show it to Mia. "This is still so funny."

Mia doesn't look at my phone. She just says, "You're not supposed to have your phone on in here. It fucks with the machines."

Feeling like an idiot, I turn off my phone. "Shit, sorry, Mia. I forgot to turn it off."

I'm worrying now, and even though I know I should stop, I ask, "How have you been feeling lately? Have you been feeling nauseated again? Do you feel weak?"

"Seriously, Alice, stop." She won't look at me. My cheeks feel hot. "I really don't want to talk about this with you. All anyone wants to talk about with me is how I'm feeling. I don't always want to talk about being sick. It's my whole life now."

"It's not your whole life."

"It is, Al. But it's not yours. Stop acting like it is."

I don't know what to say, other than I'm sorry, but that feels ineffectual, so I go to the bathroom.

The mirrors in this hospital make me look different. The shadows settle under my eyes and in the small cracks in my face and make me look old, like I could be one of Mia's hospital roommates. I don't see any of Mia's creams in here, and I wonder if she is still doing her lengthy skincare routine. I lean against the door, afraid to go out, afraid to see her. But she needs me now. She needs me to distract her. I've needed her so many times throughout my life. That's how I met her. When I was four, I got separated from my mother at the mall somehow, and I felt so scared that I just sat on the floor and closed my eyes, with one hand over my eyes, and my other arm stretched straight up in the air. Mia was with her mother, saw me, broke away from her, rushed over to me, and took my hand to help me up. And then they helped me find my mother.

I look in the mirror again and smile. My teeth look yellow in this light. I walk out.

"Let me put this on you." Mia is holding a tube of lime-green lipstick, the same one she put on herself while I was in the bathroom. I think she's trying to apologize. "It's called Envy. Boring name."

The lipstick is darker over the chapped areas of her lips. "Where do you even find green lipstick? Party City?" I ask, relieved her mood has shifted.

She ignores my question and finishes painting a green smile on my face. "There. Late bloomer, but you're finally hot."

A nurse comes in and starts a new drip. Minutes later, Mia starts closing her eyes and I can tell she's trying not to look too pained. Her face turns red. She says she feels weird, and says she thinks she needs me to leave. I hate this drug; it makes her panic, which makes me panic. She puts a small white pill under her tongue, and waits for it to dissolve there. She says it makes her calm down. She asks me to go and says she's fine, but that she'd rather I not see her like this. I protest, and ask to stay and help her, but she tells me to leave. She says she's going to try to nap once the white pill kicks in. I kiss her forehead and leave a green lip print.

At the elevator, I select the lobby floor, but when I'm in, it skips the lobby and takes me to the basement. Is Mia worse than she lets on? It occurs to me that I should write down everything I can about her, stories from all the years I've known her, or even lists of Mia things like songs she loves, the kind of gum she chews. These types of things seem insignificant but might hold weight someday.

On the way home, a man biking on the sidewalk almost hits me and I have to jump out of the way. I roll my ankle and my hand scrapes against the cement. Little drops start slowly falling from the sky. Then it starts to pour. I swear that I could hear the rain falling before I felt it.

At home, I pick tiny stones out of my wound and brush it with an iodine swab; little bubbles boil out of the cuts. In bed, I look at my hand and think about how easily skin tears and bleeds. I think about eating some vegetables, but I stay in bed instead.

I listen to the wheels of the cars driving over the rain-covered asphalt. It sounds like eggs cooking in a pan.

"I thought you were vegetarian?" James asks me when the server drops off our meals at our table.

"I am, I'm not vegan though, so I eat eggs."

"Do you eat cheese?"

"Yes. Though I'm slightly lactose intolerant. My stomach wants me to be vegan, but I can't do that to my tongue. Cheese is the greatest food in the world, along with the potato."

"The potato?"

"Yes!" I say, then take a sip of pink lemonade. "The potato is so versatile. Mashed potatoes, fried potatoes, scalloped potatoes, oh *god*, scalloped potatoes! Potato wedges, latkes, even a boiled potato is good. And then there's French fries, and chips. The potato is our saviour. The potato is magic."

"Yeah, potatoes are pretty good," James agrees, but halfheartedly. I shoot him a cold eye for his dispassionate response.

"So, you have to tell me how old you are now because it's starting to get weird."

"Okay. You're what? Twenty-four? Well, I am five years older."

"Wow, thirty is old."

"I'm not thirty yet. I'm twenty-nine and three-quarters."

"Do you ever notice that when people start getting old, they get really specific about their age? It's like when you're a child, and when someone asks you how old you are, you'd say, I'm eight and a half or I'm eight and three-quarters. So, I guess, it changes back to that once you approach thirty."

"Sure. But I'm not thirty yet."

"Want to go to my place?" I ask. He wants to.

I cleaned my apartment because it's been a while, and I knew there was a chance I'd invite him back. I rummage through my cupboard to find a glass for James that doesn't have water marks or stains. This hunt proves to be unsuccessful, so he'll have to settle for the least stained glass. "Don't worry, it only looks dirty," I say to James as I pass him the tarnished glass of water.

He takes a sip and asks for a coaster. I take his glass from him, set it on the wooden side table, and tell him I have no coasters. I wonder if I'm at an age where coaster use is expected. He moves it to the glass table in front of us.

We watch *In the Mood for Love* in my living room, and I start to say something about the use of colour and then bail out midsentence when I worry I sound like I'm trying too hard. When it's over, I put on *Point Break* to adjust the mood.

I tell James my gum has lost its flavour while trying to get up to throw it out and moving my legs from across his lap. Earlier, he lifted my legs onto his lap, and I felt the urge to move them, but I pushed myself to keep them there.

"I'll throw it out," he says while extending his arm and cupping his hand by my mouth.

"Really?" I ask, surprised yet curious.

"Yes! Spit."

I spit the green wad into his hand, and he walks to the kitchen, and then comes back to sit down.

"Wow. You took my gum. That's a big step."

We sit in silence, the back of my hand barely grazing his.

"I think you like me," James says to me.

"I might," I say as I shrug while trying to suppress a smile. "What are you trying to do?"

"I'm not trying to do anything but get to know you. And I like you. So far."

I hit him lightly with a throw pillow.

James reaches to grab his glass off the table, and I spot a dark mark on the inside of his bicep.

"Did I just see a tattoo?"

He shakes his head.

I give him a look as if to say *you're full of shit.*

"Show me. You got the tattoo so people would see it."

"It's embarrassing."

"All tattoos are embarrassing. It's too late now."

He hesitates, and then he pulls up his sleeve to show me. It's a small, plain, black stick-and-poke of a bed.

"Is this supposed to mean you're some sex god or something?"

"No! It's because I really like sleeping. Bed is the best place to be."

I ask him if he has more tattoos. He leans in and kisses me. His eyes are closed, so I close mine. He puts his tongue in my mouth, and then leans against me. As he pushes against me, my sweater is rising. I decide to be bold and push back against him, and then I surprise myself by straddling him and kissing him hard. I can hear us both breathing loudly, and for a few seconds, I'm focused on how to breathe and kiss at the same time. He starts to kiss my neck, and I think I like it a lot because I start to feel cold and hot at the same time. My skirt rises like my sweater.

We get to my room and keep touching each other and kissing. I close my curtains so the room is less revealing. He takes off his shirt. He has small nipples, and he has slight grooves in his stomach that suggest he might work out sometimes but still eats what he wants. He has another larger tattoo on his bicep, but I resist the urge to focus on the tattoo. I take off my tights, and I take off James's belt, which feels like an insane thing for me to do. I don't take off other people's belts. He takes a cue from me, takes his shirt and pants off, then his underwear, and starts to pull down mine. My skirt is still pushed up around my waist, but I leave it there. When I first started having sex, I used to shave off all my pubic hair, like I was some hypoallergenic cat. I've let it grow now, but I've been shaving my bikini line because it bothers me to see it grow out of the triangle. I hope he isn't turned off. He takes my sweater off and tries to take my tank top off, but I put my hand to his chest to stop him. I don't want him to see my bony chest. He might not like it, or he might really like it, which is not great because I don't usually look like this.

"I think I'm going to keep my shirt on. I don't think I'm ready to be fully naked in front of you."

"We don't have to do this."

I can see that he wants to. He puts his T-shirt back on.

"I want to," I say. I prove to him that I want to do this by kissing him. I bite his bottom lip and I know he likes it because he puts his hands in my hair, holding the sides of my head, securing my head while he kisses me harder.

Sex with men can be pretty all right when they seem extremely happy just to let you lie there while you make satisfied groans and open your mouth a bit. I haven't had much calcium or vitamin D lately, so I'm pretty sure my bones would turn to dust if I tried any kind of complicated movements. I hope he doesn't expect anything too elaborate.

As we continue kissing, we can faintly hear a woman singing in an operatic style. James gives me an odd look, and I explain that a soprano has moved in upstairs, and I've heard her sing a few times, but never at a time like this where the singing actually heightens the drama and romance of a situation. Usually, it happens while I'm washing the dishes or peeing. I don't believe in signs, but I do believe in taking full advantage of cinematic moments, so the accompaniment of the serenade helps to quash any hesitation I feel about having sex with James.

When he puts his finger inside me, it feels good, but I realize I don't want to be the centre of attention like that, having him focus on how I'm reacting. If we have sex, he'll be more distracted. I pull his hands away and hand him a condom from my nightstand. I want to ask him to use lube, but some guys are weird about it, thinking it means their dick sucks or your vagina is broken. But when he moves to go inside, I motion for him to stop, I reach into my nightstand, and hand him lube without saying anything. The tube makes an unsexy noise when he squeezes it, but I pretend I didn't hear anything. He kisses me as he moves back on top of me. It hurts a little at first. Then once he's fully in, it feels good, and I start to relax. I put my fingers through his hair. We have sex for around eight minutes. We mostly stick to the missionary position, probably because neither of us is confident enough to try anything too intricate. The only issue with missionary for the first time is that it's fairly intimate since you're face to face. I vacillate between looking off in the other direction and keeping my eyes closed, but I make sure it appears to be a reaction due to pleasure rather than boredom, discomfort, or awkwardness. I hope that's evident to him. I make soft sounds. He comes. I do not, but I think I still enjoy it. I pull up my underwear as I lie on my back. James rushes off to the bathroom either to dispose of the condom, or maybe because he's a little embarrassed about the whistle tones he hit during orgasm.

My back hurts a little, so I turn on my side to face the wall for a moment. I see all the familiar bumps and divots.

When I'm with James, my real life blurs. I seem to forget about my problems. This may be bad. James is obscuring reality, and once he's gone, I'll probably be worse. My head starts to spin. I become noticeably upset. James returns and asks me what's wrong.

"It's nothing," I say.

"Should we not have done that? It was probably too soon, right?" James cracks the knuckles on his hands in frustration.

I turn away from the wall. "No, it's not that. It's not you." I run my finger along my hairline nervously. "It's a lot of things." I don't want to get into it, but I'm not sure how to avoid it.

"You can tell me. Or you don't have to, whatever you feel comfortable with. I can leave if you want." He touches my shoulder in a non-threatening way, like he's a school counsellor.

"It's a lot of things." I close my eyes. He lies down beside me, but we're not touching. I think I'm giving him the impression that I don't want to be touched right now, and I can't tell if I want to be or not. "You know how you asked how I afford an apartment on my own?"

"Yeah?"

"Well, it's a two bedroom. The closed door by the kitchen that I said was a closet is a bedroom too. That's Mia's room. She hasn't been living in it for a while now. She's really sick. At first, her doctors said she would be fine, and her treatments were supposed to be over by now, but she's still doing them. I don't know what's going on. And I can't focus on anything else." I can't muster up the courage to look James in the eye, so I stare at his mouth. It's a nice, soft mouth.

James doesn't know what to say, even though there's really nothing to say. "I'm really sorry about your friend. That's terrible."

His words are generic, but I don't see how I could have expected more. James and I lie in bed for about another half hour not saying much to each other. We both stare at the ceiling. I'm not sure what he's thinking about. I wish I could take back what I've told him.

Chapter Twelve

Paper cuts hurt, but cuts from a file folder are extremely painful. Felicia, the office administrator, told me file folders are like razorblades when I asked her for a bandage. My new temp job is two days a week at a law office. They've hired me to organize their file room and pack up the files in banker boxes to prep for their move. I work alone in the filing room, which is better than working with others, but the days are so slow. Handling papers all day makes my hands so dry, and every hour, I apply moisturizer and wait for my hands to absorb it, so I don't grease up the important documents that I'm filing. I worry someone will come in while I'm waiting for my hands to dry and think I'm not working. Sometimes people come in and instead of asking my name and what I'm doing in there, they kind of jump and say sorry as if they walked in on me on the toilet, and then they take the file they need, quickly, and leave. I'm sure I could threaten to ruin some lives in exchange for cash with these documents, but I have no clue how to do that, and I guess I don't have it in me.

I wonder if the temp agency told the office that about me. Sometimes I go to the washroom in the office and just sit in there, so I'm doing something other than filing.

One day after work, James meets me at the office to keep me company on my commute home. I asked him, do you really want to come all the way here just to go back to our neighbourhood? James insists that he must walk on the side of the road closest to traffic, as if he could protect me if a car jumped the curb. I feel like a bad feminist for liking that he does this. As we walk through a tunnel in the subway station, a man wearing a cummerbund over a coffee-with-cream coloured shirt is indiscriminately mashing down the keys of a reedless saxophone. He has a fig-coloured velvet hat by his feet; the inside is glimmering with coins. As he inhales and exhales over the mouthpiece, I come to the conclusion that this man has just happened to find a saxophone. James gives him two dollars.

When James saw me upset after sex, I figured I wouldn't hear from him again. I started planning alternate routes to places to avoid walking on our street for too long. But he texted me the next day. I couldn't tell if I was happy, or if I wished he had never texted me again. I like him, but there was a small pang of relief when I figured he was done with me.

It's been close to six weeks since our first date. At first, I was resistant to seeing him often. I was slow to respond to texts, and I made excuses to avoid hanging out, but he was both respectful of the space I needed and persistent. If I gave a half-assed excuse for not wanting to hang, he didn't fight it, though he would suggest another time. His persistence makes me wonder if there's something wrong with him.

I'm still not used to spending so much time with someone who isn't Mia, and I think sometimes I ruin our dates. One afternoon we were out for drinks, and I had put on lipstick. He made me laugh, and I caught a glimpse of my reflection in my glass, and I looked so warped and garish. I didn't feel like myself, and I told him I had to go, but I wouldn't let him walk me home. He likes to go out, and I've become accustomed to a sort of reclusive lifestyle, so I'm not always willing to leave my apartment or his. But he knows that the one thing he can get me to do is go to the movie theatre. It's not that far removed from what I would do at home—sit in the dark, watching movies.

It's strange having someone in my apartment. I forgot to clean the butt mark off the wall in my bedroom once before James came over, and he asked about it, and I covered my face but told him what it was. He has this bit now where he says, "Honey, I'm home" to the mark, and he kisses it, and says things like, "Is that a new blouse? It's stunning."

I miss him sometimes after he leaves, but only sometimes. I like to examine the faint violet bruises on my thighs left by fingerprints after sex. I study them, looking for patterns, like they can tell me something crucial about James and how he feels about me.

It's the night before Halloween. Summer is dead. The trees are on fire with leaves turning shades of red and orange. I'm at Mia's parents' house watching *Hocus Pocus* with Mia. On screen, Thora Birch jumps out of the closet in her witch costume.

"I was planning to go as Laura Dern in *Wild at Heart* this year, well, before my hair fell out—it would have been perfect. And you were going to be my Nic Cage."

"Well, I can't deny our striking resemblance."

"You got me hotter than Georgia asphalt," Mia says in a bad Southern accent, impersonating Laura Dern's character.

"Next year," I say, taking a sip of apple cider.

"I hate that last Halloween we bought those dumb animal costumes. So boring!"

"We ran out of time. I thought we were kind of cute."

Mia shakes her head.

"Are you sure you don't want to come out with us tomorrow? We can leave if it sucks."

"Nah, not in the mood."

"If you don't want to go out, I can stay in with you, and we can watch Halloween movies and poison the candy we hand out to kids."

Mia tells me I cannot cancel my plans.

I abandon my apple cider. It's too sugary. Mia asks me if I have a costume and I tell her I haven't figured one out yet. She suggests I wear her lion costume from last year and makes me follow her to her bedroom to try it on.

Mia's bedroom in her parents' house doesn't have much in it. Her walls are bone white, and completely bare except for a 27-by-40-inch mounted print of Redon's *Cactus Man*. It scares the shit out of me, but she loves it.

"Try it on. The legs were a little short on me, so it should be the perfect length on you." I take my dress off to try on the costume. I'm standing in my black cotton tights and my bra.

"Jesus, Al, you're bones."

"I've gained weight in the last few weeks. I'm not even that skinny, you're just used to seeing me bigger."

She looks worried. "I hope you're eating."

"I *am*," I say, unable to conceal my annoyance. I really have gained weight. I put on the costume.

There's a knock and Mia's dad pokes his head in. He tells me there's a man named James at the door. Mia looks startled, but she doesn't say anything. I ask him to tell James to wait at the door.

Mia starts scrolling through her phone without pausing to look at anything. She tosses her phone on the bed. "Why did you invite him here? I wish you had told me." She smooths her wig while looking in the mirror.

I look at her reflection. "I didn't. I don't know why he's here." I begin to take off the costume.

"How does he even know where my parents live?" She isn't even trying to hide her irritation.

"We walked by when we were out one day. I'll tell him to leave."

"I don't want to meet anyone new when I look like this. I don't mean I can't meet anyone, but I need to have some warning."

I tell her I understand and apologize too many times. Then I promise to make James leave.

I open the door to see James holding a pumpkin and a bag of mixed candy. He looks puzzled. "Should I not have come?"

"Why are you here?"

He looks deflated, and I realize I should have delivered that sentence with more sensitivity.

"I wanted to surprise you. I thought we could all carve a pumpkin," he says.

I feel bad now.

"That's really nice, but you can't do that with Mia right now. She's less into surprises and meeting new people lately. It's hard to explain."

"No, that makes sense." He starts to back off the porch. He

hands me the pumpkin and candy. "Please tell her I'm sorry. Fuck, I hope she doesn't hate me."

I try to assure James that Mia doesn't hate him. I tell him the time isn't right. He says he understands, but I can tell he's hurt. He leaves. I'm frustrated with both of them, but I don't think I'm allowed to be with either.

Mia and I finish the movie. I suck on a few pieces of the sour candy from James until my tongue starts to hurt. We don't carve the pumpkin. Mia is withdrawn for the rest of the night.

On the way home, I notice the spot on my palm where I fell and cut my hand open a few weeks ago. My hand is nearly healed and all that's left is a faint mark. It doesn't hurt at all.

The following night, James looks in the bathroom mirror as he adjusts his poncho, trying to make himself look more like the Man with No Name. "I don't have as much facial hair as Clint."

I nudge him out of the way so that I can make sure my whiskers are painted on okay.

"So, we're going to Maxwell's house? Like . . . the coffee?"

"Yeah, but more accurately, it's an apartment."

James pours his Guinness into a glass, and I sip on my gin and tonic on the couch. We watch some slasher movie he said was the best, but it's like every other one I've seen.

"Remember: Dylan and Anne are the only people at the party tonight who are my friends. Also, people will be calling Anne *Anastasia*—she prefers that."

"Is that her real name?"

"No."

"Does everyone else know that?"

"No. But Dylan knows she's *just Anne*."

"So, is Dylan a close friend of yours?"

I ignore the question. "Honestly, you probably won't like Anne. Just remember she's one of those friends I've known for so long that I can't really get rid of her." I feel guilty for saying this.

"Why do you hate her so much?"

"I don't hate her. I just think she's self-absorbed and sort of phony." I don't hate Anne. I think most of my aggression toward Anne stems from her neglect of Mia in the last few months. Anne is the type of person who earnestly asks you who you would choose to save from drowning if you could only save one. She posed this question to me with herself and Mia as my two options when we were thirteen, the age girls are at their meanest. I said I would save her, but I don't think she believed me. I always wondered if she had asked the same question to Mia, but I could never ask her because then I'd have to admit that I betrayed her by telling Anne what she wanted to hear. The thing is, I had already thought about that scenario before Anne asked me, and I knew I'd choose Mia. And I know Anne would choose Mia too. I wonder what is worse: someone who would ask that question, or someone who would think about it on their own and come up with an answer?

"Relax, Holden Caulfield. What do you say about people who aren't your friends?"

"Come on, don't you have any friends who you just put up with? But you know you'll probably be friends forever because you've known each other so long?"

He shrugs while I resist the urge to scratch at my face paint. My cheeks twitch.

When Maxwell opens the door to his apartment, the first thing I notice is the same thing that caught my attention when I met him—he has a lot of greying hair for someone supposedly only twenty-eight years old. It looks like there are grey and black smoke clouds curling over his scalp, like some mysterious, haunted mountaintop.

Maxwell says hi to me, and he barely tries to sound enthusiastic. His expression tells me he's already bored by my presence. Or maybe he's just drunk. He doesn't have a costume, but he's wearing a grey shirt with *Vince* embroidered on it. His big joke of the night is yes, he has a costume—he's Vince!

Maxwell has a sonorous voice that commands attention. This makes him seem older, and in turn wiser, so when he says stupid things confidently, they don't sound entirely ridiculous.

Maxwell has taken a minimalist approach to decorating his apartment, or maybe he just doesn't have any furniture. He only has a record player, four milk crates full of records, a tube television sitting on the floor, a fold-out table covered in packs of cigarettes and empty bottles, and a bunch of chairs, but no couch. Alcohol bottles line the perimeter of the room.

When I introduce James to Anne, Anne pinches me on my wrist. I know this means that she's trying to tell me something, but I can't tell if this means that she approves or disapproves of James. I focus on James's face while he shakes Anne's hand, but I can't tell if he's mesmerized by her beauty.

Anne, Zoe, Claire, and Naomi are all wearing fitted white button-up shirts, with white little boy briefs, sheer black tights underneath the briefs, and black fedoras. Anne has a black cane and has attached a fake eyelash on her lower right eyelid. Oh god. They're hot Droogs, wearing the wrong hats. I don't point this out because I'll sound pretentious.

"Are you all supposed to be Droogs?" James asks.

"Isn't that obvious?" Naomi asks. I'm sure there is more to Naomi than simply just Disinterested Woman Too Cool for You, but I can only work with what people give me.

"It's from a movie. *A Clockwork Orange*," Claire informs us. She looks at James while letting her tongue explore the straw of her drink. I should have known Claire would try to flirt with James. Boundaries aren't a big concern for her. She told me once that she had a crush on her dentist, so when his gloved fingers were in her mouth, she wrapped her tongue around his fingers in a sensual way. I never know what to do with my tongue at the dentist. Instinctively it touches the tools in my mouth and the hygienist has to ask me to keep my tongue still, but I get in my head about this and I'm pretty sure it just jerks around wildly.

"She knows it's from a movie, Claire," Anne says.

"A book first, actually, if you can believe that," I say, maybe a little arrogantly.

"I haven't read the book or seen the movie," Zoe confesses. "But Anastasia had this idea, and I thought it was cute. I love your costume, Alice. I want to be a lion next Halloween."

"Mia wore this last year, An-Anastasia. Remember?"

Anne quickly says, "I should introduce you to Maxwell's new roommate, Grant. He just moved in."

"What happened to Damian?"

"He moved out, like, a month ago. I thought you were at the going-away party?" She looks at me, confused. "Anyway, he moved to Europe. I forget where exactly. He said it's too rigid here. You know how he makes video art? Well, he said the people here are uninspiring."

"All of them?" James asks.

"Damian is just so much more of a European soul," Claire explains. "He was born on the wrong continent. I feel like that myself too." Two years ago, Claire lived with her cousin somewhere in England for four months, and when she returned, she spoke with a slight English accent. She also adopted British slang by referring to her apartment as her *flat* and her cellphone as her *mobile*. She stopped this when an English girl overheard her in a bar and called her out on it. Claire continues, "I'm in the wrong time period too. I'm misplaced."

Naomi says, "Someone should tell Damian that Europe is over and has been for years."

"I don't know. I kind of think that Damian also moved because he's had sex with, like, everyone in the city, and he started to run out of options," Anne suggests.

I agree. "Yeah, and he'll probably think that his foreigner status over there will get him laid."

"It probably will though," Anne says. "To be honest, I never actually liked him." Anne will occasionally recognize arrogance and pretension. She noted this flaw in Damian; she became so enraged whenever he corrected her pronunciation. The first time they met, Anne made tacos for Damian and Maxwell, and when Maxwell asked what the pico de gallo was, Anne pronounced it *pee-co de gall-o*, and Damian laughed cruelly.

"Do you like Grant?" I ask.

"I don't really know him." Anne looks around to make sure no one is in listening distance. Only James and I are close enough to hear her. "Claire slept with Grant. Last week. Don't say anything."

"I won't," I promise. "I guess she's not back with Marcus?"

"No! Marcus got that chick pregnant, and she's keeping it!" Anne is always good for gossip. "Come on, we'll go meet Grant."

She grabs my wrist like a mother grabbing a misbehaving child. I take hold of James's hand to follow. Anne stops in the kitchen and pours us two glasses of white wine, saying she doesn't know whose it is. She leads us past two guys arguing over what to add to the playlist. We walk by a room filled with boxes, and a double bed that doesn't have a bedframe, only a box spring and a mattress.

We walk to the end of the hallway and enter another bedroom. There is a huge bed that takes up almost the entire room. The walls are bare except for a large mirror, a set of photobooth photos of an unsmiling Maxwell, and a crinkled poster of *Requiem for a Dream*—formerly a dorm room staple for *young men who know cinema*.

Maxwell is sitting on the bed with a tray on his lap with some rolling papers and a small bag full of weed on it. He's cutting up weed in a shot glass with some scissors. There are two other people on the bed whom I don't know: a lanky man with rocky bone structure in a red-and-white checkered 1950s style dress that is fitted at the waist and then flares out and ends at the knee, a neat blonde bobbed wig that makes me think of Mia, and red lips with heavy mascara to match. The young woman beside him is wearing Levi's jeans, a white T-shirt with a pack of cigarettes rolled up in one sleeve, and her dark short hair is slicked back. Her skin is so smooth, like a sculpture.

Anne sits beside Maxwell on the bed and kisses his neck, and he responds by worming away from her face and says, "Babe. Public." She mouths *fuck you* behind his head, and then notices James and I standing by the door while the two strangers on the bed stare at us. Without getting up, she introduces the man in the wig as Grant and the dark-haired woman as Talia. She tells them I'm an old friend and calls James my boyfriend.

I bite my tongue when she says *boyfriend*, as James and I have yet to discuss our title preferences with each other. I wonder if she did this on purpose. I look at him after she lets this word loose and am met with a wink, a grin. I don't think that he minds. I also think he winks too much.

"You're a lion?" Grant asks.

"Just today," I say.

"And you are a cowboy?" Grant asks James.

"I'm the Man with No Name." Grant raises an eyebrow. "You know, he's a character Clint Eastwood plays?" Grant does not understand. "Have you seen the movies?"

"Can I ask you something, James?" Grant asks while pulling up his pantyhose. He even does this the correct way—by beginning at the ankle and making his way up to the thigh. "Do you feel pressured to dress as something"—he uses air quotes—"*masculine*, *heroic*, and *powerful*?"

James lets his bottom lip fall from the top and hang there for a second, and then says, "No, I just grew up watching the movies, and have always thought the character was cool."

"But you'd probably never dress as something that didn't exude virility, would you?" Grant continues. Maxwell puts a joint in his mouth, grabs Anne's hand, and they exit the room. James and I are still standing near the door.

"Well, I went as Cher last year," James says with a grin and looks at me. I smile back, then look into my glass of wine and hope to find a portal out of this conversation.

"And would you say that you felt compelled to impersonate Cher out of love and respect for Cher as an artist, or were you mocking a strong woman, and you thought it was funny for a man to wear women's clothing?"

"Love and respect," James replies firmly.

"What are *you* supposed to be?" I ask in defence of James.

"Tal and I are archetypes of the postwar *ideal man* and *woman*." Grant looks at Talia to add something, but she just lights one of Maxwell's joints instead, looking bored.

"That's cool," James says. "Honestly, I just like the movies. And I just like Cher. No message behind either."

Grant ignores James. "Coming Talia?" he says. Talia shakes her head and continues to puff on the joint. Grant leaves the room. James and I stand awkwardly in the room while this quiet stranger gets stoned on an oversized bed.

"He's exhausting," Talia says. She hauls on the joint and then ditches the roach on the tray, and takes another joint and puts it in her bag. "He has good intentions, but he challenges the wrong people. He's a reformed bro. I think he's trying to correct past sins."

"Are you two together?" I ask as I sit down on the bed and wonder if she knows he's slept with Claire.

Talia shakes her head. "We're basically just fucking."

"I figured couple's costume means you're serious," James adds.

Talia grabs the last joint on the tray and lights it, takes a drag, and hands it to James. He accepts.

"I'm Stanley Kowalski. He can say our costumes are related, but to me, he's just June Cleaver." We nod. "I have a thing for skinny men," Talia confesses.

"Is it worth it to listen to him talk?" I ask.

"He doesn't speak during," says Talia.

I get a text message from Dylan saying he won't be able to make it out tonight. I'm relieved as I would feel the pressure to make Dylan feel comfortable around Anne's friends, while at the same time keeping James occupied. And I don't think I'm ready for Dylan to meet James.

Talia, James, and I talk throughout the night; she shares her thoughts on everyone at the party, roasting them severely and perceptively. We isolate ourselves in doorways, corners, and other nooks around the apartment. We escape undesirable interaction by making an island out of our bodies with our faces inward and our backs to other guests. The number of guests shrinks as the bottles begin to empty. Talia drinks the last bit of wine she can find. She says goodnight to us while she pulls on the now wigless Grant's skirt hem and takes him toward his bedroom. An earthy guy whips out a ukulele, so I know it's time to go.

On the way home, James says to me, "They weren't so bad." I give him a probing look, and he confesses, "Okay, well, Grant was kind of a dick. And Naomi and Maxwell seem kind of awful, but everyone else was fine. You were worried what I would think of Anne, but she seems nice. I like her."

I wasn't expecting this. What could he like about her?

"You barely interacted with her. She was fighting with Maxwell in his bedroom most of the night because she thought he caught a glimpse of Claire when she took her top off."

"Yeah, but they seemed fine."

"She's beautiful, don't you think?" I ask him but know I shouldn't. I'm hoping he'll lie to me and tell me she's not.

"She is, yeah."

My stomach drops and I feel ashamed.

James asks why Dylan didn't come, and I tell him I'm not sure why.

"Do you hang out all the time?"

I detect some jealousy in his questioning.

"Not so much lately."

"So, you know him well then?"

"Are you asking if I know him carnally?"

James laughs. "No." He pauses. "I guess I am, yeah."

"No! Completely platonic. Trust me."

I can hear an accordion playing, and it sounds close though muffled. James and I look around, and he points to a lit-up attic window in a Victorian house across the street. In the window there is a woman in her pajamas playing the accordion. James offers me his hand, and in the middle of the street, we dance a bit. I laugh wildly when he spins me around and I lose balance. The accordion stops.

Chapter Thirteen

In the morning, James and I sit on my front porch in big sweaters and wrap ourselves in my duvet while eating blackberries. The street is quiet this early. A squirrel found half of a bagel, and ran off with it triumphantly, but that's about it in terms of living company. James asks if I want to hang out this afternoon, but I tell him I have plans with Dylan. He runs a finger over his eyebrow, but I don't know his mannerisms well enough yet to know what this means.

When I meet Dylan at a café near my apartment, it looks like he's been here for hours. He's surrounded by empty small white coffee cups and a plate filled with beige crumbs. He's reading some nineteenth-century novel we read in school. I realize I remember nothing about it other than women suffering in a gloomy landscape.

"What did you end up doing on Halloween?" I ask him.

"Went to Mia's to watch movies. I didn't feel like seeing Anne or any of her friends, especially Claire. Anyway, Anne didn't even invite me and I—"

"I offered to stay in with Mia, and she told me not to, and said she was probably going to go to bed early."

"You know Mia, she didn't want to put you out. She had a good night, don't worry about it. We stayed up 'til two or something."

"So, you think she wanted me to stay with her?"

"I don't know. Probably?"

"Oh god. I'm a terrible friend, aren't I?"

Dylan looks tired. His grey eyes are bloodshot, and he hasn't shaved, but he still looks clean, like always. He looks so innocent that sometimes I forget he occasionally runs through women a little carelessly, and when Mia told me about all the saved ass photos he keeps on his phone, I was shocked. Not that it's weird that he has them, but I didn't expect it. Today, Dylan has on a charcoal wool pullover sweater that looks brand new. When not at work, he's either wearing athletic gear or expensive, high-quality basics.

"I'm saying she probably wanted you to be there because she wanted your company, but at the same time, no, she didn't want you to stay with her because she didn't want to ruin your night."

"Now you're making me feel bad." I know I sound whiny, but I want him to absolve me.

"How is that my fault? I'm just telling you what you already know about Mia. Don't worry about it. Like I said, we had a good time. How was Max's party?"

"It was fine," I say. He probably wants details about Anne and Max.

Dylan leans his chest against the table so that his face is only a foot from mine while I peel the label off the honey jar. "Alice, are you going to sulk for the rest of the time?"

"No," I say while adding honey to my tea, even though I don't actually want honey in my tea. "I just feel shitty for not staying with Mia."

"Don't feel bad. She seemed to be happy for you. I mean about James." This is the first time either of us have said James's name.

I'm making circles in spilled sugar with my finger like I'm a little kid, but when he puts his finger in it, I realize what I'm doing and stop. I grab a spoon to busy my hands. I feel fairly secure with James, but I still find it strange to talk about him, especially with Dylan.

"I didn't want to say much because I didn't know if it was going anywhere." I'm now making circles in my tea with a spoon.

"But you do now?"

"Yes." I keep stirring until the sound of the spoon hitting the mug becomes so grating that I stop and set my wet spoon on the table, forming a brown pool.

Dylan devotes himself to drinking his entire mug of coffee. Then he asks, "Is he a good guy?"

I laugh, trying to sound confident. "Are you worried about me, Dylan?"

"Yeah." He looks me right in the eye. I scratch my ankle. "Just because," he continues, "a lot of men are real pieces of shit."

"Yes, he's a good guy. Too good for me probably."

"Not possible."

I give him a look to say I don't believe that.

"I think you'd get along well."

He responds with an unnatural smile and this leaves me confused. I generally credit myself with being able to figure out what people are thinking, but I never feel entirely confident with Dylan.

"He didn't go to university?" He says this while resting his head on his closed fist with his elbow on the table.

"Don't be a snob, Dylan." Dylan thinks studying literature in undergrad for a year gives him an edge over other guys who want to talk about books. I can tell he wants to defend himself, but he knows by my tone to drop it.

"I miss seeing you, Alice. Let's make more of an effort to see each other."

He reaches toward my hand, like he's going to touch it, but he grabs his coffee mug instead. I try to think of something to say to him in response. I wonder how to say it so that it sounds genuine, since he made the effort to tell me he's missed me, but I pause too long.

In bed, with my laptop open, I'm trying to write. I tell myself I'll get to writing right after I look up Talia on Instagram. I find her account. She paints large-scale portraits in vivid reds, purples, and blues. They're quite good. She has a few selfies that somehow seem less obnoxious than the ones I take, and there are several candid shots of her that don't seem staged. I want to think these women on Instagram aren't actually as beautiful as they look online, but I've seen her in person, so I know she is. Talia wears a lot of black, but not constantly so that it looks like a uniform or a pretense. She knows when to mix it up with bursts of colour. At the party, we talked about how she doesn't want kids, and on her Instagram, I see her apartment is filled with plants, so while she doesn't want children, she knows how to be patient, tend to things, and make them grow. She has a lot of followers but follows few. I consider following her, but I wonder if she'd follow me back. I thought she seemed to like me at the party but what if she was only being kind, and if she just knows how to make people feel good. I keep scrolling and see a video of her. She's singing. She has a beautiful voice. I decide not to follow her.

I close Instagram. I open a browser and Google "jobs + my city + English degree." I don't click on any of the search results. Maybe I should go back to school and expand my qualifications.

Mia was in teacher's college before she got sick, but I don't think I could talk all day at my job or successfully motivate children.

It's been about a week since I've seen Mia. Her cousin is staying with her before she's back at the hospital again. Mia says her cousin refers to her body as a temple and seems to eat only giant salads. The drugs Mia's on give her intense cravings and she said she needed fried chicken, so I went to a fast-food restaurant with her a few days after Halloween. There weren't many options on the menu for me, but I ate all my fries and coleslaw while she worked on her bucket of chicken. It's weird not seeing her for a full week and I haven't heard from her for a few days. I type out a text asking *how are you* but realize she'll be thrown off by the impersonal, vague phrasing, so I delete it and type *what're you up to* since it sounds more casual. She immediately texts back: *my cousin brought her son and he is way too interested in my wig.* I reply *kill him?* She responds *Miss you.*

The space heater in my bedroom fails to do its job. It's well into November and cold mornings make the walk from the shower to my bedroom excruciating. On the way to work, the clouds sift a light cotton snow that disappears on contact with the ground. The next day, the snow is heavier, and a thin white layer remains.

James's uncle has a chalet a few hours from here, and he's borrowed his uncle's car so the two of us can stay there for the night. James wants me to know his uncle calls it a chalet, though he knows it sounds a bit bougie. I've never stayed at a chalet before, or even a cottage. I'm nervous to sleep somewhere other than my bed tonight. I haven't slept out of my own bed for over a year. I've tried to sleep at James's a few times, but every time I end up leaving in the middle of the night.

I don't feel right leaving the city. I don't like that I won't be able to walk to my house if I want to leave, or take the subway to see Mia if she needs me. I haven't seen Mia for almost two weeks. She was busy with her cousin, and I have less free time because of my temp job, though I guess it's James too. Earlier this week, she asked me to hang out when I was on the way to a movie with James. I considered bailing on him, but it was too late since we were almost at the theatre.

James assumes I'm hesitant to leave solely out of fear of a sleepless night.

"Don't worry, Alice. I brought a fan with me," James says to me as he watches me scan my room.

"Actually," I say, "we'll have to take mine. I've heard your fan, and it isn't loud enough, I need much more than a subtle hum."

"Okay, okay. No problem," he says as he takes the fan and goes to pack it in the car. When I come outside, I see that the car is an old rust-coloured station wagon.

"What is this?" I ask.

"It's a Datsun wagon. Not sure about the year. I don't really know much about cars."

"Will we make it there?"

"You've got nothing to worry about, ma'am," he says with a twang in his voice and tips his invisible cowboy hat.

It's a slow drive out of the city, and I begin to get a little car sick with all the stop-and-go traffic. I consider texting Mia to tell her I'm leaving the city for the night, but she'll think I'm mothering her. Or maybe she'll feel down since she's in the hospital right now. We've been in the car only thirty minutes, but James wants me to eat some of the snacks he brought.

I humour him and eat some corn nuts. I tell him they look like salted teeth.

We enter some little town coloured by cornflower-blue houses, and ma-and-pa shops, all sprinkled with snow. The downtown is only about three hundred feet long. James sees a market and says we have to stop and get some vegetables because towns like these have the best vegetables.

After the market, James turns to me and says, "There's a gas station ahead and they have a car wash. Let's give the wagon a cleanin'."

"Let's bathe the old bitch."

We pull into the car wash, and we're surprised by the soap sprayed onto the windows. It's not the usual white clouds of soap; instead, thousands of tiny dots of pink, purple, blue, green, and orange soap cover the car. It reminds me of those Magic Eye illusions you have to squint at and a secret picture like a castle will appear. I squint even though I know nothing will happen.

We see more snow as we drive further north. I spot horses outside in the cold. We listen to a mix James made on a cassette tape because the car is ancient. It's a mix of his favourite songs by the Ronettes and Patsy Cline. As soon as it gets dark, he puts in a new cassette of his favourite songs by Cocteau Twins and Slowdive.

There are no other cars on the road, and it's so dark that all we can see around us is the small bit of road in front that the headlights illuminate. White light burns in the distance. As we get close to the light, we see it's a ski hill, but the mechanics of the lifts, pulleys, and cables are not visible from this distance. There are yellow and white lights on the individual gondolas on the ski lift. Orbs of light move up and down the hills.

"I don't believe in an afterlife, but if heaven were real, I bet it would look like this." I'm embarrassed to have said this aloud. James just grins—his teeth have a slight glow in the darkness.

We pull in front of the chalet, and the headlights reveal a squat brown house. An army of tall evergreens surrounds it. I almost tell him that this is a cabin, not quite a *chalet*.

I grab my duffel bag from the back. I can't wait to get inside and take off my boots because my baby toe is getting pinched.

I start walking toward the door, but when James shuts the car door, the light from the inside of the car turns off and I can see only the night.

We follow each other's voices and he finds me, grabbing my hand. I stand on my toes to try to kiss him, but I kiss his eye because I can't see what I'm doing.

"Can you use your phone so we can find the door?" he asks while carrying a bunch of bags.

"That's so cold and unromantic. We need torches, or a candelabra, or a cluster of fireflies showing us our way. That would be best. I've never even seen a firefly."

"All of a sudden you're a romantic? My dick is hiding inside my body for warmth, so can you please just get your phone out?"

We make it inside and James cranks the heat. The hallway is loud—decorated in a tacky floral wallpaper. Carnations and daisies, I think. My mom has a Laura Ashley dress she wore in the '90s in a similar print. I go to walk around and explore, but James grabs my waist, and turns me around.

"What are you doing?" I ask.

"I have a bit of a surprise that I've been working on, so I'm going to have to insist that you wait in the bedroom for about forty-five minutes before we take a tour."

"What?"

"Just go in this room. There's *Where's Waldo?* books and some Guinness World Record books."

Nearly an hour later, after I've found Waldo on every page of three *Where's Waldo?* books, and after I've learned that in 1992, the world record for stone skipping was thirty-eight skips, I become impatient and ask him, from the bedroom, how much longer.

"Soon," he shouts. My feet are cold, so I go into the closet to look for slippers. There are no slippers, but heavy cotton robes hang in the closet. I wrap myself in the one that looks the least worn. It's much too big for me, and the sleeves run past my fingertips, so I roll them up. Minutes later, I can hear "Comme Moi" by Edith Piaf playing. James opens the door. I think I smell cheese.

"Did you make me dinner?"

He takes my hand. We turn a corner, and there is a bistro-style circular table with a cream laminate top and three-point cast-iron base. On the wall, there is a string of white lights.

"Sorry I took so long. I thought I could just heat up the dinner, but I ran into some issues. We're having ratatouille, croquettes, but meatless croquettes with potato, cheese, and vegetables inside. And there's a baguette. And profiteroles for dessert. I was going to make crème brûlée, but did you know that you have to use a blowtorch for that?"

I'm overwhelmed. No one has ever done anything like this for me. I fumble while trying to come up with something eloquent to say.

During dinner, James keeps asking me if my food is okay. I can tell he's tried hard for me. I call him Mrs. Dalloway. He tells me in detail how he had to make the profiteroles three times because he was sure he could make them without a piping bag, but after the first two attempts, he caved and bought one. I can't stop thinking about all the work he put into this. It makes me feel happy and also kind of nervous.

James asks me if I want to get into the hot tub and I agree to go in after making a comment about feeling like I'm on a reality TV show.

The hot tub sits at the edge of the deck attached to the chalet, and it looks out onto an empty snowy field. The lit-up ski hill is visible in the distance, and it looks like some glowing planet that fell from the sky.

I ask him to get me a drink so that I can take off my clothes and get in the hot tub without him seeing me in my bra and underwear, which is ridiculous since he's seen me naked. I close my eyes and don't think I can accurately picture what my body looks like. When he's back, James takes his clothes off and gets in the hot tub.

I don't remember the last time I was in a hot tub. It feels both luxurious and trashy at the same time.

"Who did your uncle exploit to be able to afford this place? This *second* home?"

James shakes his head. "He's actually not rich—he got such a deal on this place."

"Anyone with two homes is rich."

James reaches out of the hot tub to open an orange tea tin. He pulls out a joint and a lighter. It's a bit windy, so it takes a while for the flame to catch. I watch it burn dully between his lips as he inhales.

As he hands it to me, I ask, "Have you ever seen a firefly? I was hoping there'd be some here, but I don't see any."

"Of course you don't see any here. They're only out in the summer."

"Are you sure?"

"Pretty sure," James says, not as confident.

"You know we're pretty useless when it comes to science," I say.

"Does this count as science?"

"One of us needs that knowledge. Global warming will bring the end of days soon enough, and we're kind of fucked for survival."

"But I mean, if it's the end and the world is water, like that Kevin Costner movie, I can build you a boat. So, I have that, in terms of a practical skill," James says.

"No, see. You can build a replica of a boat, like just the skeleton. But your boat wouldn't float. It would only look like it could—it would be an imposter boat. When you make a set, you don't build an actual house, or a car, or a boat, you build the necessary pieces of it in order to facilitate the illusion that it is real for the audience. So, you probably can't build a boat."

"You're a real asshole, you know that?" James asks.

I shrug.

"Well, anyway, when the world does end, we can go to my brother's house. He's one of those left brain, right brain people. He'll have a good strategy for staying alive, and he'll explain to us why the world is ending, and he'll know how to turn a barbecue into a plane, but then he'll also be able to paint art for us to hang in our fallout shelter."

I play with the lighter, trying to flick the ring back to start a flame, but my hands are too wet.

James pulls out rolling papers and takes the lighter from my hand. He takes one of the papers out of the pack and lights the end on fire. He lights three more and they move up through the air. They look like low-hanging stars.

"Okay, so they don't really look like fireflies, but I tried."

The stars seem to be lower out of the city where there are fewer people. They look so low that it feels like if I put a chair on the roof and stood on the tips of my toes, I could reach them. I know that what would actually happen is that I'd fall off the roof and break important bones, and likely die.

A rush of wind comes and blows James's fireflies across the backyard, and we see them fall about thirty feet away onto the wet ground and the flames go out.

I tell James he should feel bad about littering.

When we're back inside, we set up some pillows and blankets in front of an electric fireplace in the living room. The floor is carpeted. I don't think I've seen carpet for years.

James's eyes are narrowed and he's grinning at me, making me realize how drunk we both are. He says, "I think we're great friends."

I laugh, then fake offence. "*Friends*?!"

He waves his hands to say no. "I just mean like we're a good pairing." I can tell he was about to say couple but avoided it. He probably thought it sounded too serious.

I give him a blank stare to mock him for saying something so earnest, but it breaks and I smile to show him I agree with him.

"Did you have a lot of friends as a kid?" he asks.

"I think I'm confused by your definition of friend now. Do you mean friends like us, or friends who don't have sex?"

"I said as a kid."

"Right. Not a lot but some. Always Mia. I can't even remember a time before knowing her." I pause. "You?"

"Nah, I was the weird kid. Carried around a box of spiders with me a lot of the time."

"Are you a Tim Burton character?" I take a sip of wine. "Do you think it's weird that I've never really been in a relationship before? Like, a real one." I'm intoxicated and brave.

"I just think you're guarded."

"I worried that they'd know all these intimate things about me that I couldn't get back."

He wraps his arms around me, and I think he's trying to think about what to say back to that.

"Have you ever been in love with someone?" I ask him to save him from thinking of a response.

He nods.

"Was she your girlfriend?" I ask.

"I thought so. But evidently, no. She didn't like that I told her I loved her. We were just hanging out, she said."

"Do you still love her?"

"No! Of course not."

I want to ask him what her name is and ask him if he brought her here and if she looks like me, but I don't.

He softly kisses my neck. "You always smell the same, like raspberries."

"I hate to ruin it for you, but that's just my deodorant."

"Nope," he says. "I didn't hear that. You're different. You're special."

"Men always think the women they're into are different than anyone else. They see a girl reading a book they think only they've read and then assume they're the only two people who have ever read it, especially if she's waifish with big eyes—yes, you all fall for those ones."

"Oh, come on, you think we're all that simple? I tried to compliment you and you basically called me a shallow idiot."

"Not you, just all the other guys," I say.

My finger traces the circumference of the wineglass. "I'm only telling you this because I'm a bit drunk—okay, and high—but you seem really open. I know that I can be stubborn and closed, but I don't want to be that way." I immediately regret what I've said, and I get up off the floor to start cleaning the mess from dinner.

Chapter Fourteen

I wake up, pick the crusts off my eyes, and sacrifice a few eyelashes in the process. James is a sprawled-out naked corpse beside me. A long creek of drool begins at his open mouth, curves, and collects on the duvet. I don't remember much after getting into bed last night. I know we had sex, but the details are hazy. I know James put on a sex playlist he made, beginning with Prince's "The Beautiful Ones," which I thought was a bold opener, and then I remember hearing "I Only Said" by My Bloody Valentine at one point. Neither of us came, but we were both fucked up, so it didn't matter. I look at James's watch. It's 10:19 a.m. The last time I remember looking at the time was in the kitchen at 2:58 a.m. That's the longest that I've slept without waking up in months. I look around the room—the fan is in the room, but not plugged in. I'm surprised at how comfortable I feel out in the middle of nowhere. Or maybe the wine and weed knocked me out. I can't believe how easily I fell asleep last night. I just dissolved into the night.

In bed, I ask James if he has a Facebook account. He says he does, but that he's neglected it for years. I ask him to show me. He doesn't have any photos of himself as his profile pictures, only stills from movies. The last one he posted is Patrick Swayze from *Ghost*. When he gets up to take a shower, I look through the photos he's tagged in. There's a photo of him playing beer pong, which makes me like him less, and one of him singing "Moonlight Desires" at karaoke, which makes me like him more. Then I find some of him with a woman who looks familiar. I hover the cursor over her face for the tag to appear: Beth Maynard. She was the TA in my Chaucer class. Beth was so arrogant. When students spoke in class and their interpretations differed from hers, she'd walk around the classroom as if considering a response, but instead of engaging with the comment, she'd smirk. She also wrote *This is a mess* on one of my essays. That red ink is imprinted in my mind forever. I shut the laptop when I hear him turn off the shower.

I check my phone and see that it's dead. I don't even remember looking at it last night. I search through my bag for my charger, but I guess I forgot it at home. That's not like me to forget that, or to let my phone die. I worry that I've missed calls from Mia or maybe calls about Mia. I ask to use James's charger and watch the screen while it charges. I don't have any text messages. I type *hey, you good?* to Mia but I realize I'll seem anxious. I'll just visit tomorrow instead.

After loading up the car, we begin our drive back to the city. It's a lot icier on the road today. The Datsun moves like a bumper car.

"Have you been writing?"

My mom asks, Mia asks, Dylan asks, even Anne asks, and now James asks.

"Yeah," I say, while looking for gum. I don't have any, I never do. Mia is the one who always has gum.

"Can I read it?" James asks.

"When it's done."

"Don't you want an opinion about what you've already written?"

"I'm not ready yet. And I'll probably show Dylan first. He was always my first reader on short stories I wrote in school."

And not me? I imagine James saying, though he doesn't. He is silent for a beat too long.

"Well, if you feel the urge to show me, I will gladly accept. And I know I'm no literary scholar like Dylan, but I did just learn how to read and I'm actually pretty good."

As we drive closer to the city, I feel the urge to bring something up with James.

"Did you ever date Beth Maynard?" I ask.

James glances at me. "How do you know that?"

"So, you did date her?"

"Yeah," he says. "How do you know that?" He leaves space between each word.

"Does it really matter?"

"Kind of," James says.

"I saw tagged photos of you with her."

"On Facebook?"

I nod. "I just wanted to see photos of you from when you were younger. I wasn't looking for anything else."

"Okay, I get that." He still sounds annoyed. "I did date Beth for a while, but not longer than half a year or so. How do you know her?"

"She was my TA for my Chaucer class. You liked her?"

"Well, clearly."

"Why?"

"I don't know. She was smart? Pretty."

"She was great at being condescending and totally pomp-ous," I say.

"Wow, she must have given you a bad grade."

"No, no, that's not it. She was just . . . terrible."

James asks, "When was she your TA?"

"About three years ago."

"I may have read one of your essays."

"She used to show you students' work?"

"Only the ones she thought were funny. I never really under-stood what she thought was so bad about them."

"God, she's the worst. So why did you break up with her?"

"Actually, she broke up with me."

I am kind of horrified that Beth left James. What am I supposed to think about James's taste in women? What am I supposed to think about myself?

"I can't believe you dated her."

"It wasn't for a long time, and it's not like I was in love with her or anything. It was more of a sex thing."

"Oh, god." I cover my eyes.

"Does that make it worse?" James asks as the car comes to a stop in traffic.

James asks if I want to sleep over tonight, but I tell him Gus will be missing me after being away. When I left, I filled three bowls to the top with cat food. Gus looked at me as if to suggest I was overdoing it, and I dumped one bowl back in the bag out of fear he would overeat and die. James looks like he's waiting for me to invite him over, but he doesn't ask. I had a good time with him, but I am desperate to be alone.

When I step inside my apartment, Gus appears, meows theatrically, and lies down on his back to lure me to his furry belly. I drop my bags and go to him, telling him he radiates desperation. After giving Gus some attention, I wash all the makeup off my face, throw on a giant toothpaste-stained T-shirt and a pair of sweatpants, and crawl in bed with a box of cheese crackers and my laptop and feel relieved to be by myself. I don't have to worry about saying the right thing, and if I want to eat this entire box of crackers in bed and then sleep in the crumbs, I can. I know that I really like James, but sometimes I wonder if I want to be in a relationship only because it's a normal thing to want.

Gus is apparently still feeling slighted by my absence and butts his forehead against my hand and rubs his gums against my fingers while I'm trying to find something to watch on my laptop. It was my idea to get a cat. Before we found our apartment, a friend from our dorm asked if Mia and I wanted to live with her. The three of us got along well, but I wanted to live with only Mia—we'd planned it since high school. I couldn't hide my disappointment over Mia wanting to live with another person, and I got defensive while struggling to think of a reasonable way to say no. I said, But you told me we'd get a cat and she's allergic, and I really want a cat. I knew at the time I sounded whiny. Mia sighed and said I knew you'd do this. Alice, just have the guts to say no. So, I asked Mia, if you knew that, then why did you ask me? She said I guess I was hoping you'd do something for me.

James doesn't text me before he goes to sleep like he usually does, and I wonder if he feels rejected by me because I didn't invite him over. But maybe he was relieved when I didn't invite him, and perhaps he asked me over only because he thinks I'm insecure. I put on an old season of *The Real Housewives of Beverly Hills*. I fall asleep during episode three.

The next morning, I think about visiting Mia like I'd planned to, but I need to conserve my energy. I text her telling her I'll visit tomorrow. It's Anne's birthday and she invited people to an art show. All day, I struggle to muster up the energy to take a shower and get dressed, but when James tells me he'll be over in an hour, I make myself get up. The last thing that I want to do is go out for Anne's birthday, but if I don't show, she'll hold it against me, and that seems more annoying to deal with than a night out. I'm hoping that she'll get so drunk that she won't notice me leaving early. I'm also nervous about Dylan and James meeting. I hope they like each other.

Anne is wearing heels. When she puts on heels, she looks like she is eight feet tall. Her legs stretch like headlights on a night road. She's wearing a black satin dress with a short hem and a low back. She has brown moles all down her back and curving up around her neck. The highlighter on her cheeks makes her look ethereal. She's dyed her chin-length hair a deep red, and everyone is shocked because she didn't tell anyone that she was going to do it. I ask her what inspired the new look, and she responds, "Well, I've never been a redhead before," and I think, why do you have to be everything?

The art shows I've attended before have been in crowded narrow spaces where people are hoping they're standing in the correct line for alcohol, but often they're just trapped in the throng. This space is big and white with Edison bulbs on thick black cords hanging from the ceiling, but only a few in the centre of the gallery are turned on. The canvasses hung on the perimeter of the room can't be seen. A black velvet rope separates the guests from getting close to the work. There's a pink neon sign on the wall that says *The art wants what it wants*. I point it out to James and he says, "What have you got me into?"

I look around thinking everyone looks put together in a way that's meant to appear effortless, but if you look closely you'll see what fine attention has been paid to even the most dishevelled looks. I wonder if I fit in with my green-and-blue plaid skirt and loose black sweater. I've attempted to look kind of grunge— though I would never admit it—but I think I might look more like a Catholic school girl. No matter what age I am, I am subconsciously trying to emulate *The Craft* in some way.

I tell James I'm going to get us drinks. In line at the bar, I feel a tap on my shoulder. It's Lauren. Her hair is still purple, but it's a darker shade than when we ran into each other on the subway, and it's much shorter. She's wearing a black jumpsuit cut low in the front.

Lauren, in faux-European fashion, presses her cheeks against mine. "Look, I have to get back to my friends, but I thought I'd give you a quick hi."

"Hi!" I do my best peppy girl impression, and I feel like I need a three-hour lie-down on the couch to recover from it.

Lauren says we should hang out, but this is just a polite gesture—pretending to make plans that neither party intends on following through with. She says she noticed Anne was here and then says I mean *Anastasia*, and makes a little derisive smile, and asks me if I'm still friends with her. I say yes. She says *interesting*.

She says she has to go and gives me more kisses around my head. I don't know how to receive these phantom pecks.

The crowd has grown quite large, and I've almost made it to the bar when Claire pulls me toward her and Anne. She's wearing straight-leg jeans and a lime-green sheer button-up tied in a knot above her navel and buttoned low. I can see that her nipples are pierced. Claire's hair is as big as a fanned peacock tail tonight.

"Since when do you talk to Lauren? I figured you hadn't seen her since high school," says Anne.

"I ran into her on the subway in the summer," I say to Anne. "Do you know Lauren?" I ask Claire.

"She was dating a pretty huge filmmaker for about a year, I think everyone knows who she is," Claire explains.

"She flirts with Maxwell constantly, and she acts like she doesn't even know who I am," Anne says.

"But do you act like you know her?" I ask Anne.

Anne looks surprised. "Of course. I smile at her. I don't get why people are impressed by her. She's not even pretty," says Anne.

"She really isn't," Claire agrees.

"What? I think she's pretty," I say. They both look betrayed.

"HAPPY BIRTHDAY, ANASTASIA!" I hear screamed behind me. Anne hugs a short girl with long hair and tattooed hands and a skinny girl in a pink latex dress. Anne's dress rises when the skinny one picks her up, and I pull down her dress so that her butt is not exposed.

"We got you a present!" says the short girl with glazed eyes.

"It may or may not be cocaine. But I would say that yeah, it is," the skinny one whispers, revealing a gap between her two front teeth.

"Not tonight," Anne says. "I took some other shit, and when they're mixed, I always puke everywhere." I know she's lying.

Anne is terrified of doing coke. She's done it once with Mia, and she cried the whole time because she thought she was having a heart attack. She wants people to think she does it occasionally, so she lies about it.

I see James push his way through the crowd to stand near me, and I mouth *I'm sorry* for leaving him so long and not succeeding at getting drinks. I spot Dylan making his way toward us. When Claire notices Dylan has arrived, she corrects her posture by pushing her shoulders back and her breasts forward.

Claire whispers in my ear, "Is Dylan single?"

"I never seem to know. He's hard to keep track of."

"Come on, Al." She never calls me Al, we're not nearly close enough for nicknames. "Tell me." She leans forward, trying to lure the truth from me.

"I really don't know." I'm 99 percent sure he isn't seeing anyone, but I'm trying to help Dylan out. "I think he might be seeing someone."

She is no longer whispering. "You just want to keep Dylan for yourself, don't you? I knew you had a thing for him." She says this playfully, but James overhears and looks at me. I don't think he's pleased.

I shake my head and laugh, trying to suggest that she's ridiculous.

Dylan's arrival causes Anne to go out for a cigarette. Much to Claire's dismay, Anne requests her company. Anne whispers in my ear, "I'm not drunk enough for this yet," and says hi to Dylan on her way out by tapping him on the shoulder with only her fingertips. I wonder if Dylan has to stop himself from watching her walk away. Claire hugs Dylan, which Dylan does not expect. Dylan is left with me and James, surrounded by strangers. Dylan is wearing a charcoal knit turtleneck that's not tight but also not too loose. The neck is folded down, so that it doesn't ride too high up to his chin and make him look like a creepy psychiatrist. He pushes the sleeves halfway up his forearms with his coat folded over his arm.

"I really know how to clear a room. Should I not have come?"

"It's fine. She's completely cool with you being here." I attempt to reassure him. I introduce him to James. I suddenly feel flustered, knowing I need to get conversation rolling.

"Dylan, James worked on the set of *Who's Afraid of Virginia Woolf?* that you saw early in the summer."

Dylan is stretching forward to hear me. "That's cool. Did you design it?"

"Nah, I'm just an underling."

"He's being modest. He's really talented." I make eyes at Dylan, urging him to talk more.

"The actress playing Martha was kind of over the top, I thought."

I shoot him a look as if to say *that's not what I was thinking.*

"That's kind of the role though," says James.

"I guess, but she should be more nuanced than just loud."

"I didn't think she was just loud though. And she made it her own thing, which is hard to do when everyone's seen the movie."

Dylan shrugs to show he doesn't agree but decides to say nothing more. He runs his fingers through his hair and looks behind him.

I ask them both if they want drinks, and James says he'll get us some, but Dylan says he's got them.

"I was going to get those," James says.

I pretend not to hear him.

Dylan comes back with our drinks: a beer for James with an embossed label that's so fancy I feel I should save it, and though I asked for a G&T, he hands me a two-toned drink with unidentifiable fruits and a lavender stalk sticking out. We thank Dylan for our drinks and James says he'll get the next ones. Dylan says not to worry about it but James insists. James looks at the bottle and takes a sip of the beer, and when Dylan checks his phone, James whispers to me, "Of course he bought some bougie ass beer." James's hostility toward Dylan is surprising. I mouth *please* to him to ask him to give Dylan a chance.

"Who's that guy?" James asks. He's trying. He points to a man with long curly grey hair pulled up into a high bun. He is wearing a grey Henley shirt with white denim overalls and white Doc Martens. "Is he in costume or something?" James must be referring to the monocle on his eye.

"No, that's his everyday eyewear. Calls himself Ekphrasis." Dylan grins wanly. "But his close friends call him Dean. This is his show."

"What the hell does *ekphrasis* mean?" James asks.

"It's like an artistic representation of another form of art. So, like, a poem written about a painting," I explain.

"What an asshole. He just wants people to look that up. Who's ever heard of that?" James asks.

Dylan replies, "Well, Alice and I studied it in one of our poetry classes."

I give a half nod, knowing Dylan is showing off a little.

"Sure, but the rest of humanity, we've never heard of it." James looks around. "I can't see anything. What is his art?"

"Name a medium, and he's covered it," Dylan says.

"You work in business, right?" James asks Dylan, abruptly.

"Is that what Alice told you I do?"

I'm trying to remember if I told James that Dylan was worried that his job made him seem shallow. I try to redirect the conversation. "So, Anne was his muse for a while and he painted lots of portraits of her. She said there's one of her tonight too, which is a big reason why we're here."

James asks if Ekphrasis is actually talented and I say no.

"Come on, Al, you know he is," Dylan objects. "If he were a terrible artist, hating him would be way more satisfying, but you can't deny that he really is talented."

"Okay, his portraits, sure. But come on, his video art and his installations, they're ridiculous. Don't tell me you actually understood what his aim was when he built that hut out of gum in front of that convenience store and tried to live in it for a full week. And you know his parents own the building beside the store, so he was sneaking away to sleep and eat there."

I wait for Dylan to respond, but I don't think he was listening. He's staring at Zoe who's waiting at the bar for a drink. She's wearing a high-neck cropped T-shirt with high-waisted black jeans and patent leather boots.

James asks, "So, is he famous or something?"

"I guess quasi famous, *local* famous, but I'm not sure if I would know about him if I didn't know Anne," I explain. "Maxwell isn't here because he hates Dean. He made a pass at Anne, and I think she returned the affection once. During a fight with Maxwell, she listed all the people who wanted to sleep with her, and gave him details about Dean, then next time we were all out together, Maxwell punched Dean in the face," I say.

"Did he break his monocle?" James asks.

"No, the monocle is a new development," I say.

"Maxwell is over there, talking to some girl with purple hair." Dylan points over to a shadowy part of the room where

Maxwell is looking cozy with Lauren. I look around to see if I can find Anne. She's in a group of women who are all touching her new hair. I notice Dylan keeps sneaking glimpses at Anne. I wonder if he likes her as a redhead.

Someone whispers in my ear, "I taught this sad dude everything he knows. He rips me off. He rips everyone off."

I turn to see Talia in ripped faded denim jeans, a Budweiser T-shirt, and a long black leather jacket. She hands me a drink. I take it but worry I'm getting too drunk since I had a few drinks with James before I got here. I go to whisper something back to her, but I notice the music—shoegaze covers of happy pop songs—has been turned off then I hear Ekphrasis clearing his throat over a microphone. Talia says this should be good.

"I won't say many words for I believe art should speak for itself. All the models, *muses*"—he pauses to look at Anne and she's beaming—"posed under the impression that I was painting their portraits, and indeed I was. However, they believed I was capturing their exteriority, but what inspires me isn't the physical but the interior. Housed inside the flesh and bone vessel is the soul. Now, please raise a glass and sup Bacchus's divine nectar." Everyone raises their glass and Ekphrasis toasts to the *human soul.*

The lights come on, the velvet ropes come down, and the portraits are revealed. They all look vaguely like Rothko paintings. Everyone gasps as they're expected to and rushes over to the paintings.

Talia says, "I can't decide whether it's depressing or comforting when people do exactly what you'd expect them to do. Should we grab James and get out of here, away from these clout chasers?"

"I wish I could, but it's An-Anastasia's birthday."

"Hmm, right," she says. "Are she and Maxwell over? Is she with him now?" I look over at where she's pointing and I see Anne making her flirty face while talking to Dylan. I feel a sinking feeling in my stomach.

"Definitely not," I say while not taking my eyes off them.

Talia tells me she's going to leave and says I can finish her drink. I do that even though it's whiskey and I hate whiskey.

"How long do we have to stick around?" James asks as he puts his arms around my waist. I forgot he was standing behind me.

"I don't know what's up with Anne. She's definitely flirting with Dylan, which is so weird. They have barely spoken in years." I should stop but I go on. "Do you think she's trying to make Maxwell jealous?"

"Maybe?" James says flatly.

"I think I told you they had sex years ago, but she doesn't give a shit about him anymore. She usually ignores him, so her talking to him now is clearly a ploy to piss off Maxwell, don't you think?"

I stop looking at them for a second to look at him, impatiently.

"How should I know?" he says.

My head starts to hurt, and I tell him I'm going to go get some water. I look at the lineup for the bar, and try the washrooms. Usually, there's only one stall in a gallery like this, but there are three here, and they're all occupied. I turn on the faucet in the sink, cup my hands under, and drink some water. A woman in all black gives me a disgusted look. I look into the mirror and feel plain. I reach into my bag to find my mascara to put more on. I notice my phone is flashing. One text from Mia: *I have to turn off my phone soon. I know you worry when I don't reply. I won't get any texts til tmrw when I'm unhooked for an hour.* I don't get why she's told me this since she always has to turn off her phone when she's getting treatment. I wonder if she's hinting that lately we haven't talked enough. I feel bad. I try to think what to text her back and it all seems lazy. I should have gone to see her today. I don't put on more mascara. I turn to leave right when Anne walks in.

"Hey!" she says. She touches up her neon-pink lipstick. "I love red with pink, don't you?" I nod. "Is it just me or does Dylan look really good tonight?" What is she doing? Trying to make Maxwell jealous, or me?

"I guess," I say. "I should get back to James."

She says something else as I leave the room, but I can't make it out and pretend I don't notice that she was saying anything.

When I get back to James, he's staring at a painting of a pink and red square. "This is Anne's soul," he says to me.

"What?"

"She told me this is the portrait he did of her."

"Did she say anything about Dylan?"

He takes a sip of his beer and turns to me and says, "What's up with you?"

I give him an irritated look. I spot Anne talking to Dylan again. So does Maxwell and he laughs obnoxiously at something Lauren says. He slowly tucks her hair behind her ear while making eye contact with her—he might as well have just licked her neck. That was meant for Anne, but she missed it. I tell James, without looking at him, that I'll be back in a second. I walk over to Anne and Dylan.

"Hey, girl," she says while smiling.

"Having a good birthday, Anne?" I ask, but I'm sure she notices I sound off because she just nods. "Do you remember it's Mia's birthday in a few weeks?"

"Yeah, of course."

"*Of course?*" I say. "Dylan and I are going to bring her a cake. Want to come with?"

"Al, let's get some water," Dylan says.

James approaches. "Everything cool?" He must notice Anne looks distressed.

"Yes, everything is cool! Anne is *so cool*. Don't you love her new hair?" My voice is sounding louder than I mean to talk, and it makes me feel like I'm going to fall over.

Anne looks hurt but tries to give me a pitying look and then walks away. James leads me outside and Dylan follows. James starts rubbing my back while Dylan stands a few feet away. I have a boulder in my throat. It's snowing and I realize I'm shivering.

"Did you drink too much? Feeling sick?" James asks.

"It's not that. It's Mia," Dylan says.

James and I both turn to look at him, and he looks at his phone and starts typing. Dylan says he ordered a rideshare and hopes I feel better. He says goodnight to us both. Dylan doesn't tell James it was nice to meet him, maybe because he doesn't think it was. He walks away and I wonder why he didn't arrange to have the driver meet him at the gallery. Where is he going? I'm watching him, but James hails a cab and we get in before I can see where he's going.

I expect James to ask me if he can sleep over tonight, but he doesn't. Neither of us say anything in the cab.

At home, I look in the mirror and decide that I hate how my hair has grown.

Chapter Fifteen

I wake up to my phone ringing. I can feel my hangover, it's like I've got a tight helmet on. I see Anne is calling me. She cuts me off before I can apologize for last night.

"I'm kind of pissed at you, but I need you," Anne says.

"What's wrong?" I ask.

"Can you just come over?"

"Sure. Are you okay?"

"Can you just come now? Please?"

It's snowing lightly outside. It's getting to be the kind of cold I can't stand. I notice James hasn't texted me, and I wonder if my antics last night irritated him. I text him apologizing though I don't specify what I'm apologizing for. I ask if we can hang soon. I text Dylan: *Was I awful last night?*

He responds within a minute: *I wouldn't say awful. You okay?*

Anne lives in the basement apartment of a three-storey red-brick house. The entrance to her apartment is at the back. When she opens the door in a lilac bathrobe, I see she has no makeup on. It's the first time in years that I've seen her clean-faced. She's still beautiful, but not quite flawless. I can see lines under her eyes. There are a few red spots on her cheeks and forehead, and without brow pencil, her eyebrows look less strong. Her eyes are pink, bloodshot.

"I think I'm pregnant," she says before I'm even inside.

"What? Why do you think that?" I ask as I step inside.

"I haven't had my period for a while," she says as she nervously pulls at the sleeves of her robe.

"When was the last time?" I ask.

"I don't remember. And I've been sick, not just in the morning though, all the time. I even threw up last night at the gallery. I took a test this morning, and it said that I am." Her voice breaks as she tries not to cry. "Fuck."

"I'm sorry for being a dick last night, Anne."

"It wasn't just you. Max kept flirting with Lauren, like, right in front of me, like he didn't give a shit." She wipes her face on her terrycloth sleeves. "And with Zoe too. Fuck. I could kill him. But I really do love him."

"Why do you love him though?"

"That's not so easy to answer."

"Shouldn't it be? You only say bad things about him. If someone is making you feel like shit all the time, what's the point of being with that person?"

She throws me one of her piercing looks. I bet she's thinking, what does Alice know about relationships? She's never dated anyone long-term. She looks away and clears her throat, and I can tell she's not going to go there. She needs me too much.

"You don't know about the good stuff. I just tell you about the bad things when I'm upset. Al, I have other things to worry about right now. Can we focus? I'm fucking *pregnant*."

"But you only did one test. What if it's wrong?"

"I bought three other brands too. I got scared after the one though, so I called you."

"Let's try them all. Do you have enough pee in you for three more sticks?" I ask.

Five minutes later, Anne comes out of the bathroom. I set a timer and try to get her to sit on the couch with me, but she says she's too nervous to sit. When the timer goes off, Anne looks at the three tests on the ledge of her bathtub. She gestures for me to come over. She looks frantic.

"These symbols and colours are confusing. Let's read the instructions to make sure," I say.

I pull out the different sets of instructions and then look at the plastic tests. Two lines. A plus sign. Blue.

"Okay, well, yeah, you're definitely pregnant."

Anne curls into a heap on the floor. "I don't think I'm ready to have a kid. I don't even know if I want one ever. I couldn't afford to take care of it. And obviously I'd love it, but—" She pauses before saying, "I think I would just be really depressed."

I hand her a tissue and say, "Sounds like you shouldn't have it, Anne."

She looks surprised. "That's what I was thinking, but I'm scared. Do you know anyone who's had one, an abortion I mean?"

"Yeah, do you?"

She nods.

"I hear it's uncomfortable and after it feels like bad cramps, but I think it's different for everyone," I say.

"And if I had a kid now, modelling would be done. But I mean, I think that's pretty much over anyway. Most of the money I make now is from bartending."

"You don't have to convince me. And with modelling, you did some pretty cool shit." I try to cheer her up.

"I probably should have gone to university or something, right? Maybe applied to other schools."

"Oh yeah, because look at how successful I am. Struggling to even get a full-time job answering phones."

"Modelling's not one hundred percent over with. I just mean I'm not going to be famous like I wanted to be."

"Yeah" is all I can push out.

"I know you think I'm superficial or whatever, but you don't know everything."

"I didn't say that."

"I know you, Al. I know you don't like Claire or Max or my other friends, but they're not so bad. There's a lot more to them, but you don't take the time to see that."

"I really am sorry about last night."

She nods as if to say she forgives me.

"I'm glad that you called me, but I'm wondering why you didn't call Claire."

"I love Claire, but I trust you more. For the most part, you calm me down."

I know if things weren't tense with her and Mia, she would have called Mia and not me. I'm useful to her. I'm a backup.

Anne runs her finger over a tiny scar beside her brow bone. When we were at camp, I accidentally hit her in the face with the blade of my paddle. She had to get stitches and completely milked the injury for attention. Someone started a rumour that I did it on purpose out of jealousy.

"Do you still hate me for that scar?"

She takes her finger off the scar and absently says, "Takes two seconds to get rid of it in Photoshop."

"So, you don't blame me for your career not taking off?" I worry that this joke is too much.

"No," she says. "I don't know why that happened, or didn't happen."

When Mia and I are upset, we console each other by lying together in bed or on the couch. Usually, the sad one rests their head on the consoler. I consider doing this with Anne, but I think she'd be uncomfortable. She'd likely go along with it, but she wouldn't feel soothed. We've both done this kind of comforting thing with Mia but not with each other. I remember when Claire and I first met, she insisted that I play with her hair one night when I was at her place. I didn't know what she wanted me to do, so I was just kind of kneading her hair, not knowing if I was doing it right. Then she took photos of us while I had my hands in her hair, and I could tell she was trying hard to create a *moment*.

Anne makes us cucumber and cream cheese sandwiches. This makes me think of when I made her nachos when we were thirteen or so. She got locked out of her house after school, and her parents were out of town visiting her older sisters at their university, so she needed somewhere to stay. Anne tried to call Mia to see if she could stay at her house, but she was out and didn't answer, so she came to my place. When she got to my door, she told me her dad was supposed to put a key under a stone in the garden but he must have forgot. Anne's parents often acted as though they forgot they had a third daughter. They didn't remember to pick her up when the bus from camp dropped us off, and they repeatedly forgot the names of her boyfriends.

Anne decides she'll call a clinic tomorrow and make an appointment. I tell her I'll go with her. I ask her if she'll tell Max, and she says no. I say she'll likely feel a bit ill after, and I ask her if she may want to confide in him. She explains to me that she knows that he wouldn't handle it well. I give up on trying to convince her. I'm not completely certain that it's the right thing to do anyway. Maybe I'm just used to being contrary to Anne.

I tell Anne that I have somewhere to be. I'm going to see Mia, but I don't tell Anne. I don't want to make her more upset. I feel like I am betraying Mia by concealing this.

As I'm lacing up my boots, Anne says, "I do want to see her, Al. I'm just scared, but I know that doesn't matter."

It doesn't matter, but I don't say that.

On the way to the hospital, a young girl with bright blue eyes and long yellow hair is sitting across from me on the subway train. This girl looks just like Mia did when she was a child. I almost expect her to open her palms to show me the change she stole off her mother's dresser and suggest we go buy candy.

Mia looks nearly translucent when I enter her room. She's wearing an ivory scarf around her head and no makeup. She looks weary, and I can't imagine her standing up and supporting her own weight. She keeps her eyes on her paperback even when I'm standing in front of her. One of her long legs is hanging over the edge of her bed with a sheet covering it, her toes peeking out. Her roommate is snoring in the corner with the curtain drawn.

"Do you want me to bring you some new books? You've read that a million times," I say as I sit at the edge of her bed.

"I'm fine for now," she says, not moving her eyes from the page. With no makeup on, the blue of her eyes glow, and her eyelids are like white opal. Her lips look paler than usual, though they still have a faint pinkish hue. I try not to stare, but she looks so unlike herself.

I let her finish the page she's on, and I begin to tidy up her room. I pick up food wrappers off her side tables and sweaters draped over the chairs and the end of her bed and hang them in the closet. Her eyes break from the page and follow me while I do this.

"You don't have to do that," she says.

"I don't mind." I try to sound sprightly. It's a tone foreign to both of us.

"Just stop."

I feel something hard in my throat.

"What's wrong?" I ask meekly.

"Where have you been?"

"I've been busy. I'm sorry. I—"

She interrupts me. "Busy doing what? Working? Are you still doing that temp job?" She stares at me.

"James and I went away for a night to his uncle's cabin, and last night we went out. It was Anne's birthday and—"

"I know when her birthday is," she says. Holding the book to her chest, she shuts her eyes tightly. "I called you the other night. I guess you were away."

I walk over to the bed, but I don't know how close she wants me, so I sit back down on the edge.

"I'm sorry. My phone died. I didn't know you called. I did think about you when I realized it died, but I didn't want to seem like I was smothering you." I feel terrible.

"I was having a really hard night."

"I should have told you I was leaving for the night. I'm sorry I haven't been around as much lately. I've been caught up in this whole thing with James, not that that's an excuse. I'm so sorry."

"I'm fucking embarrassed."

"What do you mean? About what?"

"About you and James." She pauses. "I think I'm jealous." She covers her eyes with her hand.

"Why?"

She drops her hand away. "Sometimes I don't know, Al. I see the looks on my parents' faces, and I see that they're terrified, even if they don't say it. And the way they always try to hug me now, just in case. And Anne, she hasn't been here for months. Am I supposed to think that we're still friends? I texted her yesterday for her birthday, and she just responded with a dumb heart emoji. You still visit me, but it's not the same. Right before you leave, you always stare at me. I know what that means."

I try to say something, but I can't.

"I know this is confusing because I've been telling you to write, and get out and go on dates, and then I freak out on you when you're away. I can't really explain it. It's not your fault." She pauses. "I just feel like I'm not going to get it back."

"Get what back?"

Her eyes are blue vats in a web of inky red. I'll never be able to understand what she's feeling, and she knows it.

As I pass my neighbour's garden, covered by the blankness of snow, I realize it's nearing December. I keep thinking it's a different month than it really is. I stop and look at the yard, focus on it, but everything is the same, all white, and I feel a sense of dread. When Mia first told me she was sick, there was snow on the ground. I remember looking at my neighbour's yard expecting to see flowers and feeling a similar disorientation. My head feels heavy, like it's too big for my neck, and I put my hands on my head, trying to secure it, make it stay up. My muscles go limp, so I hold onto the fence to stabilize myself. I start to question if this is even my neighbour's home and if I really do live next door. All the houses look warped and are starting to look the same, though unfamiliar. I try to remember what the flowers in the garden look like, and I picture red roses and yellow tulips growing along a fence. When I start to hear a '50s song in my head, I realize this isn't my memory—it's the opening sequence from *Blue Velvet*. My heart is beating too fast. I try to picture Mia before she was sick, but can only conjure famous blonde actresses. I feel a rush of tears in my eyes. Someone is looking at me through a window in my neighbour's house, and I summon the energy I have to walk away quickly to my front door. As soon as I'm inside, I sit down on the floor with my coat and boots still on, soaking my tights. I open my phone to my camera and scroll back and find photos of Mia with her long hair, before it all happened. My heartbeat slows. I take off my boots and coat and get in bed. I feel a momentary prick of anger toward James, for keeping me from her, for shifting my focus.

I scroll through my photos again, and realize I've barely taken any in the last year. Mia keeps telling me I'm wasting time. I think about how much time she has spent in the hospital and how she considers it lost time. She feels like she is behind everyone. I feel behind too, but I'm not stuck in a hospital.

I turn on my laptop to start writing. To use my time. My cursor blinks and I notice a light on my phone is also blinking. I grab my phone and see texts from James asking where I am, if I'm okay, and if I want to talk about last night. I wonder if he hates Dylan. I think I was being weird about Dylan, but I was drunk, so James shouldn't take it so seriously. I don't want to call James, even though I should. I stare at his text for a while, feeling guilty. I turn back to my screen and stare at it for hours.

Chapter Sixteen

Poppies bloom in Mia's cheeks as the hospital shrinks behind her. I tell her that her cheeks are red, and she pulls a pink wool hat over her head and ears. The ends of her blonde wig cup her chin. She's going to stay with me for one night, but she has to check her temperature frequently. If we're worried at all, we're supposed to call the hospital. Right now, she seems perfect.

While Mia counts the coins in her hand, I ask her, "Are you sure you want to take the subway? Your mom wanted us to take a cab."

She scoffs. "Cabs are for elitists."

I suggest a rideshare.

"Evil company."

"Your mom seemed worried about you taking the subway."

"She's always worried now," she says as she drops her money in the glass box and walks through the turnstile. "Kinda like you! Anyway, I miss the subway. I know it's disgusting, but I miss it." She sticks her tongue out at me. I hope the subway germs didn't jump on it.

When we get to the bottom of the stairs, we see that the platform is crowded. It's not usually so busy at this time, so I assume that there was a delay or a Christmas parade or something. I look over to Mia and she's scanning the crowd nervously. An arm of light reaches out of the tunnel and stretches across the back tiled wall signalling the approaching train.

"It's crowded, do you want to wait for the next one?" I ask Mia. I worry she'll feel overwhelmed.

Mia walks toward the masses and plunges in. I hold onto the belt loops of her long fuzzy brown coat that makes her resemble a giant teddy bear, while thinking our positions should probably be reversed. Before the last few passengers are out, people swarm in through the doors, bodychecking their fellow civilians. Mia has always been skilled at snaking her way through a crowd while I hold onto her. This was most beneficial when Mia and I went through our punk, well, pop-punk phase in high school. We would regularly attend all-ages shows where I would occasionally try to catch the eye of a mysterious drummer, but the best I could do was receive a bad line from a nerdy bassist. We are three feet from the subway train doors, and suddenly Mia stops. I bump into her and a few other people bump into me. The crowd swells around us. I hear *bitches* in my ear. Mia doesn't move. I pull her over to a deserted spot on the platform. She has a glazed look in her eyes.

"Sorry," she says. "All of a sudden, I freaked because I think I left my phone in the hospital."

I know that's not why she stopped. "I think I saw you put it in your bag."

She unzips the middle compartment and finds her cellphone. "I'm a dumbass. I just wanted to make sure I had it."

The crowd swells. "We should probably get in there—it says the next train will be here in a minute," she says.

"Hey, do you mind if we wait it out until the crowd dies down? My claustrophobia is really acting up," I say to Mia.

She looks at me and with a cheery voice says, "Yeah, no prob."

On the walk to our apartment, Mia asks me how everything is going with James. I give her a clipped response, revealing nothing, and she says come on, give me something. So, I tell her how it was awkward when James and Dylan met at the gallery.

"Oh, and you have no clue why they were weird around each other?"

I shrug. "I guess with James it's dumb jealous man shit, but I didn't think he was like that."

"And Dylan?"

I look up at the sky. "Don't pull this again, Mia. I don't have the energy to go through this with you again. There's nothing between us."

"Maybe not on your end. I honestly can't tell anymore if you really aren't into him, or you're just deluding yourself. Or maybe you just like the attention."

"I wouldn't do that to him," I say, unable to pad my annoyance.

"Whatever, Al. You have fun with your little triangle or whatever it is. I can't figure out everything for you."

I pause, absorbing what she's said, feeling insulted.

She hits me with a snowball to cut the tension. I hear her laughing, and I don't want to ruin the night, so I throw one back.

I swear nonstop while walking up the pathway to our door because it's covered in ankle-deep snow. Mia tells me to calm down, but I don't want her trudging through snow. Ordinarily

I wouldn't care, but I'm particularly nervous about Mia's comfort tonight because this is the first night she's stayed with me since getting sick. The moment she steps inside, I ask her to take off her wet socks and put on a dry pair. Mia shoos me away from grabbing her mismatched socks. I scold her for not wearing proper winter boots. She's wearing a lavender sweater with daisies all over it and loose-fitting acid wash jeans cut above her ankles. We're both distracted from our footwear argument when Gus trots in from the washroom with his eyes barely open and *prrrooowws* at us, and then lies on my feet with his belly facing the ceiling and his paws over his head like he's waiting to receive a double high-five.

Mia squats down to cat level, calling Gus to come to her. He looks at her but doesn't move from my feet. She makes clicking sounds with her tongue. She raps on the wooden floor with her knuckles to try to attract him. She moves from her crouch to a sitting position. She tries meowing. She lies on the floor, sprawled out. Finally she shrinks into the fetal position, and extends her arm, reaching out to him, still calling, with a less confident "Come here, kitty." With her eyes still on him, she says, "He doesn't recognize me."

"Sure, he does," I say as I lift him into my arms, carrying him like someone might carry a baby. "He just needs to smell you. Their memory is all based on smells, I think."

I sit down beside Mia, she straightens up and crosses her legs, and I place Gus into her lap. He leaps out and runs into my bedroom.

"See! He doesn't know who I am. I probably don't even smell the same. I smell like a hospital. Or like death or something. Animals can smell that."

"He'll realize you're you. Give him time."

Mia walks toward her bedroom and I follow her. She opens the door and walks in. "It's so cold and stale in here." She taps on Elton's bowl and sprinkles food into it. She collapses on her bed.

"I turned up the heat before I left—it should be warm."

I walk to her drawer and pull out a pair of thick grey socks with a red stripe around the top. I sit at the end of the bed, and pull off her wet socks, and replace them with the grey ones.

Mia sits up and picks up her phone. "So, did I tell you that Charlotte has been emailing me?"

Charlotte lived in our dorm and was known for being strict about the theme parties she threw. She once kicked a boy out for an anachronistic costume at her *Gatsby* party. We used to hang out with her even though I suspected she was friendly with me only because she was close to Mia. We both haven't seen her in a year or so.

"Really?"

"Yeah. She's been asking how I am, and all that. She wants to see me." She balances her phone on her knee.

"Are you going to let her? I thought she hadn't contacted you since your diagnosis."

"Yeah, she hadn't. I guess I'll see her, but it'll be a little weird. She's going to tell me about life after school, and her cool new job, and her boyfriend's awesome dick, and I'm going to tell her that I've discovered freckles I didn't know about on top of my bald head."

I ask what Charlotte's new job is. Mia says she did an internship at a book publisher and they hired her as an editorial assistant. Charlotte is a rich kid, so she could afford to do an unpaid internship. I remind Mia that I used to edit Charlotte's essays in school, and they were awful before I helped her. Mia gives me a consoling look and tells me she hears the pay is terrible.

"I told her I was staying here tonight, and she asked if we want to hang. Do you want to?"

"Sure, why not?" I say, though I do not want to.

"You're usually the one providing the reasons why not," Mia says.

"True, but maybe I should make some literary world connections. Network or whatever." My face gets hot as I imagine Charlotte with her shiny hair, excitedly telling me about her new job.

Mia texts Charlotte and we plan to meet her at ten. The wind shakes the windows while we wait for the pizza we've ordered, and we can barely hear the knock on the door. The delivery man is wearing a coat and hat made of snow even though he had only a short walk from his car to our door. "Your doorbell is broken," he says.

When I open the pizza box, I look at the glistening cheese and feel I've never been hungrier. Mia and I used to order cheese pizzas when we had sleepovers, and I can still remember the feeling of dough and cheese getting stuck in the brackets and wires of my braces. I run my tongue along my teeth. In less than an hour, Mia eats four slices and I eat five. "I'm impressed," she says. "You're looking healthier."

I don't say anything because I don't want to talk about my weight. My clothes aren't as loose, but I didn't think others would notice. I'm back in a B cup, but it's still pretty roomy in there. I could probably wear the A, but I have only one A cup bra, and James has seen it too many times.

Once, we were kissing in the kitchen, and then James propped me up on the counter, and started to take off my tights, and then he took off my underwear. He started touching me, and we started to have sex. It was daytime, and even though the curtains were pulled across the window, it was still bright in the kitchen. I wasn't comfortable getting completely naked, so I pulled the top of my dress down to my waist and left my bra on. As we started, the cupboard door behind me was mimicking the rhythm of our movements. It let out a loud *bang* with each thrust that James delivered because my bra strap was tangled around the cupboard door handle and pulled the door open when I moved forward, and then slammed it shut when I moved backwards. At first, we tried to ignore it since it is a mood killer to address minor distractions like this while you're in the middle of sex, but it was just too much to ignore. James tried to subtly brush my shoulder and back to unlatch me from the cupboard's grip, but it was quite a complex entanglement. So, James had to stop, and focus closely on undoing the intricate snarl. Every second was agony. Time really slows down when sex is delayed. But he couldn't seem to do it, so finally he reached behind me and unhooked my bra, pulled it away from my shoulders and chest, and the bra hung limp off the cupboard handle. As he took my bra off, I covered my breasts with my arms, and he said, "Don't worry, they're nice." And then he continued from where he left off. At first, I kept thinking, they're nice? And I felt confident in that moment. But then I got distracted by the way they shook in the light. They didn't look nice to me at all.

"Time?" Mia asks.

"Eight thirty-seven," I tell her as I pull at bits of melted cheese from the last slice of pizza. It's bubbled yellow and brown. "Shouldn't you take your temperature?" I ask.

"Later. I guess we should get ready, right?"

"Yeah, I guess," I say.

"Do we even like Charlotte anymore?" Mia asks.

I shrug.

"Fuck it. I'll get ready." She gets up and grabs her bag from my bedroom and walks into the bathroom.

I bend forward while sitting and collect the fat of my stomach in both hands to determine how much I've gained from that pizza, as if my stomach grew with each swallow. It's more than what was there a month ago, but less than what was there six months ago. Sometimes, James grabs the fat on my hips during sex, and he seems to like it a lot and gives me compliments when he does this, telling me I'm sexy. I feel pulled out of the moment when he touches me there since I'm so used to trying to draw attention away from my hips. I reach around to touch my back, and feel that my spine is still slightly protruding but not sharp like before. I think I like that, but I'm not sure. It seems I change how I feel about my weight hourly.

Out of the corner of my eyes, I can see Mia in the bathroom, putting makeup on. I wonder if I should put more on too. I enter the bathroom while Mia aggressively applies blush.

"Hey, Mia, you may want to take it easy on the rouge. The one bulb is burnt out, and I don't think you realize how much you're putting on."

She drops her blush brush in the sink and starts wiping her cheeks with the back of her hands. "Why don't you change the bulb?"

"I haven't had time to get a new light bulb," I say, taken aback. "I mean, I remember when I'm out, but I never know the wattage or voltage or whatever."

Mia pulls herself on the counter and stands on it. She closes her eyes and touches her head and I can tell she's dizzy. I don't say be careful, even though I'm thinking it. I just decide I'll be ready to catch her if she falls. She reaches up to one of the fix-tures and unscrews the dead bulb. "Sixty watts, one hundred twenty volts."

Crack.

"Fuck!"

Mia's open blush container has fallen on the floor, and the powder is staining the cream-coloured floor a warm coral. She climbs off the counter. I pick up chunks of powder and empty it back into the container, dropping in bits of cat and human hair in the process.

"Leave it. There's no point." She rubs concealer under her eye vigorously. I can see something else is going on, and pain shoots down my back. Still on the floor, I ask what's wrong. She puts her hands up and says, "I just want to look normal."

"You look good, Mia."

She looks down at me incredulously. I feel like I'm not con-vincing because I'm sitting on a bathroom floor. I wouldn't trust someone who was sitting on a bathroom floor either. I rise to sit on the counter.

She shakes her head. "I haven't seen Charlotte in so long. I don't want to talk about any of this or have her tell me I look good when I don't."

I instantly feel relief when I realize we won't be leaving the apartment.

"We don't have to go." I look at Mia.

We both stare at the streaks of pink on the floor.

I break the silence. "Let's not go. I'm not going. Blame me. Tell her I ate too much pizza, and I'm sick. I bet in an hour that won't even be a lie."

Mia picks up her phone and sends a text. "Okay, I told her we're not coming." She pauses. "Let's just watch something?"

I smile because that's all we do now, not that I want to do anything else.

Gus runs across the floor and leaps into the bathtub. He makes a high-pitched noise and pokes the shower curtain with his paw and looks at Mia. Mia reacts to this by pulling the curtain in front of Gus so that it's separating the two of them. She then lightly taps her fingers on the curtain, and seconds after the tapping begins, he lunges forward with his head still behind the curtain, but with his front legs jutting out. Mia laughs, and they continue this game.

"See! He remembers you. He doesn't do that with me," I say.

"You don't play *Psycho*?" she asks, while continuing to tap the curtain.

"Never." Even though she's turned away from me, I can see that she is smiling because her ears lift up slightly.

My phone vibrates. It's a text from James asking me if I want to hang out tomorrow. I begin to compose a response when my phone rings. It's Anne. *Anne!* I completely forgot. I am a bad friend. I pick up. I leave the bathroom and walk toward my room.

"How are you? I was just going to call you," I lie.

"Really? What for?"

"I just, I wanted to see how you're doing. How are you doing?"

She says she made an appointment and tells me the date and asks if I can meet her at her place to go with her. I say of course. I hope I don't have to work my temp job that day. I'd forgotten Anne was pregnant.

"James, Dylan, or your mom?" Mia asks, standing in the doorway of my room after I've hung up.

"Anne."

"And?"

"It's nothing. I—" I trail off.

"Oh, come on. You know you're going to end up telling me, so just tell me now," Mia says. She's right, I will end up telling her, I always do. I think I do it partially because I know Anne shares my secrets with others.

"She's pregnant and wants me to go to her abortion appointment." I can't make out Mia's expression. "What?" I say.

"I'm so sick of Anne doing whatever the fuck she wants, acting so careless about everything, and nothing bad happens to her."

"I don't think you're being fair."

Mia gives me a puzzled look. She's usually the one defending Anne. "But it's always like this—she has a problem and she has an easy fix!"

"Mia, you sound like a right wing nutjob. She's pregnant and doesn't want to be. This isn't like you."

"And what if I can't ever get pregnant? What if this shit is changing my body, and even if I get well again, I can't? I had to sign forms before I took one of the drugs because it might cause infertility."

I tell her I didn't know that.

"You know I don't care about getting married, but I've always wanted a kid."

I just stand there uselessly.

"God, I'm being a piece of shit. This has nothing to do with me. I'm sorry. Don't tell her I said any of this. I don't actually think that. I'm an asshole."

I'm about to tell her I won't when she cuts me off.

"I don't want to think about this anymore. Can we just watch early *Simpsons* or something?"

She leaves my room, and I'm left alone, trying to picture her with a pregnant belly.

Mia is struggling to stay awake, so I suggest we go to bed. She complains that her sleeping clothes smell of the hospital, so I bring her a baseball style T-shirt from summer camp and old glow-in-the-dark pajama pants with stars on them. The pants end four inches above her ankles. Mia puts on my sweatpants instead. I step into the short pants, and they are an inch too short for me.

"Can I sleep in here? I think there's something wrong with the vents in my room; it's still so cold."

"Of course." I grab her thermometer. "You should take your temperature." I put the thermometer into Mia's mouth. She's hairless and soft and looks like a baby. "Ninety-eight point six—you're perfect!"

Mia takes five pills: two white ones; a half-blue, half-white one; a violently red translucent one; and a blue one. She shelters her eyes from the bright light coming from the ceiling. I plug in the blue lights, turn off the overhead light, and then crawl back in bed.

"I'm sorry for being weird and awful tonight," she says as she stares up at the blue lights.

"You weren't!" I turn to face her, feeling some guilt as I say this because I think what she said about Anne was cruel.

"I'm scared about what's going to happen," she says.

I rest my head against her shoulder. "You'll be fine. And once you're all better, you'll have all these wise things to say." I wish I hadn't just said *all better*. I've always hated when my mother said that. I've never trusted anyone who spewed baseless optimism. I try again. "People get over bad things, and then they're okay after, so I figure this is your bad thing, and then you'll be fine." I don't believe this myself.

"A lot of people don't just get one thing. It's a constant slew of shit. Bad is always a possibility." She turns to me. The low lights make her blue eyes look black, like overgrown pupils.

"But so is good," I interject.

"Good isn't what keeps you up at night. Maybe I'm actually narrow-minded for not having the capacity to believe in something bigger. Or I'm cynical."

"If you think you're cynical, what does that make me?"

"Okay, forget higher power. I'll settle for magic beans. Where science fails, magic usually picks up the slack. Maybe we can pick up where we left off with our witchcraft."

"I've been looking for an excuse to wear black lipstick again."

"I hope we get to look back at this conversation and laugh at how dramatic I sounded."

I squeeze her hand. "Do you think you're going to go back to teacher's college when you're finished treatment?"

"I don't know. I think it's safer not to make plans."

Lying under the blue lights, I wonder where we'll be in a few years, and I can't picture anything. Maybe we should just stay in here.

"Mia?"

She doesn't respond. I touch her neck, but I'm not sure what I'm feeling for. Half a second goes by, and I see her chest rise and fall. Movement under her eyelids. I've always stared at her eyes. The perimeter of her iris is a deep blue ring, and there is a lighter blue that surrounds the pupil in ripples and looks like approaching waves. But it's her eyelids that have always fascinated me, the way they move when she reads or sleeps. They don't move differently than others', but hers were the first eyelids that I ever watched. When we were about six, we were studying butterflies in school. We studied the chrysalides and the morphing from caterpillars into butterflies. The butterflies fluttered their wings slowly behind the plastic wrap enclosures. I thought Mia's eyelids moved like their wings, and I would just watch her, especially when she read or drew pictures, thinking that maybe she was a butterfly or some kind of human-butterfly hybrid. I'd also watch her eyelids when she slept, because her eyeballs would move under the lid and I thought there were caterpillars in there.

I lie awake under the blue lights. Mia doesn't smell like she usually does, like the coconut body wash she's used since high school. She smells more like chalk or latex. She's smelled like that for a while now.

The reverberation of the fan sounds faintly like a heartbeat.

Chapter Seventeen

I'm on hold with the airline to ask them to move his first-class window seat to a first-class aisle seat so he can "be the first one off the plane" since he is "a very busy man." He waves at me to get my attention and points to a bruise on an apple. He waves his stubby finger to say *no*. I buy fruit for the men in this office twice a week. There are only men except for the temps who do administrative work here. I work here two days a week and another woman named Trina works the other days. I've never met her, but she leaves me instructions in precise cursive on sticky notes. I nod to note the bruise and push down the urge to strangle him with the cord of my phone. I picture running my finger along the wavy impressions the cord would make on his bruised neck. I hope my three-month contract isn't extended. It would be hard to turn down the extension because I need the money, but I'm unravelling here. I keep telling myself only two days a week for three months, and I'm free.

All the seats in the waiting room are full, but no one is speaking. I'm pretty sure a Lilith Fair compilation is playing. There's something comforting about the obviousness of this music selection. A young man offers his partner a granola bar and she sternly reminds him she can't eat anything for two hours before the procedure. When he starts to open the plastic wrapper, she grabs it from his hands and puts it in her bag. A woman likely in her early thirties seems to be alone and stares at her unpainted nails for what feels like a long time. Anne doesn't say a word.

Back at Anne's apartment, I ask her if she's okay.

"I'm having cramps, but I'm fine."

"And mentally?"

She shakes her head slightly. "More than anything else, I'm so fucking relieved."

We watch a few episodes of *The OC*. I tell her I used to have a big crush on Seth, but now I think that Ryan might be a better partner. I pour her a glass of water before I go.

James calls me, but I don't answer because I'm on my way to meet Dylan at some expensive store I've walked by many times but have never been in. He wants me to help him find a new winter coat, which is something he can do on his own, and when I asked him why he wants me there, he said he needs a woman's opinion. Then he reminded me I never went to the Erwin Blumenfeld exhibit like I promised, and now it's over, so I owe him. I text James to tell him I'm leaving to meet Dylan and I'll message him later. I stop to consider that I've done this a lot lately and wonder if my chances are running out with James. I've seen him only once since the night at the gallery, and I know I was being distant. I cut the night short because I wanted to visit Mia at her parents'.

Outside the store, there is a tired-looking man dressed in a well-worn Santa costume ringing a bell incessantly to get passersby to donate to charity. When I drop a dollar in the bucket, I try to give him a look of compassion because I know this job probably sucks and listening to a bell all day must be hell on the ears and take a toll on his wrist, but he refuses to make eye contact with me. I wish I could take my dollar back and drop it in again, forcing him to acknowledge my goodwill.

Inside, Dylan is wearing a cashmere sweater. Or at least it looks like he is—that's the most expensive fabric I can think of. His jeans are cuffed neatly above his immaculate boots. This suddenly makes me conscious of my salt-stained boots. He even looks cool in his winter hat as he knows to wear it pulled back a bit, so that his hair shows in the front. This isn't an easy look to cultivate. I look like Joe Pesci in *Home Alone* when I wear hats in the winter.

He puts on a grey peacoat that hits mid-thigh.

"That's nice. Get that one," I say, announcing my arrival.

He turns to look at me and smiles. "This is my old coat, Al."

"What's wrong with it?"

He shrugs. "Just sick of it."

A woman with mannequin posture, chunky gold bracelets, and a bun slicked impossibly tight comes over to offer her assistance. I immediately stop slouching and suck in my cheeks to make it look like I might belong here, though I know I stand out. Dylan tells her we're just looking.

Dylan does a kind of a model pout when he looks into mirrors, and it seems unconscious, either that or he doesn't think other people notice, but I want to laugh every time he does it. I can never tell him because he is one of those handsome people who try to seem confident but are, at times, unexpectedly insecure, so they can't bear to discuss the embarrassing things they do.

I grab a coat for him to try and he says "too showy." It's navy blue.

"So, Alice," he says as he looks for his size on the rack.

"So, Dylan?"

"You never asked me what I thought of James," he says while putting on a coat.

"I didn't know I had to, Daddy."

He leans forward against the rack and balances his chin on the back of his hand and looks at me. "He seems like he likes you a lot."

"I think he does." I really hope I'm not blushing.

He nods and puts on another coat that's black and goes past his knees.

The sales woman walks by and mouths *hot* at me and winks. I smile back or at least try to. I wander over to the other side of the store because I don't want to talk about James, and I can tell Dylan's not finished talking about him. I look back, and Dylan is looking at me in the mirror. I grab a coat and bring it back to him.

"How about this one?"

He wrinkles his forehead.

I exhale, frustrated. "Okay, it's not too showy. It's black."

"It's a woman's coat."

"Oh." I wince, defeated. "I'm not good at this."

"Try it on."

I make a pained face at him.

"Come on. Humour me. We're having fun."

I roll my eyes and put it on. He makes me do up the buttons. I put my shoulders back. "Kay, I look, like, kind of rich, right?"

"You look good. You should get it."

I look at the tag. "Fuck me. Four hundred dollars."

"That's not even bad. That's how much winter coats cost."

"Dylan, I don't even work full-time right now."

He looks around and says quietly, "I can get it for you."

I punch him in the shoulder. "Are you nuts?"

He laughs. "What? 'Tis the season. And your birthday is coming up."

"Not for months! And we usually just take each other out for Thai."

He grins and rubs his neck. "Twenty-five is a big birthday."

"Jesus. You are making a lot of money, aren't you?"

"I'm still very junior, but I'm doing all right."

"Okay, no. This *Pretty Woman* moment is not happening. But you're sweet for offering, and maybe a little insane too."

He opens up his mouth to interject, but I say, "Nope! I won't hear it. Buy the coat you're wearing. You look hot."

He gives me a curious look.

"The lady, the sales woman, she said you look hot."

He looks in the mirror again, but I don't let him linger long enough to do the pout, and I pull him toward the cash register, so I can get home.

The feathers in James's pillows poke out of the cases; they prickle and scratch my face and neck, so I bring my own pillow from my apartment. This is the third time I've successfully slept through the night at his apartment. Although the fan is facing away from me, the breeze still reaches my toes, so I pull them under the blankets. I look over at James, and he's still sleeping. His mouth is hanging open, and the only reason I don't drop anything inside his mouth is because it's his birthday today—his thirtieth, so he has no time for pranks anymore. The sun forms a pillar of light over James's body; he looks encased in a golden panel. From the shade, I watch his face twitch, and one eyelid cracks open. I kiss his mouth, and both his nipples, and then I kiss down his stomach, pretending like I'm going to give him a blow job, but I blow a raspberry on his stomach instead. He laughs wildly. I point to the ceiling, and he looks up to see *Happy Birthday, Old Man* written on a piece of cardboard taped to the ceiling.

I wrap my leg around his hip and kiss his mouth again.

He tells me I'm cute, and then coughs to the side. I feel his body quiver underneath mine. "I think I'm sick," he says.

"No! You can't be sick on your birthday," I say as I squirm away from him. I wipe my mouth on my shirt, furtively.

"The light is so bright; I feel like I may throw up." James covers his eyes.

I push myself up to stand on the bed, teetering as I attempt to close the curtains.

"Hey!" I react to him grabbing my left butt cheek.

"You're standing over me in tiny underwear."

I lower myself down to sit on his chest. "Yes, I realize, but you're sick. I can't get sick."

"But it's my birthday."

"I don't think I've ever had sex on my birthday," I say.

He grabs my ankles, and strokes them, then says, "Well, miss. There's a heavy fine for that—it's sex with me."

"That's your approach? Sex with you as a punishment?"

"Yeah." He looks around. "Okay, I didn't really think about it. Are you seduced?"

"Perhaps I will be later."

Harry is James's close friend. He has an impressive beard and hair to match. Most of his head is just hair and beard. Harry's girlfriend, Nina, has very fine hair, and she's wearing it in a braid—it looks like an orange shoelace drooping over her shoulder. Her head bobbles a little, side to side, when she walks. She's more than six feet tall and at least three inches taller than Harry. I've met her three times, and she only ever says *hi* or *yes*. I like Nina, but not because I have a strong connection with her. I just don't find her offensive in any way. She may be a cyborg.

Harry and Nina treat James and me to a movie for James's birthday. When we leave the theatre, I gasp at how cold it is outside. Conversely, Nina is hatless, and gloveless while eating her leftover popcorn, and wearing a cropped leather jacket. She's not shivering. Cyborg.

Harry has wrapped a scarf around his neck so tight that I'm worried he'll choke, although this does not deter Harry from wanting to discuss what we've just watched as we walk down the street.

"So, that was amazing, no?" He's not really asking a question.

"Are you kidding, it was terrible!" I say.

"You've got to be joking, Alice. It brilliantly summed up the fear of intimacy following the pain and humiliation of rejection," Harry says.

"I know that's what it was attempting to do, but it didn't deliver. It was completely hollow; the characters never said or did anything interesting, they just made gloomy faces for three hours. How many times do you need to show the tops of trees swaying in sunlight?"

"He's a genius though. A true auteur," Harry says as we struggle to weave around three teenagers linked at the arm, taking up the entire width of the sidewalk.

Harry grabs Nina's hand and stops at the subway entrance. "Look, Alice, I have to go, since this is where the subway entrance was built. I think you're great, but I also think you're wrong on this. We'll talk another time?" Harry puts out his gloved hand. I give him my mittened hand.

We let the cab driver know our destination. He turns on some Bon Jovi song, winks at us, and then turns back around. We smile at him out of love for his enthusiasm, not out of our love for Bon Jovi. He sings along in a better voice than I expected. He's driving a little too fast. I watch the lights of the city elongate into beams of white, yellow, red, and blue, painting scenes with our speed. I feel a light warmth on my hand and look to see James's hand resting an inch from mine. His body radiates warmth, even on cold evenings. At night, he falls asleep before me, and I'll lie there shivering, and latch onto him to feed off his heat. He calls me the leech. Sometimes I'll wake up and have to wiggle away from him because the heat becomes too intense.

James puts his hand over mine.

"I know you don't want to talk about this on my birthday, but it's twelve-oh-six a.m. so it's not my birthday anymore."

The driver has slowed down as if he's trying to match the slow rhythm of the Cranberries song that he's selected. The cold from outside has chilled the window. I rest my head against it.

"I'm not sure why you're sometimes unreachable for days. I don't get it because it seems like we have a lot of good times together. Have I done something?"

His hand is still on mine, and I'm starting to get too hot. But if I pull it away now after he's said all this, I'll seem aloof. I take too long to respond, so he starts again.

"Is it Mia? You feel like you can't let yourself be happy?"

"I'm trying. But you don't understand." I don't know how to tell him that as good as I feel with him, I'm still not entirely there with him in those good moments. And it's not only because of Mia.

"You don't have to deny yourself good things—that's not how this works."

"I have no idea how this works. So, I'm just going with what feels right."

James moves his hand away. He doesn't say anything for the rest of the ride back to our street.

We drive past my apartment, and I think how nice it would be to sleep alone in my bed, with Gus warming my toes while he vibrates by my feet. But I know I should stay with James tonight. He peels away my clothes soon after we get inside. I don't feel like having sex. I'm doing it only to be able to go to bed and avoid conversation. I keep trying to avoid his mouth by turning away my head and positioning my neck and breasts closer to his mouth to suggest he kiss them instead. After a while, he notices what I'm doing and tells me he's not actually sick, he was only stuffed up this morning. He slips his tongue in my mouth, and it's warmer than usual. I wonder if he really is sick. I won't see Mia for a couple days to be safe. The thought of this makes me angry at him, but I try to suppress it since I know it's unfair. He stops kissing me. He asks me what's wrong and suggests we talk. I say I'm fine and inch toward him to kiss him. He says forget it and walks to the bathroom, shutting the door behind him. I can't get that Bon Jovi song out of my head.

The next day, I spend an entire day looking for a job that is both interesting and something I'm qualified for but find nothing. That same day, I receive a letter with red type on the envelope about my student loan. I apply to a bunch of administrative jobs. I can't live off part-time pay much longer. I decide to devote the next two days to writing. I wake up early, shower, put on a bra and clothing I would wear to an office, thinking it will put me in an efficient mindset. Feeling constricted distracts me so I take off my clothes and my bra and put on my sweatpants and a big T-shirt.

I read the first few pages of my manuscript. I like them. I imagine my book launch. Everyone who has ever wronged me will somehow be invited—though not by me because I've forgotten about them. They show up and I look surprised to see them. I receive their compliments, but I'm humble and act as if it's nothing. I tell them they look great without really looking at them, and they tell me I look incredible, and I do. Somehow my hair has transformed and looks just like Helena Bonham Carter's in *A Room with a View*. It's thick, full of vitamins, and looks like several expensive wigs stitched together. I can't quite picture what I'd be wearing, but it's devastating and it has a cape. I'll have thrown away the red satin dress in the box—it was never right for me. Everyone has their own panna cotta and snobby French fries seasoned with a rare pink salt. I make an incredible speech that makes my editor cry with pride. I don't do a reading because they're awful. I try to picture my makeup and wonder if a cat eye looks smart—I decide it's sexy and literary. I try a few makeup tutorials on YouTube, but I can't quite get it to look right on both eyes. I discover my eyelids aren't ideal for a cat eye.

The next day, I try to continue where I left off in my manuscript, but I decide I need to read the last chapter again. I don't like it so much now.

The best-before date on the milk carton was three days ago, but it smells fine. I stand on the step-stool to grab a mixing bowl from the top cupboard and hear a knock. As I open the door, white flowers are shoved in my face.

"Will Mia like these?" Dylan asks me.

"You can't bring flowers to the hospital. Allergies and bacteria. Put them in a vase and we'll take a picture of them. She's only in for the night, so she can get them tomorrow."

Dylan looks disappointed. "I feel bad for Mia. In the hospital on her twenty-fourth birthday. That really sucks."

"Yeah. She'll like the cake though. But I do feel like you're trying to outdo me with the flowers."

"You caught me. Trying to take your place as Mia's favourite."

Dylan and I make a cake together, and I think it would have been easier for me to do it on my own than both of us trying to find counter space in my tiny kitchen. When the cake is in the oven, Dylan dries the mixing bowl while I wash the hand mixer.

Dylan tries to get a conversation started about a book he just read. He's trying really hard, but I'm monosyllabic. He senses I'm not in the mood to talk books, so he changes the subject.

"You know you can talk to me about Mia stuff, right? Because you don't really. And you never text me, I text you."

"Are you giving me shit?"

"No, I'm just saying that you *can* talk to me if you need to. I'm not sure you have anyone else to talk to about her?"

I wonder if that was a dig at James, but I decide not to explore it. The bubbles gather around my wrists in the sink like a bracelet.

"You've been distant ever since she got sick. Maybe I can help if you'd just talk about it."

I wish he'd stop. I turn to him and say more bluntly than I intend, "I'm worried she'll die."

He looks so soft right now, like I could push my hands against his face and sink right in.

"Alice, her treatments are working."

"Are they though? They keep changing, and I feel like that's not good. And she keeps needing all these blood transfusions, and she's said something about her platelets being low, and sometimes she's too weak to have visitors or even talk on the phone, and then other times she seems fine. She's not even supposed to be in there right now. It's in-between treatments, but she had to go in for a transfusion and they want to keep an eye on her for the night."

"I think you need to trust the doctors."

"I feel like I'm not being told everything. I think her parents know things I don't. I think Mia knows too."

Dylan shakes his head. "They'd tell you, Al. I get that you worry about her, but don't start inventing new things to fear."

"I just don't know what I'd do without her."

"She'll be okay. You don't have to feel low all the time. It doesn't have to make everything bad."

"I don't know how to feel good when she's going through this. We need each other."

"I know you're close," Dylan says, "but Mia never seems like she needs anyone."

This comment irritates me, so I turn on the faucet and let the sound fill the break in conversation.

On the subway, Dylan reminds me about his birthday in second year. Mia got his roommate to let us into his room and take his clothes, so we could arrive to our Victorian Poetry and Prose class dressed as Dylan. Mia wore his grey Nike sweatpants and his old basketball jersey from high school. I tried to wear his jeans, but they didn't fit properly, so I wore a pair of his sweatpants and one of his fancy grey pullovers. Mia wore his blue sweatband and I wore a white one. When we got to class, Dylan was already there and he covered his face when he saw us. We both hugged him while his hands were still over his face, and he said I hate you guys. Throughout the day, we pretended to be Dylan, well, an exaggerated version of him and said things like, I know this sweater is expensive, but you can't compromise on quality, and Girls back home don't get me.

"God. We were so annoying. Why did you like us?" I say to Dylan.

"I think it's a Stockholm syndrome thing," says Dylan.

We open the door to Mia's room. She's sitting in front of the window with a wrapped gift in her lap. She's wearing an ankle-length white floral dress. Her mom is standing in front of her IV pole, blocking it, so it looks like Mia's not even attached to it. Her bright red lips break into a wide smile when she sees us. She's glued on dramatic thick fake eyelashes. The sky is dark, and the city is lit up like a birthday cake behind her.

Chapter Eighteen

I've always denied looking like my mother even when others have noted a resemblance. It's not that I don't think she's pretty, it's just that I've resisted being like her in any way because I find her unartistic and ordinary. I know this is insufferable of me. I don't have enough faith in my creative abilities, and I worry if I'm like her, I won't be able to achieve anything more than her. She struggled as a single mother to make enough for us, and it took her about twenty years, but now she can afford to pay for wants, not only needs. She's got her career and she's a good parent, but I don't want what she has. When she opens the door, I see my eyes and mouth. I'm worried about the wrinkled loose skin on her neck and jawline. I remind myself to moisturize my entire body daily.

"How was the bus ride?" she asks.

"Do you want me to say it was good?"

"I'm asking you because I want to know how it was."

A rough start.

She tells me she has a list of fun holiday tasks for us. I feel fairly confident that hell is just a place where you have to untangle Christmas lights with your mother for the rest of time.

I decorate the tree while she makes a green bean casserole. I yell to her from the living room, Did we really need to contribute to the death of another tree? She yells, It's tradition. When she comes in with a platter of cookies, I say you didn't need to make so many cookies since it's only the two of us. She crosses her arms and says, It's tradition. I bite the head off one shaped like an elf. I tell her it's delicious, and she says they were better last year. She starts to move some of the ornaments on the tree around and I ask her if there's a problem and she says no. She adds some ornaments to the back of the tree even though it's facing the corner of the wall. I ask her why she would bother putting any back there, and she says it's nice to cover the whole tree. She removes the tinsel I've put on the tree and says I hate this stuff. I ask her why she has it, and she says because I know you like it. I hold my tongue.

I catch her staring at the top of the tree. "What is it now?"

"I just prefer the angel to the star."

"But you're not religious."

"That's not true. Besides, it's nice at Christmas."

"Nice to be religious?"

She frowns at me. "You know what I mean."

I smirk and she catches me.

She asks me to go out and get potatoes for the mashed potatoes. Yellow, she says. They have to be yellow. Yukon gold is best, but if you can't find them, just make sure you get yellow ones.

I shop at the shitty store because it's less likely I'll run into someone from high school. My hair is down and I don't take off my sunglasses, which may actually be drawing more attention to myself. The woman wearing felt reindeer antlers at the checkout looks familiar. She might be a younger sibling of someone I went to high school with. She looks at me curiously. I pay in cash so she can't see my name on my credit or debit card.

When I get back home, I hand the bag to my mom. She sighs.

"What? They're yellow!"

"They're small. They're so hard to peel."

"You didn't say anything about the size. I'm going to prove you wrong and peel them myself. They'll be fine."

She lifts up her hands as if to say *by all means, go ahead*.

The potatoes are difficult to peel, and I've cut myself a few times, but I don't show that I'm in pain because I don't want to hear about how she's right. I keep catching her furtively sneaking glances across the kitchen at my slow peeling.

I hate Christmas music because I used to work at a mall and it plays all November and December. An exception is Mariah Carey's *Merry Christmas* album. We play Mariah every year while we exchange gifts. The Wham! Christmas song is also great.

My mom gifts me a rice cooker and a couple of sensible sweaters. One is angora, and I almost tell her I'm not going to wear a bunny, but I hold back because I know it must've been expensive.

I bought her red socks with snowflakes on them because her feet are always cold. I know she'd wear only white socks out, but she says these are fun for around the house. I also give her a necklace with a pendant of her birthstone, amethyst. She looks surprised and I think she thinks it was a lot of money, but I spent under fifty dollars for the necklace and socks.

"Are you good for money?"

I nod as I bite the skin on the sides of my thumbs.

We stare at each other, both nodding. She looks as if she might want to start talking about jobs, so I grab my phone to turn up Mariah, trying to remind her that it's Christmas, so let's keep it light.

She sings along, off key.

During dinner, she says the potatoes are good, though she wished we had more. I don't say anything, thinking just let the small potatoes go. I tell her thanks for making me a vegetarian shepherd's pie since I know she prefers them with meat.

As a tradition, we watch *Little Women*, the one with Winona Ryder. I make fun of my mom every year when she talks about how Eric Stoltz is so handsome in this movie. I tell her his character is the definition of a wiener. We both agree that Jo forgives Amy too quickly for burning her manuscript. I leave the room before Beth dies, telling my mom I need to go to the bathroom. She says she'll pause it, but I tell her not to. In the bathroom, I text Mia, *what did Santa bring you, little girl?* She texts back immediately: *a dependency on cream puffs . . . and indigestion xox.*

When I'm back I tell my mom the new bathroom renovations look good, even though it looks like a soulless bougie hotel that doesn't match the rest of the house. My mom says she wishes Jo ended up with Laurie, and I disagree. She's surprised and asks if I like Bhaer better than Laurie. I say I think neither are right for Jo. My mom tells me Winona Ryder introduced Christian Bale to his wife. His wife was Winona's assistant. I already knew this, in fact I told her this years ago, but I pretend it's new information and act surprised. She says not bad for an assistant. I'm definitely not going to tell her about James.

Lying on the bed I've had since I was eight, I touch my full stomach, grateful that my mom didn't mention that she's happy to see more *meat on my bones*. She painted my room white recently.

She said it took several coats, including primer, to paint over the mint-green colour I painted it in high school. She left everything I had up on the walls in a cardboard box except for my old Bright Eyes poster, which she taped to the walls after the paint dried. I told her I don't listen to them much anymore and she said, Well, how would I know that? I choose their fourth album to listen to on a streamer, and I immediately think it's still so good. I think about the two half hand jobs I gave on this bed, giving up both times. I was attempting to catch up to Anne and Mia, and so I tried hooking up with some guys I wasn't really interested in. The guys I actually liked were the mysterious, quiet ones who dated older girls at other schools, so I settled for making out with gross dudes who figured they could get me off by just stroking my nipples. I hear creaking in the hallway and think, shit, I forgot to bring a fan. How will I sleep? My mom knocks on the door, I tell her to come in, and she brings in a fan, plugs it in and turns it on.

A few days later, I head to the hospital. Mia's unhooked, and she doesn't have any makeup on, but she's wearing her blonde wig. She looks exhausted and confirms she is when I ask her. She says she has an hour until treatment begins again and asks if I want to go outside and sit in the courtyard.

The courtyard is between the old building of the hospital and an addition built a few years ago. It's named after a family of wealthy donors, money not organs. The walls of the hospital surround the small courtyard, so there's nothing really to look at. There are two wooden benches and one feeble-looking tree. When we sit on the bench, I think it's probably too cold to be out here, but I don't want to spoil the moment. I want to do what Mia wants.

A bird is chirping on the skinny tree. It shits white down the flimsy trunk.

"Anne came to visit yesterday," Mia says.

I turn to her but she's staring forward. "And?"

"She wouldn't come close to the bed, like she was afraid to catch it from me."

"She didn't hug you?"

She shakes her head. "She can't handle it. I wanted to ask her, are you here because you want to see me or because you want to forgive yourself?"

I tell her I'm sorry. I say that Anne's red hair looks stupid.

"Nah," she says. "I like it." She turns to me but I can't read her expression. "How were those couple of days with your mom during the holidays?" Mia asks.

I shrug. "They were fine." I ask how her holidays were.

"Okay, I guess. My dad doesn't get super emotional in front of me. My mom cried a lot, but she thought she was doing it in a discreet way. She'd hide behind her napkin or wineglass, and close her eyes, but I could see her shaking. And one day she kept getting up to go to the kitchen to check on the pies, even though they had finished baking an hour earlier, and they were just sitting on the counter. I knew she was just trying to hide her face."

She looks like she's going to say something else about her mom, but she doesn't. I try to think of something to make her feel better, but I come up with nothing.

"I got a lot of gifts this year," Mia continues. "December birthdays blow because you get screwed for gifts, but this year, I got a ton. I think everyone is worried it's the last gift they'll give me so they're trying to make it really good."

She's joking but I say no quickly, without thinking. "Think we should go in? It's pretty cold out here," I say.

"It's worse than I thought it was." She takes my hand, and I follow her.

At night, there's a snowstorm, and the power goes out and I wake up when my fan turns off. I'm not fully awake yet and don't realize the power is out and I plug in the blue lights, but they don't turn on. I pull the comforters off Mia's bed and bring them to mine as the cold seeps into my bedroom.

Chapter Nineteen

Over breakfast at an overpriced café, James asks, "Do you want to get married?"

"Are you proposing? I think it's too soon," I mock him. "I mean, in general, eventually, to whoever."

I tie my hair up into a nest-like bun as I reply, "I don't really see the point, but if I had a bunch of money to throw away, and I wanted to have a big party, then maybe. But I wouldn't do it until I was financially stable."

"Aren't you romantic," James says.

"I don't know, the whole idea of marriage to me is cultish. You swear to love someone and stay with them forever? You can't promise to feel something forever."

"I think for some people that feeling lasts, and not just because they made a promise."

I know this is a sweet thing to say, but the cynic in me wants to make fun of him. I know I have a problem responding to earnest or kind sentiments without hostility, so I try to think of something to say, but he's not looking at me anymore. He's looking right over my head.

"It's been so long," says a woman behind me. Her voice sounds old Hollywood, all breathy, and makes my arms and neck feel staticky.

James seems stunned. "Kate, are you back in the city?" He zips up his hoodie to his neck and then unzips it back down to just under his ribs.

What the hell is he doing?

"You see me, don't you?"

He leans forward, searching for words. "I mean, why are you here? What brings you back?" Some horrible laugh that I've never heard before escapes him.

She bubbles up into a cluster of tiny giggles. "Aren't you going to give me a hug?"

She doesn't move; she makes him come to her. He bangs his knee on the table in the process of rising, but he doesn't appear to notice. I've never seen him like this. I resist turning to look at her.

James settles back into his seat after a hug that's probably stroking the shaft of some erection of the past, and I'm studying his face to see if he blinks.

"So, what are your New Year's plans for tomorrow night?"

"Don't really have any," he says.

Actually, we do—a Steve Buscemi marathon, followed by sex right at midnight.

"Do you remember Billie? Gorgeous ginger with the big mouth?" she asks. "Well, Billie's having a party at her fiancé's. He's loaded and is supplying the hooch." Did she just say hooch? "You should come." She says the last word like she's taking a big bite out of a juicy steak. Or maybe I'm hearing it this way only because I hate her.

James is taking off his hoodie now. He is rubbing his bicep. Who in the fuck is sitting across from me?

"I'll see what's up tomorrow night. But that sounds pretty cool." He keeps nodding. I want to wrap my hands around the back of his head and slam it right into his sunny-side-up eggs.

"You can come too." She lays a single finger on my shoulder. I picture turning my head and biting it hard like a pissed-off cat.

"Free hooch is tempting, but I have plans," I say as I keep my eyes focused straight ahead, just past James, denying him any eye contact.

"This is Alice," he says, sounding alarmed.

"I'm Kate."

She pivots into my eyeline, and I'm forced to gaze at her. I look up, and it's a humbling sight, like looking up at the top of a mountain from the bottom, feeling pathetic and mortal. She's beautiful. She knows it, and she smiles because she knows it. She looks at me like I'm so easy, it's almost comical to her. I've been sized up and there's nothing for her to worry about. She doesn't even have to do anything, except look like that.

I hear the humming of words between them, but I'm not even sure what they're saying. I'm absorbed by the rising heat in my spine. Her neck is impossibly long, like her face is a piece of art propped on a pedestal. When she leaves to go back to her table, she moves gracefully like a ballerina en pointe, but I'm almost certain that it's some rehearsed, premeditated dance that she's counting out in her head.

As soon as she's out of view, James asks, "Is your food good?"

"Are you done?"

"What?"

"Are you done eating?"

He frowns. "What's wrong?"

"I want to go."

"Okay. Okay, I'll just go up and pay."

I walk ahead and turn down a narrow street that hasn't been plowed. James is calling my name. I'm trying to pick up my pace, but he catches up to me.

"What the hell is up with you?"

"What do you think? I could have got up and left, and you wouldn't have noticed."

"What? Kate?" He takes a second to look at me. "I just hadn't seen her in a long time, and I was surprised. What did I do wrong?"

"You should have seen yourself. I didn't even recognize you. You were mesmerized!"

"Mesmerized? Come on, Alice, that is bullshit. I was just talking to her. Did you want me to ignore her?"

"I guess you felt you had to ignore one of us."

"I haven't seen her in years. And yeah, I'm a little uncomfortable around her because we were close, and I—"

"You told her you loved her."

"Yeah, I did. You can't get mad at me for feelings I had then, and when I didn't even know you, that's irrational! You're acting like a total bitch." He says the last word quietly, like he hadn't fully decided that he wanted to say it.

I say nothing for a moment, so I can absorb what he's said to me, and because I want him to feel the silence.

"If you saw what I saw in your face, you'd be upset too."

"I don't know what you're talking about, but if you're going to go there, then let's talk about Dylan."

"What about him?"

"Let's talk about how he looks at you, *mesmerized*. Or how he talks to you. How you talk about him."

"I am so sick of having to justify my friendship with Dylan! We're just friends, and do not have those feelings for each other."

"Don't you think that if it comes up so often, then maybe there's something to it?"

"No, I think that everyone's a fucking idiot."

"Everyone but you, right? I'm used to that line of thinking from you."

"I need to be alone tonight—maybe even tomorrow night too, so then I'm not interfering with your plans, and you can go to your party with free hooch and girls with big mouths."

I see a bus ahead, and it's going the opposite direction from my apartment, but I run up to catch it.

"Alice, come on." When he realizes I'm not going to respond, he yells, "You just keep going, don't you? You can find a problem in anything."

I get on the bus. I look at him out the window. I consider going right to Mia and telling her what happened. It's what feels most natural, but I keep thinking about what she said, how she can't figure out all my problems.

I show up at his door without calling or texting, hoping that he's home.

Dylan opens the door, and I'm met with a smile that quickly collapses into a frown. "Have you been crying? Is Mia okay?" He pulls me inside. He's wearing grey sweatpants and a black sweatshirt.

"No, it's not Mia. It's James. We had a fight. He's an asshole."

I think he's going to hug me, but he puts his hand on my shoulder. He asks me if I want tea. I nod.

We walk across his dark hardwood floors and I sit on the grey couch while he puts a kettle on.

As I'm retelling the story, I'm finding it difficult to explain what James did. I keep having to say, You had to be there, you had to see the way he looked at her. I can't articulate it well, but I'm supposed to be good with words, so if I can't explain myself, maybe that means I'm a bad writer, or that my pain has no foundation. Sometimes I feel that way when I'm really down, like I can't explain it, but I know it's there. This though, this isn't quite like that. It feels moveable. I know I've overreacted about Kate.

"You're overreacting," Dylan says. "Sorry, but it sounds like he got flustered when he saw an ex-girlfriend." He cuts me off before I respond. "Don't say I had to see how he looked at her again because it doesn't matter. You were upset, so maybe you skewed things in your head, and saw something that wasn't there. Or maybe you saw something that existed before. You said he hasn't seen her in years, right? It's confusing, seeing someone you cared about. You're upset because he loved someone else before you, and that doesn't fit into your version of an ideal relationship, so you're pissed about that."

The kettle hisses, and Dylan gets up to make us tea.

Dylan waits for me to say something else, but I don't. The black tea scalds my mouth, but I force it down, though I'd like to spit it out.

"So, what are you going to do?" he asks.

"James doesn't trust you."

"What?" He puts his mug down. "What do you mean?"

I regret my choice of words because I know that's not what James said. I try to explain. "I should have said that differently, but basically he thinks there's, like, something between us or whatever. You know that typical jealous bullshit. I told him that neither of us think of each other that way, and I'm pissed off that he even brought it up. It's just so stupid."

Dylan doesn't respond, he's just running his fingertips over the back of his head.

I keep talking because I'm uncomfortable. "It's annoying, everyone says that about us. I feel like a broken record, you know."

"Yeah, *everyone* says that about us. Even Mia—" He cuts himself off.

I open my mouth to say something, but my heart is beating so fast.

"I think he's right, Al." He looks in my eyes for half a second and then looks away.

My mouth is dry and my heart speeds up even more. I feel like if I say anything, I'll puke.

"It happened slowly. I don't want you to think I was always keeping this from you," he says.

All I can get out is "What?"

"Are you going to make me say it?"

"I should go," I say without looking at him. I notice my tea is still steaming. I grab my bag and walk to the door. My legs feel stiff. Just keep moving, I think. I turn the knob of the door.

"Your boots."

"What?" I say, looking back but not right at him.

"You forgot to put on your boots."

I look down at my socked feet. I put on my boots but don't tie the laces.

"I'm sorry," he says as I turn away. He hasn't got up.

"I'm really sorry," I say, as I head out the door.

If I'm honest with myself, I've always hoped that Dylan had feelings for me. It was something I held onto, a secret wish I turned to occasionally. After Anne told me he said he wasn't attracted to me, I forced myself to stop wanting anything with him. I think it was a method of self-protection: don't want the person who doesn't want you. It took some time, but I started to feel okay about having him in my life as a friend. Though something was tucked away, something I convinced myself I no longer needed or wanted. The trouble is that I don't develop feelings for people easily, so it was tough for me to shake them entirely. Every time someone suggested that Dylan had feelings for me, I brushed it off, but a part of me wanted it to be true. I felt almost entitled to it even if I wasn't sure if I really wanted it anymore since I had spent so much time telling myself I felt nothing. And that's an ugly thing—to want someone to love you even if you're not sure you want them. But I never thought I'd have to confront it.

Part of me wants to go to Mia now and tell her everything, and ask her what to do, but I'm so exhausted.

A few hours later, I get a text. It's Dylan.

Can we just pretend that didn't happen? I'm sorry.

Less than an hour later, I type *I'm sorry too. Don't worry.* I erase *I'm sorry too* and just send *Don't worry.* My stomach knots. I know this is vague and could mean a number of things. I don't know what I mean.

I stare at my phone for the rest of the day, hoping to receive a text or call from James. I've totally fucked things up. Why do I want someone to think of me and only me, to see me and only me? Maybe that's it—I set myself up for failure, so I can bail out. I type *sorry* to him but don't send it when I picture him yelling at me in the street. Then I think of all the times I've left him waiting, left him wondering. My face gets hot.

I send the text.

I send another. *I want you to meet Mia.*

Ten minutes later, he texts me back. *I'm sorry too. But we should talk. Need to be alone tonight but let's meet tomorrow night.*

I don't want to put this on Mia, but I need her help. And I know she'll feel hurt if I tell her too late. But I have to tell her in person. I'll go see her in the afternoon tomorrow before I see James.

That night, I sit on the floor of my bedroom with only the blue lights on. I pull my curtains to the side just a bit to look at his windows for signs that he's up, but his windows are dark. If he were looking at my window, he'd see the corner of blue light and know that I'm looking for him.

I wake up to Gus meowing by my ear. I didn't feed him last night. I give him food. When I get back to my bedroom, I see my phone light up on my bed. It's on silent, but I can see someone's calling. I figure it's James, but no, it's Mia's dad.

"Erik?" My chest feels constricted. Everything feels too tight. Like my bones could burst through my skin. I feel like I'm moving at a very fast pace even though I'm sitting still. He's breathing heavily.

"Alice." His voice breaks. "She had an infection—"

I throw my phone to the ground.

Chapter Twenty

I've always thought that during the winter, this was the quietest place in the city. In the summer, it's a crowded beach; in the winter, the water is partially frozen, but the ice is not thick enough to walk on without getting pulled underneath. The ice is dusted in snow. The sky is white now too.

Mia's parents took Mia, Anne, and me to a beach when we were twelve or so. Mia and Anne were much taller than me, and I stood out when I walked with them, or likely they stood out while no one noticed me. In our bathing suits, they looked even taller, the tops of their thighs came up to my ribs. Mia was the first in the water, running right in, not testing the temperature with her toes, swimming until it was deep enough to put her head under the surface. Her hair sticking to her neck and chest when she broke through the surface again. She called out to me and Anne. Anne was sucking on a green lollipop and bit into it to speed up the process. She chewed the candy and threw the stick on the sand, running to Mia without glancing at me. I grabbed the stick and folded it in half and folded it again and again until it broke. Mia called my name, telling me to join them. I shook my head and dug my toes in the sand, feeling how the heat of the surface breaks when you dig deeper and it becomes cool.

I hadn't been in a body of water since those girls pushed me under a few years before, during that school trip to the lake, and I was nervous to go in again. I stayed on the sand, wrapped in a towel while Mia and Anne argued over who did better handstands in the water. Mia said we need Alice to be a judge. I still said I wouldn't go in. Mia promised I'd be safe. Then she said we won't go deep. We can't even go that deep to do the handstands anyway. I said fine. On the way into the water, a freckly boy making an elaborate sandcastle with his younger brother told Anne she was pretty. Anne smiled and turned away, embarrassed, running into the water. The same boy then told Mia and me that we were too fat for our bathing suits. Mia said nothing, but she walked through the sandcastle, kicking sand at the boy in the process. I didn't know what to do, but I wanted to contribute, so I took the boy's hat off his head and threw it. It landed only about five feet away, but I felt bold. Mia then ran to the water with me trailing behind her. She won the handstand contest. Her legs stood straight out of the water, knees touching and toes pointed while Anne's legs wobbled, her toes spread.

On the way home, in Mia's parents' minivan, we sat in the very back, in the three-seater, so no one was left out. Mia sat in the middle, and Anne and I kept peeling the skin off Mia's sunburnt back, trying to see who could get the bigger piece. It started to hurt Mia, so she asked us to stop. I put the biggest sheet of skin in the pocket of my shorts. As it got dark outside,

Anne fell asleep on Mia's shoulder, and Mia fell asleep with her head on Anne's while I stayed awake. Mia's bare arm against my bare arm created such an intense warmth that we both started to sweat.

The bench I'm sitting on has a thick layer of ice on it, like it's being saved for another time, for someone else. I know it's cold, but I can't really feel anything. I drank the half bottle that was in the freezer, left by Mia or maybe Dylan some night that feels so long ago. The label was peeled off, but I think it was vodka. I drank it to mute my thoughts, but that didn't really work. I know she's gone. I will never see her again. I want to run away, but there's nowhere to go where this isn't happening.

After I threw the phone, I called Erik back, my hands shaking, my face wet. I just heard a ringing in my ears after he told me she was gone, and it's still there now. I wanted to say something, but I had nothing, so I just hung up.

I felt an urge to go to her bedroom, but I stopped in front of her door. I've opened that door so many times. I remember seeing her, writing essays in her bed, with opened books all around her; practising doing the splits even though she never totally got there; listening through the vent to the fighting couple who used to live in the basement. I used to crawl in bed with her to gossip, or to show her articles I hated, or when I had bad cramps, to tell her it felt like someone was twisting rusty screwdrivers in my ovaries. When it spread into our thighs, we called it "pain shorts." Looking at her empty bed over the past few months made me feel lonely, but I convinced myself she'd be back. I knew if I opened that door, I'd get in her bed and never leave again. So, I drank what I could, left the apartment, and got on a subway train and rode to the end of the line.

A few years ago, Mia called me into her bedroom. The bed was made, smooth all over, and she sat on top of it with three objects in front of her, spaced perfectly apart: a laptop, a cellphone, and a knife. I gave her a strange look, and she made me sit down beside her on the bed and took my hand in hers. She told me that the night before, when she was out with Anne, she saw the guy I was dating kissing another girl. We had dated less than two months, and even though we said we were exclusive, I didn't care because I knew it wouldn't last.

Before I could tell her that, she told me she thought of three options for dealing with this. The first was to break up with him through email. She said she took the liberty of composing a first draft. It was very Mia: direct and balanced with a few cutting remarks. The second option was to block his number and stop speaking to him entirely. The third option was to kill him, or just cut him a little, she said. The third option was just for flair—she was trying to make me laugh. I chose option one and two, editing the email a bit. I also blocked his email address. That night, she was supposed to go on a date, and she was on her way out, wearing a purple slip dress over a black turtleneck, when she saw me lying in bed, and though it wasn't unusual to see me in bed before nine, she figured I was down and decided to stay at home with me. I didn't feel much for this guy and I don't think I was even sad at all. I was kind of relieved, but I didn't tell her that because I was happy she was staying in with me.

I don't know how to do all this without her.

I'm a coward. I run from knowing everything. I avoid thinking about the ocean or space—they're too big. I can't grasp death. The immensity, the finality, if you don't believe there's a place where someone is waiting for you. I don't know what to do with something so immovable. To know you can see someone only by looking back.

When we were kids, Mia and I went to our friend's birthday party. We all played hide and seek. Mia ran and looked for a hiding spot, and I ran beside her, trying to keep up. She said, Alice, you can't hide with me. We're supposed to hide alone. So, I let her run ahead, but I kept an eye on her. I noticed she was headed to a wooded area, and I didn't want to lose sight of her, so I followed her but from a distance. She looked back, so I hid behind a bush. After I moved from behind it, I couldn't see her anymore, so I went into the wooded area. I looked for her for what seemed like hours, but I went too far, and it got dark. Eventually I heard adults calling my name and saw the light from their flashlights. As they were leading me back to the house, I said we have to go find Mia—she's still out there. They said no, she left.

I feel so tired. I think I could sleep here. I feel exhaustion moving through me, like my blood is thickening or just not pumping. The cold is creeping in, and I'm shaking. My palm has been resting on the icy bench. I can't stand the feeling anymore, and I lift up my hand, but it's stuck to the ice, and it burns when I tear it away from the bench. I put my hand on my cheek. The numbness makes it feel like someone else's cheek, or hand. I can still bend my fingers a bit, but the cold is becoming too much. I should leave.

Acknowledgments

I really never thought I'd actually have the privilege of getting my book published. If I say this is a dream come true, my editor, Deborah Sun de la Cruz, will cringe at my use of cliché and lack of originality, so I definitely won't say that. I cannot thank Deborah enough for her brilliance, creativity, enthusiasm, kindness, patience, endurance (honestly, she never gives up), and for challenging me—this book exists because of her. If I had a kidney to spare, I'd give it to her—she doesn't need it, but maybe she could keep it in a jar and think of how grateful I am.

So many people are involved in the life of a book, and I am grateful to them all. I want to thank my agent, Maria Massie, for believing in me and this book. There are endless people at Penguin Random House Canada I want to thank, starting with Nicole Winstanley, publisher of Penguin Canada, who has been a wonderful support. Big thanks to Marion Garner who offered invaluable guidance to me early on and throughout this whole process. I want to thank Kristin Cochrane for all her support, as well as

Barry Gallant and Scott Sellers. I'd like to send a substantial thank you to my publicist, Dan French. Thank you to the entire Penguin Canada team, especially Alanna McMullen, David Ross, Bonnie Maitland, Meredith Pal, and Anne Hardy. I also want to thank Brittany Larkin, Erin Cooper, Terri Nimmo, Maureen Simpson, Ann Jansen, and Sue Kuruvilla. Thanks so much to the Office Services team and the Warehouse teams. Okay, I actually need to thank literally every single team at Penguin Random House Canada—thank you all! A special thanks to Kate Sinclair for creating a perfect cover and book design. I am so thankful to all of my colleagues who gave me feedback on earlier drafts. Thanks so much (!) to Anne Collins, Pamela Murray, Lauren Park, and Margot Blankier. A tearful thank you to Melanie Tutino for her thoughtfulness and great eye. A massive thank you to Danielle Gerritse who provided excellent editorial notes (and emotional support) and has been a major champion of this book.

I am so fortunate to have a very cool family who accepts and celebrates my sense of humour (which I know is not for everyone). I'd be so lost without good people in my life. A few of my family members read early drafts and I thank them for their feedback . . . and love! Derek O'Donnell, my romantic roommate/barely-recognized-by-the-government spouse, thank you for always being there for me with your big muscles and generous heart, and always making me laugh like Dr. Hibbert. Rachel Mahrer, my mother, you are a tiny woman, but I know you'd summon the strength to carry my much larger body over vast rough terrains to get me to safety if you needed to—thank you for all (all is a lot) you've done for me. Larry Jackson, my father (dad), thank you for supporting me and for never making me eat the hospital food. Thank you to my brother, Ben Jackson, for looking out for all of us and for never making me feel like the dud child even though you're better at almost everything. Thank you to my grandmother Sue Jackson for always letting me sit in the La-Z-Boy. Thank you to Morgan Sheppard (one of my keen readers!), Levi Theodore Jackson, Karen Yoworski, Ari Mahrer, Jon Mahrer . . . okay I can't list every single family member who's been kind about my book, but really—thank you all!

Thanks to all my incredible friends who have been so lovely, especially when I've been weird and cryptic about my writing—if you didn't know this book existed, please know it's not you, it's me! Extra special thanks to Ashley Sepers and Danielle Roach, two of my longtime friends who read an early draft and provided feedback. And thanks to Renata Kaveh for kindly letting me use her studio.

Thanks to Doretta Lau, Anne T. Donahue, Haley McGee, and Anna Maxymiw for their lovely blurbs. Thank you to Crissy Calhoun for the copyedit and to Marcia Gallego for the proofread. Thanks to everyone in the creative writing classes I've taken. Thank you to Mr. Mahnic (John Mahnic) who told me I was a good writer when I was a dumb teen. Sorry to all my high school math teachers.

A major thank you (and wow I can never fully express my gratitude) to the many doctors and nurses who've helped me over the years.

And thank you thank you thank you to all the readers.